THE GIRL WHO HAS ALREADY DIED

ALESSA WINTERS

To "A Brand New Chapter Writing Group" who listened to this ENTIRE thing.

To Allen, because why not.

CONTENT WARNING

There is some body horror in this book, as well as generational trauma.

A LOT of dealing with complicated feelings about someone, while mourning them at the same time.

THERE IS sex in this book. Mom, please skip those chapters.

THE FIRST BOOK in this series is "The Girl Who Brings The Dead" and this book won't make much sense without reading it first.

1

Contrary to popular opinion, Alette is not a nice person.

She's kind, sure, or she tries to be. She's polite, because she believes that if she isn't, she'll have to face consequences she'd rather not deal with. She's many things, things that make people assume she's nice.

But a nice person wouldn't do the things she does. And when she comes to the crossroads of things she's done in her life, she evaluated them, and then once and for all decided to cross off "nice" on the list of descriptors of herself she keeps neatly in her head.

So when she sits in front of her laptop, waiting for a video call with the College of Europe to start and feels the beginning frisson of nerves, she squashes that down. Squashes it down so it sits underneath her confidence, somewhere back behind her spine, along with all other emotions that she would rather not deal with.

It's somewhere near her grief.

Grief at losing her aunt, at losing the one person who

looked at preteen Alette and thought she could be someone worth teaching. Grief for being so suddenly without the one stabilizing force in her life. Grief for being so suddenly thrust in the wind, to where she has no protection, no way of dealing with politics, no tools or shielding from the stranger magics that Aunt Frisse dabbled in.

Grief for knowing that's what the College wants to talk about, and fury that they want to judge. That they want to take apart all of Alette's memories of her aunt and weigh them against what is good and ethical and make decisions.

And fury that her aunt kept so many secrets.

Alette breathes out, a controlled exhale, and sits up straight, tossing her long black braid behind her. It thumps against her aunt's computer chair. This room is the best for these meetings, completely soundproofed to the outside world and yet actually has decent internet, compared to the rest of the place.

All the magic around the complex slowly started failing at the death of Aunt Frisse, and so did some of the modern amenities that Frisse magicked into working. Good Wi-Fi is one of them. Most of the rooms, besides this one, have unreliable Wi-Fi now that she's gone.

All of this unknowable magic, all of the techniques and threads woven into the very grounds of the place, and all Alette can do is look at them and see the magic fraying apart, unravelling and twisting away from her grasp.

Her aunt was a genius, a lightning rod of an intellect, and Alette just can't keep the place together.

"What's wrong?" Even though her back is to the door, she would recognize Axel's footsteps anywhere, even with all the changes that have happened with him.

She doesn't look over at him.

After the battle one month prior, when Aunt Frisse fell and Axel sustained an injury that all but erased his substantial magic, he no longer looks like the picture of him she keeps neatly in her head. No longer looks like the Axel she's known since they were very young, ever since he learned that he could use his alchemy to change his very appearance.

And worse, he feels different. Like she had gotten so used to his magic and his general powers, that the lack of it scrapes like a loose tooth against her awareness.

"Nothing," Alette says, crisp. Or, rather, as crisp as she could, but her voice quavers all the same. "The College is late."

Axel drags a chair over, the feet scratching loudly against the linoleum. "It's still uh...thirteen minutes until the call time," he says, and sits sideways in the chair next to her, coming into her eyeline.

His face is wider than it was before, his hair no longer perfectly straight but curly, coarser. Still black, but the texture of his mother's wild red curls from Alette's dim memory of her.

"That's late for them," Alette responds.

Axel flips a coin in his hands, deft. When they were children, it was his way of keeping focused during classes and during the long hours of magical training, but now it's almost a nervous tic. Almost more of a tell.

Now, with Aunt Frisse gone, he's the closest thing she has to living family. More of a brother than even her brothers, who she hasn't seen in over a decade. And here she is, almost too nervous to even look at him and think about how much he's changed.

"Did you sleep?"

The College had, of course, scheduled the call for 1:30 PM their time, all the way in Helsinki, leaving them to look presentable at 3:30 in the morning. Alette is sure it's intentional.

"No," Alette says, enunciating as cleanly as she can. "Didn't seem worth it."

Axel looks at her, and there are circles under his eyes, circles that she knows for a goddamn fact that he would have magically erased away, if he still could.

She just holds his gaze, still a little ashamed that she's so prickly.

"Oh well," he mutters with a loose shrug. "Want a 5-Hour Energy?"

Alette hasn't touched caffeine since her aunt died.

"No."

"Suit yourself," he grumps, and it's just enough of his old attitude that it soothes something inside of her.

Her laptop beeps, and the waiting symbol on the video chat pops up. Still no one for them to talk to, but still, Alette controls herself on her exhale.

Axel notices, of course, then tosses the coin at her, which she fumbles. "Stop being nervous."

She throws the coin back at him, and he catches it easily, smoothly flipping it between his fingers. "I'm not nervous."

"Stop lying," he shoots back, and even though his face doesn't look like him anymore, the tuck of his chin she would know anywhere. He's about to do something very annoying. "Or I'll call that guy you saw five months ago and say you want another date."

Alette briefly closes her eyes. There hadn't been anything wrong with the guy five months ago, but that was almost part of the problem. After all but working full time with her aunt, almost any guy she tried her hand at was just...interminably boring.

"We are about to talk to the College and you're bringing up old dates?" Alette says, and the waiting symbol mocks her. "Axel, they could throw us in prison. They could take away all support, they could burn her research, they could—"

"They could also give her the Nobel Peace Prize of magic—"

"—That doesn't exist," Alette interjects.

"—and give us pats on the heads for defeating a powerful and dangerous demon who fucking wiped a town off the map," Axel says, just talking louder over her. "We don't know."

Her laptop beeps again, and she focuses on that, instead of her broken best friend and the threads of magic she can see warping in the very walls and the pounding of her own heart.

"That's the problem," she murmurs, when nothing changes on the screen, "we don't know."

Instead of answering, Axel tips his chair back, leaning his feet on the computer desk.

"I'll tell Lyra you're not sleeping again, and then she'll get concerned," he says, after nothing changes with the screen for too long for him to be silent. "She'll want to come over and check out the magic and then she'll get distressed and then Melekai will be pissed again."

It's a weak threat. Lyra, a powerful necromancer in her own right and the only reason why Alette's still alive—or, rather, alive again—would probably be kind about it, and Melekai...now that Lyra brought him back to life as just a human, would just scowl at her, all intensity and terror gone from him.

Another bit of nerves frays at her.

She knows that Aunt Frisse told the College that they knew a necromancer but didn't know exactly how in depth she went with them, and Alette is fairly certain that Lyra would not be terribly happy to be ordered to Finland to be examined.

"Oh no, then I'll have to get brunch with Lyra, what a trial," Alette says, and out of the corner of her eye she sees Axel crack a smile. "And then you and Melekai could go off and mope together."

"I don't mope," Axel says, cheery, "but if you stop being so tense about this, I won't snitch on you. And if you actually go home and sleep after this."

"That's not fair," Alette says, and the screen in front of her briefly turns black, before the grand ballroom of the College fills the screen.

She sits up.

All members are sitting in throne-like chairs, their faces almost entirely obscured in shadows, because if there's one thing that all magicians love, it's theatrics.

Axel doesn't move his feet from the desk.

After a few seconds of silence, one of the magicians— probably Korhonen if she had to guess by the stuffiness in his tone—clears his throat.

"Did you gather all of the honorable Doctor Joyanne Frisse's research?" he starts, and yes, it's Korhonen, complete with the giant stick up his ass about titles.

"Yes," Alette says, because not answering would be worse. "Or, rather, what we could find."

"She hid things," Axel says, and there, beneath his casualness and his idle motion, she could hear an undercurrent of fury, so closely matched to her own.

Because hiding things was all that her aunt did.

Going through her research revealed more of her aunt than Alette had ever known. That she had a daughter only a little bit younger than Alette, with someone who wasn't Alette's uncle. That she paid off several people, so they wouldn't come questioning her business. That she hadn't only ran aboveboard experiments, but instead experiment after experiment that no guiding College would ever allow.

Alette estimates they've found maybe a third of them.

Korhonen peers at them through the computer screen. "Did you find her research on the demon named Terese?"

Axel shifts at the mention of the name.

"Not entirely," Alette says, refusing to blink, refusing to shy away, refusing to back down. Because while they're entirely in the right to ask about her aunt's sketchiness, she's not going to be ashamed of her.

Even though the shame definitely winds its way around her nerves and her grief.

"We only found mentions," Axel says, after she pauses for too long, "referring to other projects in relation to it, like a set of constants she already knew." When he wants to, Axel knows how to sound the part of the intellectual, even though he usually leaves it to her. "We don't...we didn't know."

It's too much of a confession for Alette, but she inhales, controlled.

Because they didn't know. Because her aunt had them go through the entire affair, had them take down a rogue demon who was possessing a live person beyond the laws of physics and magic...without telling them that she might've had a hand in it.

Maybe.

All they found were mentions. But mentions, by themselves, look damning.

Alette refused to talk to anyone for four days after that came to light. Lyra had seemed to already suspect, Axel destroyed things and threw plates against the wall, but Alette refused to leave the compound.

"She told us you were aware," another College member, one whose voice rings a bell but isn't immediately familiar, says. "That the three of you could handle the fallout."

And now Aunt Frisse is dead, the body that was once the demon Terese is missing after running away, and Axel is without any powers.

Axel glances to Alette, like he's hoping she'll take control of the conversation, but Alette clamps down her lips so as to not speak ill of the dead.

"Yeah, that was a lie," Axel says, and the fury coats his voice too. "I can't do any alchemy anymore, after one of the blasts." Predictably, this causes the College to stir in their chairs. "And we don't even know where to begin."

That right there is the other reason why Alette didn't want to take the call.

"And that necromancer?" Korhonen asks, voice just as crisp as before. "Can she help?"

That answers another question, on whether or not Aunt Frisse had told them about Lyra.

"She's uneducated, mostly," Alette says, soft, which feels meaner than it actually is. "She has very little practice of magic and does not know much theory."

"We will invite her to study," another one says, and there's a threat inherent in his voice, "if she tells us what she can do."

Alette privately doubts that Lyra would deal well with that sort of interaction, if her constant butting of heads with Aunt Frisse was anything to go off of.

"You need to find the body of Terese, and find her soon,"

Korhonen continues. "We need to study what happened to her, to understand what Dr. Joyanne Frisse tried to accomplish, if it is, in fact, anything. To see if there is still a human in the body, or just a demon laying low."

It's a concern that Alette has had, but absent any other interaction with the body, she has no way to know.

"And you need to manage the fractures in the magic of the area, Alette Jyotshi," he continues, and Alette sits up taller, "She was your mentor, she was your relative, the responsibility falls to you."

Axel makes a noise of protest, but one look towards the camera shuts him up.

"We will be sending someone to follow your progress," Korhonen continues, "work with them to your fullest potential."

The screen goes dark, leaving them in the dim room,

Axel sits back, finally putting his feet on the ground. "Okay!" he says, and even Alette can tell he's faking it. "Find the possibly dangerous human, balance magic—whatever that means—and break it to Lyra that she has to go visit Europe. That's not too bad."

Alette carefully takes off her golden glasses and folds them up, then presses her thumb between her eyebrows.

"I don't..." she trails off, and she sounds weak.

She should, theoretically, be okay with sounding weak in front of her best friend, but she's not.

Axel stands, like this isn't a big deal. "Go home and sleep," he says, despite the fact that they both know they're going to get an even longer email with instructions later, that this is going to be a much more complicated task than either of them think. "We'll go over to Lyra and Melekai's in the morning."

"I'll just run tracer scenarios," Alette says, instead, "see if there's something we can grab on for our search for Terese, see if we can find her."

It's fruitless without more information, of course. When Terese had gotten up and left the hospital, she had left no trail. Left no indication where she was going and how she was going to live, and all they knew is that one evening she was in a coma, and before they had a chance to get back to the hospital in the morning she had woken up and escaped through the window.

Even though she had been on the fifth floor, and no security cameras picked anything up besides her crawling out of the window and into nothing.

And no body had been found on the pavement below.

"Nah," Axel says, easily, "you're going back to your apartment and actually sleeping."

Alette freezes.

She hasn't left the compound, not beyond groceries and the trips to Lyra and Melekai's house, since it happened.

"I know you say you sleep on that couch, but you haven't been," he continues, fingers drumming on Aunt Frisse's computer desk. "So go home, clean out your fridge from whatever nightmare you've left in it for this long, and crash on your own bed."

"I don't need to," Alette says, then her own words are punctured by a large yawn, which makes Axel crack up. "I'm fine."

Her best friend looks at her, really looks at her, and it's only years of training and mentorship with Aunt Frisse that makes it so she doesn't shift in her seat.

"But you have a point about the fridge," she says, because if she can pretend it's her point then she can still take the win. "And my plants have probably died."

She hasn't left the compound for a very specific reason,

beyond the grief and the nerves and the fury, but something in this moment, after an unsatisfying video call and the vague threats and her best friend trying to take care of her, something solidifies inside of her.

Maybe, just maybe, everything could be handled better from out there.

2

The moment her car leaves the bubble of Aunt Frisse's failing protections, twin shadow shapes blur along the edges of her vision, keeping pace with her perfectly sensible sedan, even as she guns the engine faster than she usually goes.

She knows by now that if she looks straight at them, they look akin to giant dogs, like the hellhounds of old, cloaked with shadow and soot and grinning at her with giant teeth like they could bite her in half.

But instead, they just run along her car like it's a game of cat and mouse.

Her heart sticks in her throat, though, and she keeps her eyes on the road.

They first appeared in the month after Alette was raised from the dead.

At first, she ignored them, blaming their appearance on long nights and stress with Terese destroying parts of the magical web around them. She had always had an overactive imagination, or that's what her aunt always said, and maybe some trauma of actually dying spurred her brain into imagining monsters from the deep.

But then they continued appearing. Every time she glanced out a window of a car, they were there, running along. Sitting patiently at stoplights with tails wagging and fangs grinning, only to start running the moment she started moving again.

Axel never saw them. Or, rather, he never commented that he saw them, and she knows if he saw them he would never shut up about them, so she assumed.

Shortly after they started appearing, then...other people started appearing.

Melekai the demon had called them Wights, and none of her research gave her any sort of answer to what they were.

She pulls past the gates of the compound, and the Wight with curly black hair is standing, casually leaning against the aged chain-link fence, and the two shadow dogs circle around him, before continuing to follow Alette's car.

His brilliant blue eyes track her motion as she drives away, and she knows he can run to keep up with the car just as easily as the shadow runners, but he stays in place, not even visible in her rearview mirror.

She still doesn't know that particular Wight's name. He's by far the one who appears the most to her.

But giving him a name would give too much legitimacy to all her confusion about all this.

She never asked to be able to see them, though according to Melekai they were always there. Just existing next to her world, interacting with it, but never in a way she could tell.

One of the shadow runners veers close to her car, and it's

only years of driving safely that makes it so she doesn't swerve, but her hands tighten against her steering wheel.

Melekai and Lyra had said that the Wights wouldn't hurt her. Melekai had even worked out a deal with them to protect Lyra, in case something happened to him, and that's about as close to trust as she could fathom from the demon, but something about them itches under her skin. Like she shouldn't trust him, that she should be warning everyone to run as far away as possible, except no one else can see the threat and no one else would pay attention to her rantings.

There've been a few times Alette's wondered if she's crazy, but this takes the cake.

He's under the first stoplight her sedan idles up to, pale in the glow of the heavy January fog, but he doesn't say anything, and she doesn't roll down her window to let him. He just watches her, eyes solemn.

When she could first see them, he wouldn't stop chatting at her. Sometimes in French, sometimes in English, but always chatting. Chatting through her car window, muffled gleefully by the glass and metal, but still talking.

Goosebumps rise up her arms.

There's no one else around, not that she can see through the mist, so she coasts her car to an abandoned gas station parking lot, the pavement cracked and pebbled beneath her car's wheels.

This far north, the sun won't rise for a few hours, and everyone else is asleep. The gas station parking lot is empty, like no one knows it exists.

That's silly, of course, and Alette knows it, but sometimes, when faced with someplace new, her mind seizes on the idea of everyone who's moved through there, everyone who has or has not passed in an area, and how it leaves a place different.

Like how she can tell if Axel's been into the compound's shared kitchen or not. Or how she could tell when Lyra stopped by, even if she had been deep in research the entire time and missed her. Or, before, when her aunt left her food and her favorite coffee and she didn't notice.

It had, like all of this, started when she was raised from the dead, and now she knows this little forgotten corner hasn't seen any other humans in too long.

Alette exhales, her car idling in the parking lot, only illuminated from a nearby streetlight.

Before she loses any will to try this, she shuts off her sensible sedan and delicately opens the door.

The mist swirls around her coat, and she swears she can feel the very magic of the gritty parking lot swirling through the spells she wove into it with her golden needle.

The two shadow dogs find her first, and they circle her in the trot of pleased animals who caught their prey, but they don't get close to her.

Still, she rests her hand against the secret pocket she sewed into her jacket, where her needle case is neatly tucked inside.

One of the dogs shies away at that, but the other stays in her orbit, never venturing a step nearer.

She doesn't see him walking, but between one blink and the next, the Wight appears, and the mist doesn't swirl around him—it envelops him. Welcomes him, like it knew he would be there, and it knew it could accept him.

He regards her, for a second, as if she truly caught him off guard by stopping the car. His hand rests on the scared shadow dog's head, and it relaxes, sitting down, its edges becoming clearer.

Once it's not in motion, it looks something akin to a

cattle dog, a heeler, instead of a nebulous mass of shadow and movement.

The Wight's not speaking, he's not saying anything, so Alette steels herself.

"Why are you here?" she asks, and it's so late at night it's into the early morning.

The dog still circling edges closer, but she doesn't let herself look at it.

The Wight's gaze sharpens, and for a second she steels herself for some sort of attack. Some sort of something thrown at her, in case he is just as magical as Melekai was.

"Things are broken," he says, and his voice is raspier than the last time he chatted at her, the Quebecois accent deeper, "can't you tell?"

She stills, trying to read his face, but it's just as inscrutable as before.

She knows better than to attempt to answer a question she doesn't understand.

"What do you mean?" she asks, keeping her hand over her needle case.

His head tilts at her, and she's seen that motion in Melekai, both when he's a demon and now. "I would think you could tell?" he says, voice trailing off, and the scared dog stands back up again, like it's about to start pacing once more. "How parts of the world aren't working how they should. How magic that should be eternal is fragmenting apart. How systems are failing."

It's a close echo of the words of Korhonen, and she shivers, despite her coat.

"The very nature of magic is falling apart, and you're the only human magician who can see us, see all of us, who actually knows what we are," he continues, and it's logical if she squints at it. "There are things happening that I cannot control and we need help."

"Who's we?" she asks, quick.

He looks caught, for a second, and both the dogs growl, until an idle hand quiets them. "Me and my kind," he says.

She's tired, and the exhaustion coats her throat, crunching in her eyes. "I'm not sure why you think I could help." It's not saying no; she knows better than to refuse when someone asks for help that's close to her own goals.

But she also knows to not agree recklessly.

He hesitates, and for a second, his hand plays with the mist, swirling around between his fingers, like he could command the very part of nature it represents, and Alette watches, as sharp as she can this early in the morning.

She knows next to nothing about the Wights, and every little detail she can safely observe she files away into the neat little part of her mind, in the quickly growing folder of things she couldn't see before she died.

"Some magics need more than just Wights to maintain them, and the great magician who lived in the compound did more than you know to hold the region together," he says, and she swallows past the initial hurt, of hearing him speak of her aunt.

"You're right, she did more than we know," Alette says, and a car drives by on the road, headlamps dim in the mist, disappearing. "And she told me none of it."

His eyebrows raise, and every emotion seems so evident on his face that she has to look away.

"Can you meet me later," he starts, and she shivers again, despite not being the slightest bit cold, "and I will show you?"

She should push for something different, push for some real answer, but it's now close to four thirty in the morning, so she remains silent. Let him give her more information, instead of demanding it.

"Do you know Placer's Cabin and Shaman's Point?" he asks, and she nods once to confirm. "Have you been there since the necromancer brought you back?"

She hasn't, the time taken up entirely by racing around and the exhaustion of chasing Terese. "No."

"Meet me there thirty minutes before sundown, two days from now," he says, his voice dipping into his accent, rich. "Bring your tools, they'll be useful."

"Call off your dogs," Alette says, enunciating as clear as she can with her lack of sleep. "I don't appreciate being hunted."

"You think they're hunting you?" he says, and his face splits into a smile, wide and handsome. "If they were hunting you, you'd already be dead."

Then, deliberately, like he's letting her see, he turns around, walking back into the mist.

3

Her sensible apartment has a thin layer of insensible dust over everything and the air is overly stuffy, but she ignores it in favor of taking off her shoes, then carefully hanging up her coat.

The warmth of the magic leeches away from her the moment she swings it off, but she plucks her needle case from the breast pocket, tapping it neatly against the wall.

It takes a split second, but her apartment blossoms into light, dim with the early hour, but traces shimmer through every little spell she wove into the walls, every little thread and etching she carved into place.

It glitters as she steps barefoot through her kitchen, each rune flaring as she gets closer, lighting her way towards her bedroom. As if the very magic she put in place could tell she needs to sleep.

Back when she was learning the basics of home-based magic, her and her aunt had gone over books in exhausting detail to find the right thing to mesh with Alette's particular type of magic, and the results have left her apartment unreally aware of her own mental state. Like it can tell what she needs at any given moment.

Even though she hasn't been there in a month, all the magic twists to her touch.

Her aunt had insisted that Alette do every little bit by herself, every little etching and marking, and now...now it's just as whole as the compound used to be.

Like the events of the month never happened.

The magic trails her footsteps in front of her, down her little hallway, past her craft room and her sewing room, stopping in front of her bed.

"I get the hint," Alette murmurs, setting the needle case on her side table, sticking her phone next to it. The glow from outside her room fades, and her bedroom door softly swings shut.

Inelegant, she flops onto her bed, her mind buzzing, as the magic dims the lights in her room.

It's so late, there's no one she could text, no one she could talk to, and the magic silence she put in place is complete, leaving nothing for her brain to latch onto.

She stares up at the ceiling in the dark, still wearing her glasses, and wills herself to attempt to sleep.

AXEL (10:02 AM): College grunt is here.

AXEL (10:31 AM): College grunt is here and College grunt wants access to your files.

AXEL (11:42 AM): A, are you actually sleeping?

ALETTE JOLTS AWAKE, and it takes her a few moments to actually quell her heartbeat enough to realize that her phone is actually ringing, and no one's actually called her in forever, so she scrambles around until she can press the speaker button.

"Hello?" she asks, then coughs, her mouth feeling like something dead crawled into it.

"Are you actually asleep?" It's Axel, of course, not very many people actually have her number.

"Now I'm not," Alette says, squeezing her eyes shut. She hadn't even gotten underneath blankets, and now the pale January sun is streaming through her window. "What's wrong?"

"Wait, really?" she knows Axel enough to know that he's delighted. Unironically, absolutely delighted, no matter what the reason for the initial call. "That's awesome!"

It's less awesome now that she's having this phone conversation, but she swings her legs over the side of the bed, and the room glows anew, bright and cheery.

"What do you need?" she asks, fumbling around in the sheets to grab her glasses, because he wouldn't have called her if he didn't need something. "Are you safe?"

"I'm on my way over, the College goon kicked me out for a few hours," he says, and she takes a few heart pounding moments of frantically scrolling through her text messages to find context. "You're going to hate him."

"You can't come over unless you bring food," Alette says, glancing in her mirror. It increases in brightness, showing her just how much a mess she is, and that won't do. "Why would you ever leave the complex to an outsider?"

"Because he threatened to blow up my car if I didn't," he says. "And I checked, he's official, he's real."

Alette gives her phone an irritated look, before sitting on

her bed and at least brushing out her braid. She doesn't like people seeing her without actual time put into her appearance, without everything in its place, but Axel's seen her worse.

"I tried to delay until you could get here, I did, but they pay a lot less attention to me without the magic," Axel continues, and she can hear his car revving in the background, "said he'll deal with that later."

Alette pauses in the re-braiding of her hair. "Wait, does he think he can?"

"Who knows," Axel says, and she hears his turn signal click in the background. "Wants me to pick you up," he says, voice fading in and out as he passes that one place the signal gets bad. "Said he needed to speak to someone who could actually do something."

Alette raises an eyebrow at her reflection in the mirror. Even without his powers, Axel's not exactly someone she would want to underestimate.

"He really just sent you to gather me?" Alette asks. "That's beneath you."

"Gee, thanks," Axel says. "I already got food, I'm two minutes away." The phone clicks off.

There goes the possibility of neatly taking care of her makeup or anything beyond changing out of her slept-in clothes.

It's two minutes of panicked redressing and shoving her clothes in her laundry, before her doorbell rings. She had coded her door to open to his magic, and now his magic is gone, so of course he can't just waltz in like he normally does.

She jerks the door open, irrationally irritated with her apartment's magic, and Axel greets her with a raise of takeout bags.

Next to him sits the shadow dog, the heeler, from the night before.

"We're gonna have to redo the lock," he says, forced cheer underneath his words, "I can't believe it didn't recognize me."

Alette stares down at the shadow dog, who sits expectantly, as Axel stomps inside and puts the food on her table.

"The clerk at Zerelda's didn't even recognize me," he continues, taking out takeout container after takeout container. "They thought I stole the 'real' Axel's card so I had to pay cash."

"Shoo," Alette whispers to the dog, who, despite being cloaked in shadow, just wags its tail. "Get."

It thumps its tail, but doesn't move, so she resolutely shuts the door, turning back to Axel's chatting.

If the Wight sent her the dog to make sure she goes in two days...she's not sure what she'll do.

"And then one of the waitresses said I might look like my own second cousin, which was a trip, and"—Axel shoots her an odd look, as she's standing with her back against the door—"and then I just got too much coffee. You're a mess."

"When I only get two minutes to wake up, I am," she replies, sitting at her dinner table with as much dignity as possible. "How long did they give you to 'collect me'?"

"An hour more than necessary," he says, pointing at her with a plastic fork. "They really made us stay up super late and had someone already on her way."

"Of course," Alette says, then pulls one of the takeout containers towards her. "I'll get the lock reset today."

"It's bullshit," Axel says, but he digs into his food. "I'm still me."

"I'll code it to your genetic signature this time," Alette says, not looking at him. "Sorry I wasn't there."

"I'm just glad you actually slept," he grouches. "I'm gonna tell Lyra..."

They trail off, as they both eat, and Alette's insides twist at the food, at everything.

She still hasn't decided if she's going off with the Wight.

Or what she should tell Axel.

Two days is a while for her to ruminate on the decision.

"I was planning on researching the broken magic," she says, which sounds appropriate and technically accurate. "Did the goon give any indication of what that was?"

"Not a smidge," Axel says, morose, "just that the entire area's off balance. Put a tracker on my car, though." He gives her a significant glance. "I recognized the rune, but I can't do anything about it."

This, at least, is a solvable problem. "Want me to—"

"No, I want you to look for the non-obvious one," he interrupts, "make them think we can't actually do it."

Abandoning her breakfast, she pushes herself up, and of course the dog is still at her door. She sidesteps him—her? —to go to Axel's oft familiar car.

It's still a functionable car, despite all the alchemy he had put into it before, but the body is real and the engine is real, if a fair sight uglier than it used to be.

The rune glares obviously on its hood, like it's meant to be found. Like they want them to take it off and feel like they're secure. Anyone with even the barest hint of magic in their systems could see it and tell that it's there.

Alette's done the same in magical investigations before.

Axel follows her, carrying the two cups of coffee. "This definitely could have waited until after breakfast." He tries to hand the coffee to her.

She just shakes her head at him, and the dog circles around her, shying away from the car.

And she stares down and tries to feel. Slows her breathing. Grasps her needle case, feeling for the gold, like it could connect her to the world around her.

The car gives off the same taste that Axel's magic used to, of course, gently present against her awareness. It's faded, but still there.

There's a trace of someone else, something harsher, and it takes her a second to realize that it's the necromancy energy that Lyra throws off in spades. Of course, she had ridden in it several times.

"Did they actually touch it?" Alette asks, staring a bit too hard at the rune. This close, this concentrated, it's like a beacon.

"No, just stood near it and waved his hands," Axel says, leaning against her door frame.

The dog runs up to him, but Axel ignores it, which he absolutely wouldn't do if he had any sort of awareness of the dog.

"I figured it was safe to putter around and then come here with their little 'order.' They already know where you live and can't get in without a battering squad," he continues, grim. "We can't go to Lyra's."

"Not with your car," she murmurs. Leaning close to it, like she could smell it.

The Mustang took a beating in the last few months, though Axel had meticulously cleaned and repaired it after each time, first with magic and then without, and the stranger's rune sticks out like a sore thumb.

Something buzzes at the edge of her awareness, and she crouches down, inspecting the tires.

She gives him a questioning nod as she pulls out one of her golden needles—a nice all-purpose 75/11 she had made back when she turned twenty, with a slender ballpoint tip, and it may as well sing in her hands.

There are types of magic that she does, and then there's the types of magic she's good at.

She exhales, pulling power out of the world, until her needle has its string, and—carefully—runs the tip along the treads of the front left tire. Not enough to puncture, just enough to draw the string across it.

The dog shies away, then circles back, like it's trying to learn.

Gossamer, the string catches, tugging at the faintest of magics.

"He kicked the tires," Alette says, still crouched in the dirt of her own driveway, "probably had it prepped on the toe of his boot."

Axel huffs. "It's so freaking weird to not see the magic when you do that," he complains. "It just looks like you were scraping the needle on my tires like a crazy person."

"You're not inherently wrong," Alette says, and gets a half-hearted grin in return.

The dog shoves his nose into the rune, then, sniffing, immediately circles to the front right tire, almost a picture-perfect parody of pointing.

She checks, and that one has a rune as well.

So. Useful, if she could figure out how to better communicate with them and stop them from scaring the shit out of her.

"Do you want me to take them off?" she asks, stowing her needle and brushing off her hands.

Axel tilts his head, regarding his car. Alette knows it must gall him to have another unknown magic user influencing his project, but...

"Not yet, in case he checks again," he says, voice sharp.

"I'd much rather he thinks I know nothing than I know anything."

Because while Axel may be annoying, while he may be a show off, people often forget that he's just as smart as Alette. And he does nothing to change that perspective.

"And I definitely played up the whole 'oh poor me pity me' card with him, hopefully he'll fall in love and find a way to fix me," Axel says, then throws her a wide grin, the grin she's seen him use dozens of times, "or I'll just bug him until he does to get me out of his hair."

"Want backup?" Alette asks, standing and watching the dog sniff around the car. "I can pull the library wingman— it's been a while since you pulled a guy instead of a girl."

The dog sniffs along the door handle, on the bright places where Lyra obviously got into the car, then at the driver's side, right at the spot Axel always closes his door with his foot.

Each motion of the dog is cloaked in shadow, like it's partially made of vapor, but when it stills it's more distinct.

"Not yet," Axel says, bouncing his foot, then gives her a look. "Are you okay?"

She finally tears her eyes away from the dog, and he's raising an eyebrow at her.

"You usually don't lose focus like that," Axel continues, gesturing at his car, "but you went full eyes unfocusing and everything and you only do that when you're upset or you're plotting."

And that's the problem with having a best friend who has known you for over fifteen years.

"I'm plotting," she says, and the dog loses interest in the car and settles to pacing around her again, shadows trailing behind him.

She doesn't know why she thinks the dog is a him, but it might be.

Axel gives her another strange look. "Wanna let me in on that plotting?"

"Not yet," Alette says. "But I want to borrow your car in a few days, if they let us out." She throws him a glance, but he's shrugging. "Let's make him think I'm doing some investigating."

He nods but crosses his arms. "And me?" he says, echoing the unspoken. "I wouldn't be much use investigating."

She's half tempted to tell another lie, tell another falsehood. "Take my car and plan with Lyra and Melekai," she says, because if things go wrong, she wants the necromancer in easy distance of a car.

Not that she thinks Lyra would necessarily want to confront the Wights that currently protect her, but still. Bringing a necromancer to a fight is a bit like bringing a nuclear bomb— incredibly destructive and not very well understood.

"Sure," Axel says, but his brow is still furrowed. "You can tell me if anything's bothering you, you know that, right? Even if I can't blow up your problem, I'll still listen."

It's a bit too much emotion, so she looks away. "Of course," she says, and the dog shies closer, putting his nose in Axel's hand, but Axel doesn't react. "I just don't want to talk about it in case I'm wrong."

"You can be wrong, that's totally cool," he says, and he relaxes, best friend emotion moment over. "Eat breakfast first."

4

The dogs keep pace back to the compound, and outside its gates stands the blue-eyed Wight. He nods at her as the Mustang passes, as the dogs peel off and circle him instead.

Axel doesn't say anything, just a ball of seething frustration the closer they get to the headquarters.

A familiar rush of runes and magic hits Alette as they cross the threshold, sour in its decay. She's going to have to try to find the plans written up, to redo them herself, somewhere between all the runaround from the College and Terese and whatever it is with the Wights.

Axel's Mustang rumbles into the parking garage in an easy, practiced motion. "You're gonna hate him," he says, grim, "he's gonna push all your buttons."

"I'll be sure to not let it show," Alette says, peering at the marks on the concrete poles. They waver, slowly dying off without her aunt's magic.

She at least knows those ones are in her aunt's records. Given enough time and energy, she could easily do them.

"I'd pay you money if you blew up at him," Axel says,

still dour. "Dr. Frisse would tear her hair out to see what he's doing."

This draws Alette's attention, and she blinks at him. "That bad?"

He looks like he's about to say something, but just nods instead.

With that in mind, each click of the elevator just serves to increase Alette's dread. The elevator used to be completely silent, used to be completely untraceable, but now it sounds like it needs a rather involved maintenance check.

The elevator opens with a squeak, revealing the grand mahogany doors of the ballroom/workroom/spell room, and Alette doesn't let her steps falter.

She laid dead in that room for fourteen hours.

She knows that Axel hasn't forgotten, not really, but sometimes she wonders if anyone picks up on how terrifying it is for her to walk through the doors. See the tables, feel the sluggish magic from where Lyra let go a ton of energy, and know that if she hadn't, Alette would not be still alive.

If she could, she would avoid that room forever.

"Brace yourself," Axel mutters, which isn't a good sign, before throwing the doors open.

Inside is...

Sterile.

Gone is the flow of magic, the swirl of the thousands upon thousands of spells cast over years, leaving just the stale smell of recycled air, carpet glue, and dust.

The carpet is rolled up in the corner, and the table and chairs shoved to one side. The spot where Alette laid dead is haphazardly leaning against the wall, a chair against it.

And in the middle, stands a completely average looking

man with blond hair, an overly starched shirt, and thick glasses, waving his hand in an absentminded circle, swirling the remains of the magic in the room away.

Alette pauses at the door, heart in her throat, before a cold sort of fury settles in her bones.

Because as much as the room terrifies her, it was her aunt's, and how dare they take away something so distinct as her magic.

The man doesn't look up as they stand there. "I am just making the space appropriate for other magicians," he says, to the question they didn't ask. "Joyanne did everyone a disservice by keeping it so messy."

"Joyanne," Alette starts, and Axel gives her an alarmed look, "had things exactly how she wished."

This catches the man's attention, and he deigns to give Alette a bored look. "That's right, you were related by marriage." He snaps his fingers, and the swirl of magic dissipates, like it's nothing to him. "My sincere condolences."

Alette strides in, blowing past Axel, her boots clicking against the bare concrete floor. They echo, which they never did before in this room.

Aunt Frisse hated the echo in large rooms.

The man doesn't even raise an eyebrow at her. "I'm Gurlien Banks, you were her prodigy, correct?" he says, as if that's not information that he would have already received. As if he didn't have files on both of them, full of their achievements and failures and everything in between. "Can you tell me the last spell she put in here?"

"You can't tell?" Alette bites out, and Axel breathes out, behind her. "I was under the impression that the College would send someone accomplished."

He regards her, then snaps his book shut. "I can tell that it was a portable spell," he says, standing up straight, because no College goon is ever able to resist showing off their knowledge. "I can tell she used gold and glue for the paint, which makes me think binding. I can tell she didn't finish the spell here, instead taking it with her. I can tell that it was large, covering an unusually wide area of space. What I cannot tell, is what it was used for, or why, and given the nature of all of her...experiments..." he casts a long look to Axel, like he thinks her best friend is one of them, "it's best to have an exact view into her mind."

Alette considers lying. Considers refusing to tell him, considers locking him out and fortifying the walls with everything inside of her.

But.

"It was a trapping spell, for the demon," she says, as neutral as she can, "we wanted to stop her and neutralize her."

"Then why didn't she just drag her here?" he asks, turning back to the bare spot. "And why not use bronze, if she wanted to neutralize? Gold just adds to the volatility of demons, and could've just as easily doubled her power, instead of neutralizing."

Alette had asked the same question, when they built it, but wasn't given an answer.

"Do you have any other questions about the compound?" she asks, instead switching over to sickly sweet, "This room is by far the most chaotic, I assure you."

"She also did some big magic here," he says, which isn't wrong, "and some magic I am completely unsure of the background to. Something experimental, around there." He points to the table, where Alette laid dead. "Whatever happened there, that needs to be discussed and that needs to be authorized."

Alette and Axel exchange a quick look.

"We weren't always here," Axel says, because he thinks of lies faster than her. "She often did magic without us."

He raises an eyebrow at the two of them, then tucks the book into a bag, where it instantly disappears. A childish, showy piece of magic, telling them more about him than he probably realizes.

"Show me the grounds," he commands, and it sticks in Alette's side. "I want to see the damage she has done."

They lead him to the back of the compound, where the building backs into the rock and mountain outcropping, where the worst of the magical damage is.

Even walking out there creeps under Alette's skin, and if she concentrates and breathes out through her nose, she can almost physically see the damage, like a red-black haze over the seam of nature meeting construction.

The moss that used to grow over the stone has died off, greying and crumbling away, like the very building is killing it off. The ivy that grows everywhere has curled away, falling off the building where it used to climb up its side.

The dirt alongside is darker, drier, and no snow has fallen on it, and no ice has melted into it.

Gurlien gives it the same glum look that Alette gives it, the same glum look that had crossed Lyra's face, and the same look that Alette is sure Dr. Frisse would give it.

"Something's wrong here," he says, dry. "I take it this didn't used to be like this?"

"Nope," Axel says, bouncing on his feet, like he can't concentrate, "used to be the prettiest place on the property."

"And when did you notice?" he asks, still to Alette, just...ignoring Axel. Like he's someone to be dismissed.

That also sits poorly with Alette.

"Three days after she died," Alette says, tucking her hands in her pockets so she doesn't pull out her needle case and start fixing something that would take too much. "We were...in the hospital before that."

"When you lost the demon Terese," Gurlien supplies.

"When we left the hospital to come home," Alette says, with more emphasis, "it could have been instant, but we were...not here."

"You're naive," Gurlien says, blunt, "if you think an enemy to your aunt couldn't do this."

He bends over, rubbing his hands on the dead moss. It reeks, both physically and magically. Not of demons, but of decay.

"The demon Terese didn't do this," Axel mutters, looking like he wants to kick something, "her magic left bubbles of just death, where nothing changed from the moment of death."

"That's advanced, to know that," Gurlien says, like he thinks that's a compliment.

"You forget, we know a necromancer," Alette snips, and Gurlien's eyebrows flash up. "She can tell us if something is done by demons. And this isn't."

Gurlien pulls out a ruler, an actual ruler, out of his bag, measuring the area of decaying ground. "The College will want to speak to her, if that's the case." His words are a threat, and Alette doesn't miss them. "I doubt heaven and earth itself couldn't stop them from getting their hands on her."

Axel exhales, explosive, looking wild-eyed at Alette, who feels frozen in fury. "You realize she's her own person, right?"

Gurlien waves his dismissal. "If this isn't demonic, then

this is your aunt's protection magic doing this? Fading away as she died?"

Alette can't move, can't make herself respond.

Because he's right about that.

"No wonder this area is falling apart," he murmurs, and it rankles something deep in Alette, "if your aunt's death disrupted things this badly."

It's too close to the Wight's words from the night before, and Alette shivers.

"Have you seen anything else?" Gurlien asks, wrinkling his nose at the entire area. "Any other evidence of magic breaking down?"

"No, I've hardly left here," Alette says, but instead of coming out defiant, it just sounds small.

"You need to," he orders, and her hackles go back up. "If this is this bad—and it certainly seems to be—then the entire area is compromised and may shake apart."

"Yeah, we wanted to ask about that," Axel interjects, and Gurlien still doesn't look at him. "What exactly did you mean by that?"

Gurlien straightens, staring down Alette. "It means that your aunt almost tore apart the entire western seaboard, and now her magic is trying again."

5

He leaves with a promise to return shortly after, and the moment the doors click shut behind his back, Alette flips him off.

"Oh, fuck him," Axel says, joining in on the rude gesture, "fuck him and his prejudice and vagaries and that snooty attitude."

"Aunt Frisse couldn't tear apart the entire western seaboard," Alette spits out, making quotation marks with her hands, not caring how immature she looks. "She doesn't have that amount of control."

"And she lived here, she wouldn't want it to be destroyed," Axel says, then groans, pressing the heel of his hand into his eyes. "Wanna go to the bar and get shitfaced?"

Alette does, she really does, but instead she just pushes her thumb into the bridge of her nose, trying to think.

"None of her research showed her trying to tear apart the world," she says, turning away from the window and letting her feet guide her back to the now-sterile great room, "she was trying to fix it, trying to fix whatever happened to Terese—"

"And that threat, if he thinks Lyra's gonna like that—"

"She's going to blow her lid," Alette finishes for him, and he nods. "She's going to blow up and then the College will want more information.

The great room is empty, devoid of anything that made it what it used to be, and even the table has been magically cleaned, no longer masking Alette with dread at its mere sight.

Tentatively, she touches it, and not a hint of the malaise remains.

"Did he get into her research?" Alette asks, spinning and looking at Axel. "Not the files, but the stuff in the conservatory, near all the plants?"

"Not while I was here," he says, but she's already pacing towards the door. "We need to make some sort of actual plan, here. We need to talk to Lyra and Mel, we can't just blindside them with this."

"Mel's going to hate it even more," Alette says, not stopping.

"And we need to figure out what we're gonna do!"

"Gonna do for what?" Alette asks, finally rounding back towards him. "We can't kick him out, we can't bar him from any room, we can't stop him from doing all—this—to every single place in here!"

Axel crosses his arms, but she can see the moment his brain kicks in. "What exactly did he do?" he asks, then waves his hand. "All I see is the furniture gone and the carpet rolled up."

Alette stops short.

Because of course he can't tell.

"He took everything that made it her place," she says, struggling through the weeds to find the proper words, "every little smidgen of magic, every little thread, every little scrap of a wind that suggested that my aunt existed in here, and now it's gone. And he wants to do it to everything, and then—" she cuts herself off, a knot in her throat.

Axel rubs his eyes again. "Let's go over to Lyra's," he says slowly. "We shouldn't bring her back, he might track her, but let's go grab your car and go talk to her."

Not able to speak, Alette nods.

～

ALETTE (4:52 PM): We're coming over, important news.
    LYRA (4:53 PM): Did you find her???
    ALETTE (4:53 PM): No.

～

IT'S a quick drive to go get Alette's unmarked car, then a longer one to Lyra's tiny mobile home, and Alette seethes through all of it. By the time they pull up the winding dirt and gravel road, she's in a proper bad mood.

The shadow dogs veer off once they hit Lyra's driveway, whimpering in fear as they run off to the mountainside, and Alette still doesn't know why they're following her—she still has two whole days to decide whether to help or not.

Driving seems to have smoothed over Axel's frustration, but it always does.

"If anyone has to fight Melekai, I'm nominating you," Alette says as he turns off the car.

"I don't want to be punched by Melekai," Axel says. "He may not be a demon anymore, but now he works out, and that's worse."

Alette rolls her eyes, then, with as big of a sigh as she can muster, opens the passenger's door to her car.

The drapes are tightly pulled shut, but Lyra's cat's head peeks up on the windowsill, watching them as they walk up, and that visibly cheers Axel up even further.

Before they can knock, Lyra yanks her door open, nodding at them to come in.

The mobile home is tiny, with one large armchair and one rickety kitchen chair, but somewhere in the last month Lyra found a few camp chairs and has them set up near her little kitchen table.

In the velvet green monstrosity of an armchair, Melekai sits, and he scowls at them almost reflexively.

It has none of the potency it used to, though, now that he's fully human. Now that Alette doesn't see a monster predator every time she glances at him, instead just a mildly annoyed hipster whose eyesight is so bad it turns out that he needs glasses even more than she does.

"What is it?" Lyra asks, and she walks with a slight limp to one of the camp chairs, extending her hand to Melekai so he can hold it. "You've barely left the headquarters, much less stopped over for a visit."

"Remember the College Dr. Frisse used to talk about?" Axel says, pacing the tiny kitchen. "They're being huge dicks right now."

Melekai scoffs.

"One is here, and he says magic is 'broken', whatever that means, and he's blaming Dr. Frisse for all of it, aaaaand he may want to talk to you and make you go to Europe for a bunch of tests and shit," Axel continues, and Melekai bristles.

"We haven't told him where you live," Alette reassures, as quick as she can, "but they're being properly awful."

She almost misses the look between Lyra and Melekai,

more significant than their usual fondness. "Go on," Lyra prompts.

Alette finds herself almost unwilling to do so, uncomfortably perched on the kitchen chair. Lyra's cat plops himself in her lap not at all gracefully, and Alette makes her hands unclench enough to stroke the cat's soft fur.

"He wants to take away all of Aunt Frisse's magic from the area," Alette murmurs. "He says it's breaking it apart."

Again, the significant look.

"What?" Axel asks, unsettled.

"We found something," Melekai says, finally speaking. He's still not quite used to talking around other humans, and rarely does. "We think you should see it."

LYRA WALKS them a half mile away, where her work once was, now long destroyed and in the process of being rebuilt.

But instead of the lingering taste of Terese's explosion, instead of the brilliant bitterness of the necromancer powers Lyra used inside, it's...decaying.

The plywood against the shattered windows is molded over, curling inwards like pieces of paper, edged in a toxic black crud.

Around it, the very magic in the area is crackling, halfway between audibly and inside her gut.

"Well, this is bad," Alette says automatically, instead of anything useful. "Aunt Frisse never came here."

"Whatever it is, it doesn't feel like demon energy," Lyra says, leaning against Melekai, who has an arm tucked around her, "not any one that I've ever met, at least."

"It's not," Melekai says, confident, and Alette peers at

him. He's fully human now, nothing extra about him, so how he would know for certain, she has no idea.

"What are you feeling?" Axel murmurs to Alette, his eyes narrowed at the peeling plywood.

"It's like static electricity," Alette whispers back, eyes tracking the sparks back and forth. "Something's spinning it all up and causing mayhem." It's partially inside the old convenience store, partially outside, like a maelstrom manifested in the middle of a few walls.

"I think it started last week," Lyra says, and Melekai nods absentmindedly in agreement. "It was just a bit of feedback, before, but it's worse now."

"And all anyone normal would see," Axel starts, "is everything just looking like shit. Like it got too wet and it's too gross now."

One of the shadow dogs creeps along her peripheral vision, hackles up, slinking low to the ground.

"Have you gone in?" Alette asks, and doesn't miss the flatly unamused look from Melekai. "It's a perfectly logical next step."

"I dunno, A, even without magic-o-vision, it still looks like it'll give you tetanus," Axel says, but still, he edges closer, nudging a piece of gravel out of the way with his boot.

It does nothing, just rolls over like a normal chunk of rock, but still, the shadow dog shies away, then lifts its head and howls.

Alette flinches, but nobody else reacts, not even Lyra or Melekai, who are examining a few fragments of still-broken glass.

The howl echoes through the trees, spreading through the mist and the dreary sky, bouncing off rocks and cliffs and dirt. The hair on Alette's arm rises, and far away, another howl rises to match.

Alette exhales, and the howl cuts off, and the dog watches her with red eyes glinting, teeth shining in the muted light of the sunset and the fog. Like its call was just to warn her off, to scare her away.

And it almost works.

Something settles deep in Alette, that this shadow dog might be trying to stop her from doing something. Might be giving her its own sort of order, just like the orders from Gurlien and from the College and—

"Well, I'm going to go in," Alette says, pulling her needle case out and selecting a wickedly sharp pronged needle. It's modeled after a certain type of net needle, but it glistens with gold.

It's her most offensive weaponry type needle, and if she holds it just right, she can also swipe it at someone's face and probably take out an eye.

Both Melekai and Axel raise an eyebrow at her choice, but she ignores them and rebuttons up her jacket, forcing the strings of protective magic into their place, and the hem of her jacket glows gold.

It's showy, and Lyra gives her a thumbs up.

"Breaking out the big guns, are we?" Axel asks, sarcastic.

"I have the gun in the car if you really want one," she snips back, then steps into the crackling spiral.

When dealing with unknown magic, charging directly into it is rarely the correct idea, and Alette knows this, but still it takes her breath away.

Sparks play along her skin, snapping up her hair, frizzing it out despite the braid. Her coat swirls around her, flapping in some unknown wind.

Shivers race down her arms, ending in her fingertips,

and a spark arcs down her needle, snapping into the dead air.

Whatever happened here, whatever magic had been expelled, is long gone, replaced by whatever the heck this is. There's no trace of Lyra's familiar energy, nothing of the demon that was Terese, not even anything of Melekai's power.

Alette takes another step in, towards the peeling plywood over the windows, and between one heartbeat and the next, the strange electricity occludes her sight of the others, enveloping her wholly.

She stills, but all she can hear is the crackling around her. No cars driving by, no idle banter from Axel and Lyra, nothing, as if she has disappeared from view.

Out of the corner of her eye, she sees the glint of the shining white teeth of the shadow dog, creeping closer. It's low to the ground, like it's avoiding the wind and the electricity, but still wants to be near her.

Alette takes the moment to lock eyes with the dog. She's fine, nothing is hurting, nothing is harming her, nothing is stopping her from breathing or from moving, and when she takes a deep breath she can still feel her magic inside of her, still feel the threads of the world seeping through her.

She should have brought her linen, should have planned ahead with some physical thread—she could have gotten a lot of readings.

The dog snaps his teeth at her, too far away for it to be a threat, and she nods at it.

"Right," she says aloud, but her words are taken by the swirling storm.

Maybe if she speaks, Axel and Melekai would be able to hear her, without the sound of the storm to block her out.

That settles something inside of her, and she glances in the direction she knows them to be standing.

"I am unharmed," she starts, as another spark snaps across her hand, stinging her fingers, "I can't see out of the storm, but I am fine."

The dog growls, then whimpers, and Alette takes another step inwards.

It's foolish, and she knows this, but her aunt also would never lose the opportunity to study something strange, something new, and after her magic at the compound was stripped away just earlier that day, it firms up a need inside of her to...to do something. Anything.

So, she opens the palm of her other hand to the electricity in the storm, and the sparks fly between her open hand and the needle, creating a bridge of crackling energy.

Her hand goes numb abruptly and she shakes it out, but the feeling doesn't return. Her braid whips behind her, strong enough to thump her on the small of her back, then on her shoulder.

The dog's growl raises in pitch, and it's joined by another, as the heeler shadow dog creeps alongside its friend.

It whimpers at her, darting close to her but shying away as the electricity snaps out at its nose.

Alette's feet slide closer towards the center of the maelstrom, outside her control, kicking up gravel and shards of glass, and her breath catches. Her aunt taught her to notice when the moment changes. To notice when things go wrong, and to know when to get out. And that moment comes now. The electricity snaps at her, sending pins and needles down her spine and sparks behind her eyes, and she gasps. The air is harsh all of a sudden against her throat, dry and acrid.

She turns against the wind, against the course of magic, the needle in her hand growing hot and then molten, sizzling against her fingers. But she throws her shoulder into the wind, to get away from it, to step out of the sparks but her feet don't move, the muscles in her legs trembling, and—

The heeler dashes close, snapping its teeth on the leg of her pant, and drags. The cloth rips, tearing sound loud against the din of the sparks, and Alette can't even hear her own heartbeat, hear her own gasps.

The dog fixes its teeth around her bare leg and pulls. Unaware that she's falling, she hits the pavement, and there's pain, somewhere beyond the sparks and the snaps and the numbness, but she's sliding out along the asphalt.

Suddenly, as suddenly as it all began, the sparks stop, and the silence is deafening.

Alette gasps, sitting up, and immediately there are hands on her, bracing her behind her head, guiding her.

Her eyes snap open, and she's outside the maelstrom. It still rages on, just a few feet away, sparking and crackling, but she's back in the misty sunset and the cold damp air.

Axel leans over her, and he's speaking, she can see his mouth move, but can't hear anything, and she just shakes her head at him.

Lyra's face swims in front of her, bracing her by the shoulder, and pain blossoms on the back of her head, on her ankle, and, frantic, Alette looks down.

There's a perfect set of bloody teeth marks on her ankle, gashed open.

The shadow dog in question sits, quivering, on the far side of the parking lot. The bigger dog hovers over it, snapping at the very air.

Her hand throbs with something vicious, and she drops

the needle, now a molten mess, and it drips to the ground. Blisters rise on her fingertips the moment she does.

"...get her to the hospital, something—" fades into her hearing, and it's Lyra, she'd bet money on it.

"Wait," Alette manages out, and sits up straighter, by herself, not leaning on anyone. Tentatively, she reaches a hand to the back of her head, and it comes away red.

"Yeah no, you're gonna need medical care," Axel says to her right, and, practiced, he starts to check her eyes for a concussion, like they used to do when they were teens and still learning their powers.

She follows his hand, but her eyes keep on straying down to her hand, to where she had gripped the needle tight, before she looks back over at the maelstrom.

It still crackles.

6

After a short explanation to the group and a sincerely annoying trip to the emergency room where they dug gravel out of her skull and gave her stitches on her ankle along with some mediocre pain medicine and put salve after salve on her fingertips, they finally release her to her friends.

Axel looks like he's about to vibrate out of his skull from energy, and Lyra looks like she's about to throttle him, but Melekai stares at her, eyes unamused.

"So, that was stupid," Axel says, the moment they get back to her quiet little sedan. "I don't know—"

"Like you haven't done stupider," Alette snaps back, well and truly in a horrid mood. "At least I got answers."

"Did you?" Melekai interrupts, voice flat.

"Well, we know it's not friendly," Alette says, which is a much weaker answer than she would have preferred. "We know it has enough energy to melt gold, but only if it's against flesh." Her other needles, safe in her case in her breast pocket, were untouched and fine. "We know it causes numbness and loss of muscle control."

"And apparently teeth marks," Lyra says, deeply skeptical. "We saw you just fine, but you just...fell."

It's dark now, properly night, and as they pull out of the hospital parking garage and towards Lyra's house, Alette just closes her eyes and wishes she was home.

Only to get thumped on her shoulder by Axel, who's driving and should absolutely not be doing that. "Hey, no, no falling asleep tonight," he says. "Do we have to set up some sort of watch so you don't conk out?"

"I wasn't falling asleep, I was being annoyed," Alette says as they wind up the gravel street towards the mobile house. "I told you everything."

She didn't, she wasn't about to mention the shadow dogs currently keeping pace with the car, and she can just feel Melekai's eyes boring into the back of her skull.

ONLY FIVE MINUTES after they drop Melekai and Lyra off, her phone buzzes in her pocket.

Clumsy with her bandaged fingertips, she pulls it out.

LYRA (7:21 PM): This is Melekai. What aren't you telling us?

ALETTE (7:22 PM): Get your own phone.

LYRA (7:22 PM): No.

LYRA (7:22 PM): I will delete the messages if you don't want her to know yet.

It's an unexpected kindness, and tears prickle at the edges of Alette's eyes, but she's not about to cry over this.

Axel glances over at her, but he knows her well enough that if she doesn't want to talk about it, she won't.

The temptation to talk to him is great, as the probable

one other person who might actually know anything, but it galls something inside of her.

ALETTE (7:23 PM): I don't know what you're talking about.

LYRA (7:25 PM): Shadow wolves or shadow lions?

LYRA (7:25 PM): Bite was too low for a shadow bear.

LYRA (7:26 PM): When did you start seeing them and how often?

Alette glances out the window, where the heeler shadow dog sprints along the car, teeth glinting in the light of the streetlamps, and she tucks her phone back into her pocket.

Instead of taking her to her apartment, however, Axel drives past the exit, going to the headquarters.

"More medical supplies there," he mumbles when she shoots him a questioning look.

She half suspects it's so he can keep a better eye on her, but she doesn't call him on it, instead choosing to watch as the two shadow dogs leap and bound next to the car, through the woods and the dark, until the grand gates of the compound rise in front of them.

The Wight with the curly black hair and brilliant blue eyes stands at the gate. He watches as the car passes, locking his gaze onto hers, and the two shadow dogs circle him instead, and he rests a hand between the ears of the heeler who pulled her out.

Alette refuses to crane her neck to watch him as they pass through the gates.

THE CAR ISN'T ALONE in the parking garage, with an unmarked black SUV parked in the spot closest to the elevator.

"Fuck," Alette says, fervent, and Axel nods along, "why the hell is he here right now?"

"No, this could be good," Axel says, and she shoots him a disbelieving look. "What, maybe he's seen this before."

He's not wrong, but it still settles poorly with Alette.

"And I might conscript him to help keep you awake," Axel continues, which is worse, "or who knows, maybe he'll snap his fingers and be able to make you better."

True healers are rare, almost as rare as necromancers, so Alette doubts it. "He'll just find a way to blame it on my aunt," she says.

Axel gives her a long look, before unbuckling himself from the driver's seat.

Before he can race around to the other side of the car, Alette gets herself out, despite the pounding in her head and the unsteadiness in her ankle.

"Man, I wish that Lyra's stuff worked on people who are still alive," Axel says, easily steadying her. "That'd just be...convenient."

Alette doesn't deign that with a response, instead striding towards the elevators with as much confidence as she can muster.

Gurlien is back in the sterile conference room, this time sitting on the floor, cross-legged, papers in neat piles around him, and he doesn't look up when she arrives.

"I see you found one of the breakages," he says, somehow managing to convey how deeply uninterested he is. "Not very intelligent to just dive fully into one, now is it?"

"Oh, so you knew they were dangerous, just told us to deal with one and didn't warn us?" Axel bursts out.

"I had full confidence your schooling would have prepared you," Gurlien says, nonchalantly flipping through a stapled packet, and with a flip of her gut, Alette recognizes them as bank statements. Her aunt's bank statements. "Clearly I was mistaken. Perhaps...perhaps we should leave the investigation to more experienced hands, than to those who would needlessly jeopardize themselves."

Alette and Axel very pointedly do not exchange looks.

"How goes the search for Terese?" Gurlien asks, voice calm. "Do I need to remind you how pressing that is?"

"I know," Alette says, then hesitates, "we don't have many leads, but we investigate those we have."

"Hmm."

And with that, he returns to his neatly sorted pile of paperwork, telling the story of Alette's aunt through her bank papers and financial trails.

AXEL DUMPS her on her favorite leather couch with a pillow to prop up her ankle, then settles into his own favorite armchair next to her, fixing her with an uncomfortable stare.

She knows that stare, he's concerned and thinks she's full of shit.

"I'll set a timer on my phone, every thirty minutes," she says, digging it out of her pocket with her uninjured hand, her fingertips grazing on the lump of gold that was once her curved needle.

She pulls that out too, and it clatters onto the wood of the coffee table, now a blob of inert material.

Axel whistles, peering close at it, then poking at it with his hand.

"Think we could forge a new one out of it?" Alette asks, staring hard at the chunk of metal. "It'd be a shame to lose it."

"Would you say the magic in there was more circular or more architectural?" he asks, which of course is the question that he, a former alchemist, would think of. "Any right angles, that sort of thing?"

"It was a tornado."

"Circular, then," he says, then prods the metal again. "Think we can still access the old magnifying spells she put in the basement? I wanna check out the molecular structure. See if it's still actually gold, or if it just looks like it."

"Only if he didn't take those down already," she says, and she's way more bitter than she should be.

"Tomorrow," he says, something grim and determined in his voice. "Let's do it tomorrow."

The day, Alette realizes with a jolt, that she's to meet the Wight at Shaman Island.

That she still doesn't know if she should go. If her ankle would let her, if her head would let her.

Axel snags her phone, setting the timer himself. "Thirty minutes, eh?" he asks. "Let's see how long it takes to get some pizza."

THE NEXT MORNING, after many hours of no sleep, she leaves Axel snoring in the armchair and finds herself stumbling down the stairs in search for food more filling than the now-cold pizza. She opens the door to their coffee room and kitchen, and Gurlien stands over her aunt's favorite coffee maker with a puzzled expression.

A small fission of triumph wells up in her, that he would be so confused by it. It's a hilariously confusing contraption, with steam and espresso and many other gadgets, and not magic at all.

Alette's successfully operated it twice, and that was enough for her.

"Good, you're awake," Gurlien says with too much confidence. "I wanted to discuss the breakage without the regular around."

"He's just as trained in magic as I am," Alette says, pulling out a bottle of iced tea from the fridge. Her family may gall at that, at her drinking something so westernized as iced tea, but she loves it.

"Not anymore," Gurlien breezes by her statement, "and I don't want him to think he has a place in these discussions."

This stops Alette short, with her pounding head and her aching ankle. "He does, though," she says. "He was just as hurt by Terese, more so than I, and Aunt Frisse helped raise him."

"And it's a tragedy, now, isn't it?" Gurlien says, then thumps the coffee maker, as if that would make it work. "You're going about this all wrong, with the magic in the area."

"I'm sure we are," Alette says, the barrier between her and her temper brittle.

At this, he appears to hesitate.

"I want to say this kindly," he starts, "but you're too tied up with preserving your aunt, instead of helping the world as a whole."

Alette crosses her arms, leaning against the fridge, so she doesn't throw the bottle of tea at him.

"Charging into a volatile storm"—he gestures at her hand, still awkwardly bandaged and still throbbing—"only demonstrates that you're not looking at this properly. You're looking at it bit by bit, item by item, instead of as one big picture." He finally gets the coffee machine to turn on, and Alette silently curses it. He doesn't deserve good coffee. "You can't unravel a mess if you only look at each individual string and pull indiscriminately."

"Then how would you do it?" Alette asks, and her voice is tight, her own throat choking her.

"Sanitize it," he says, light and easy. "Eliminate it all, with any magical quirks or beings or flows. Make the entire area forget that magic ever existed."

Alette has never wanted to slap someone harder.

"It'd be a pity with all the local character, any ghosts or spirits or Wights, but it'd be better," he continues, and Alette's brain latches onto that.

Wights.

Someone else actually knows about them, besides just Melekai.

"Wights?" Alette asks, skeptical, then. "Wait, ghosts exist?"

"You were raised in a world of magic, young lady, a world of demons and people raised from the dead, did you think that other spirits weren't real?" He nods to Alette. "I'll email you sanitation spells, they should be possible with someone of your...capabilities."

As if this is just a normal office conversation, he starts to brew his own coffee, which means he slept there overnight, and a new fission of anger blossoms in Alette.

"Why this approach?" Alette asks, swallowing down the anger with a swig of her iced tea. Might as well learn something, even if she can't give words to her feelings. "If there are other spirits"—her mind immediately conjures up the dog, shying away from the maelstrom, but dashing in to pull her out—"shouldn't we leave them alone?"

"Do you think this is the first time something like this has happened?" he asks, watching her a bit too closely.

"That someone has torn a hole into the world and left it hurting?"

It's a salient point, one that she had wondered, in the early moments of them trying to deal with Terese, but no research had been available to her.

"I hadn't found any sources," she says, instead.

"It's happened three times, in all of recorded history," he says. "This is the fourth. The first two times, the broken magic spread through the rest of the world like a virus, crossing Ley Lines and rifts in the world and points of power, breaking them down, rendering all magicians useless or dead for a generation."

"And the third?" Alette asks, hating that he's actually giving her actionable information.

"The third, we sanitized." He gives her a discomfited look, like he's just as uncomfortable with the idea as she is.

Aunt Frisse would hate it. Would hate it with a fiery passion, would fight for every inch of her area to stay how it is, to stay exactly as magically weird and funky as possible.

"I'd do it myself," he starts, "but it takes at least two, as the magic would...most likely kill a single person. Especially if it's a large break, or a large disruption."

"Grim," Alette says, out of a lack of anything else to say.

"But I wouldn't do anything for a few days," he continues, gesturing with the cup to her head, "the local magic would think you're too familiar, and you probably wouldn't be able to do a single thing."

And with that, ankle and lack of sleep and traumatic head injury be damned, she's going to go to that trail with the Wight.

Nobody's going to tell her she can't.

"I'll need your help this afternoon, with her bank accounts, you're listed on her will—" he starts.

"Actually, I can't," she interrupts, "pre-existing engagement."

He gives her an odd, sidelong look, then shrugs. "The next day, then."

"Take me home," Alette says, tossing Axel his keys the moment she gets back into the couch room, and he startles awake. "I have some ideas."

He takes a second to look groggy, so she tosses him a 5-Hour Energy drink, and he rolls with it. "Ideas?"

"I'm going investigating," she says, and something solid sits in her stomach. Something akin to resolve. "I'm going investigating and I don't want this absolute asshole to know what I'm doing."

7

They chill at her apartment for a few hours, reading some old scrolls that Aunt Frisse made her store in her apartment attic and Axel fiddles with some old surveillance equipment as the sun inches steadily downwards. They don't find anything, but it's still useful.

It'll take her one hour to drive to Placer's Cabin, and when Axel starts to drum his pen on her table a bit too loudly, she pushes herself up.

"Investigation time?" he asks, not looking up but continuing to tap his pen.

"Investigation time," she confirms, before hesitating. "I'm going to look at Shaman's Point." Better to tell him, so he knows where to go if she needs him, even if she doesn't want to tell him why.

Even if he'd probably believe her.

His face screws up in confusion. "A, that's a tourist trap."

"And if everything is all screwed up, maybe its name will actually mean something," she says, then shrugs, her mind racing. "I doubt our goon will know that it's nothing. Maybe he'll think it's named after an actual shaman."

"It's named after that guy that got really high and thought he could fight the tides," Axel says, which is true. "But sure, don't wreck my car, clean it if you get it muddy."

She takes a moment, leaving him in her kitchen, to put on her armor. Her tailored wool skirt that hits mid-calf, with her own protections woven in along the seams, along with a pair of lockpicks that she made a few years back. No nonsense wool tights that fit over her bandage, so she doesn't freeze to death. Her favorite boots, ones she wrote spells inside to make her surer footed and relatively water-proofed, that stabilize her throbbing ankle quite nicely. Then a long sleeve shirt and a wool vest, gold embroidery mixed with spells to give her insight, to give her an edge on figuring things out. She fixes the end of her braid with a strip of linen muslin, in case she has to do a reading and can't find anything else.

She looks like a caricature of a librarian, but it's far better to be laughed at than to be unprepared.

"It's a tourist trap," Axel reminds her as she strides out. "The clerk at the souvenir shop is going to think you're insane."

She grabs her coat, swings it over her shoulders, tucking her needle case into the breast pocket next to the glob of gold, then grabs an extra bobbin of plain cotton thread from her table. While cotton thread can't do anything strongly, it can do most things well enough, and until she knows what she's up against it'll be good.

Axel's eyebrows steadily rise.

"I'll be fine," she says, pointed.

"Sure," he says, skeptical.

She gives him a nod and tosses him her car keys, then strides out, and both of the shadow runners are at her door now, sitting and waiting.

She hesitates a split second, then pushes forward.

The other dog, now still, is larger. More Doberman shaped.

They both watch, eyes blood red, as she starts Axel's car and pulls away from her apartment, before kicking into a run and becoming little more than a blur of shadows and glinting teeth, even in the full sunlight.

THE DRIVE to Placer's Cabin is peaceful, if full of ice and slippery roads. It has obviously snowed there more recently than her place or the headquarters, despite being closer to the ocean.

But she winds the behemoth of the Mustang up cliffside paths and back down, keeping an eye on the sun setting.

Not like she's going to miss it—she'll be exactly ten minutes early—she knows better than to cut something like that too close.

This close to the ocean, the very magic seethes with the power of the waves. Of the salt and the wind, pulling at her from even inside the car.

Too soon, though, she pulls up to Placer's Cabin, at the tiny little parking lot that's empty besides the store clerk's car, and steps out. The wind scours her cheeks and ruffles her hair, though her braid lays heavy along her back.

The dogs nip at the wind, pacing around her.

She takes a deep breath, at the beauty of the landscape and the expanse of ocean in front of her, and feels.

Magic, more than she's ever thought was at this place, swirls around her, and if she reaches out she could just grasp it in her hands, not even needing a needle. It flows, towards the peak on the beach, reaching towards the small cluster of trees at the end.

Shaman's Point.

A tidal island, it's only reachable by foot in low tide. The place where that one guy tripped balls and stayed for a few days.

The Cabin itself was built as a tourist stop, to sell trinkets to people wanting to see the beauty of the land, but not many tourists come up here in winter. Grimy snow clings to the edges of boulders and the tallest tips of trees, and the parking lot has the skin of ice of a really bad plow job.

It's a common hiking spot, a place for people to meet before spiraling off to any of the number of trails nearby, and the Cabin sells junk food to hungry hikers most of the time.

The heeler shadow dog dashes out towards the beach, then circles back to her.

"Are you herding me?" Alette asks it, idly horrified that she's talking to a shadow creature. "I'm here, I said I would be here."

It tilts its head at her, then dashes back off towards the strip of sand.

Of course it's low tide. Of course this Wight is going to make her go out to a tidal island half an hour before sundown, in the fading days of a grimy winter.

She pops the trunk on Axel's Mustang and pulls out his favorite survival kit. It's a light backpack, but there's some food and a blanket and a flashlight and a gun, just in case.

Not that she knows whether or not guns would work on the Wight.

She adjusts the bag so it's closer to her body, instead of being built for someone Axel's size. After he got his magic taken away, after he could no longer just conjure up something he needs...he got a bit obsessed with safety items. Made her store a similar bag in her car, made Lyra leave one next to her door.

It's far from the worst coping mechanism, so Alette didn't comment on it.

Her hand grazes her needle case, and both dogs shy away.

"Where's your owner?" she asks them, taking the moment to lock Axel's car and wave hello at the bored store clerk. "He's the one that asked me here."

There's another gust of wind, and the magic seethes with it, taking her breath away.

There is so much more than there was before.

Furthermore, this is so much angrier than it was before. It sits below her gut, below her appreciation of the beauty, below her frustration with being summoned, but it burns all the same.

She pulls out her trustworthy Moleskin, jots down those thoughts as notes. Before, it had only given her the vague feeling of beauty, none of this...

One of the dogs snaps at the wind, and she catches a glimpse of the magic in its mouth.

"You'll have to forgive them, they used to love this place," the Wight says, from behind her, and she doesn't jump only by sheer willpower. "It's the knot they hate the most."

Alette folds up her notebook, tucking it away, and the Wight crosses towards her from the cluster of trees next to the Cabin.

"I see you are still alive," he says, almost cordial, with a glance to her ankle. "I apologize if they injured you."

"They got me out," she says, shifting. Not quite wanting to say thank you, when her head hurts so badly and her fingers throb.

"This one," he says, resting his hand on the head of the heeler, "was quite distressed by having to bite you."

"Thanks?" Alette says, a bit off-kilter, "I'd rather not have that happen again."

"They only bite when given an order to," he continues, which, again, is useful information and would have been useful information earlier, "or when needed to complete an order."

She eyes him, unsure of all of this again. Of going off and investigating when she's still pretty injured, with a man she doesn't even know.

"You're going to have to explain things," she warns, short, then strides towards the strip of sand, so she's out of glimpse of the clerk. "I don't appreciate half answers."

"I don't suppose you do," he says, but his ice blue eyes are trained on the small cluster of trees as they walk towards the beach proper. "Did the Grand Magician ever teach you about Ley Lines?"

"Only that they exist and that we cannot change them," Alette says, rankled a bit, but she keeps up with him. She's not going to let him walk faster than her, hurt ankle be damned.

The sand is soft and damp beneath her boots, like she could lay in it and be cushioned enough for sleep.

He gives her another sidelong glance, before his eyes flicker back to the trees. "Yet you went into one yesterday, and I dare say it changed with you in it."

"Was that what that was?" Alette asks, staring hard at the line of trees, as if it could give her the patience and the steel to do this hike ahead of them. "I think it hurt me more than I hurt it."

There's a subtle shift in the air, and all of a sudden her skin crawls.

Or, rather, doesn't quite crawl, but reacts. Like how it feels when she unexpectedly brushes against a fabric of an unusual texture, rests her hand on velvet she didn't know was there.

She stops, and she's barely to the line where the tide would begin to come back in. Her boots sink in the damp sand.

The Wight's blue eyes flicker to her, an ever-so-slight motion. "No," he says, unsettling in his calmness, "I think you definitely had the bigger impact."

Alette takes a deep breath, and the air still smells of salt and wet rocks, but there's something else, something solid, bothering along the edges of her awareness, and the Wight just watches her. Watches as she processes.

"There are other magicians," she starts, then falls silent, as the wind and seething magic around her pulse at that sentence, "there are others you could've contacted about this."

He shrugs, nonchalant. "We tried."

"What happened here?" she asks, instead of following his train of thought. "This used to be a calm place."

"The demon called Terese, in her mad escape to stop her pain, tried to combine the Ley Lines and twist them together until they made something she could use," the Wight says, and starts walking again. "The Grand Magician—"

"My aunt," Alette interrupts, and his eyebrows flash up at her tone. "She was my aunt, not some stranger."

He inclines his head. "Your aunt tried to untangle it, but despite her powers, she was missing something."

"I don't have anything she didn't have in spades," Alette says, discomfited, but she follows him anyways.

The little glimpses of magic get brighter, like the rainbows cast by the edge of a cut piece of glass, and the two shadow dogs nip at them as they trudge towards the line of the sea.

For lack of a better term, Shaman's Point is on some sort of peninsula, and they have to walk on a thin strip of stone and sand jutting above the surf. The water churns in the wind, tossing a spray up them at their feet.

"Do you have a plan for getting off the island?" Alette asks, pitching her voice up to be heard over the wind. "The tide is quick here."

"I know exactly how quick the tides are," he shoots back, that asshole, and the two dogs shy close to him.

If she looks hard enough, they even leave footprints in the sand.

"Your dogs, do they have names?" Alette asks, and the heeler turns and stares at her, his teeth glinting in the light of the waves. "If they're chasing me everywhere, can I refer to them as anything?"

They're halfway to the Point, and she's asking about the dogs. Instead of anything else she could be focusing on.

"Grey," he says, pointing to the larger one, "and Spot." The heeler nips at the air at his name, splashing in the shallows.

"Original," Alette says, because naming dogs after their physical appearances is apparently still a thing when you're an unknown entity of magic.

"I'm Zoel," he continues, with another sidelong look to her. "Any Wight in the area, say my name and they will know where to find me." And he hesitates in his even strides to the beach, and tilts his head at her, expectant.

Because after all this time, of him appearing in front of her, chatting at her, terrifying her with everything that is unknown, apparently he never knew her name.

"Alette," she says, after a brief internal struggle of whether or not she should reveal her actual name to a magical being.

He nods, satisfied, and continues on his walk.

"Well, Alette who does not think she can affect Ley Lines and thinks her dead aunt is better than her, tell me what you see."

"Well, Zoel who made his dogs follow me across Vancouver and Northern Washington, I see a beach and some trees." Still, she takes a deep breath as they near the island point, and the glimmers of magic—actual, visible magic, not just the feeling and taste of magic - grow brighter.

It's not quite like static electricity, not like the mess she saw yesterday, but the air is still charged. Like all it would take is one motion to set off a chain reaction.

Her head throbs, and her fingertips burn.

"And something is refracting light," she continues, and he nods, like she's a student who needs encouragement, standing on the sand and stone between the peninsula walkway and the island itself, "like the very nature of magic is splitting it into colors."

"This goes without saying, but it really shouldn't do that," Zoel says, then, with the confidence of knowing what he's getting into, steps onto the island proper.

Both the dogs whimper.

He rests his hand on the larger one—Grey's—head, and the dog pushes up against him, a blur of shadow and flashing red eyes.

"It's safe for you," he says, and it takes Alette a split second to realize she's hesitating, still on the stone peninsula. "You don't have to worry about it sparking up like the one yesterday."

"Do you have any primary sources?" Alette asks, taking care of her ankle while stepping on the island itself. Wind whooshes past her, and her ears pop. "If I'm going around solving these things and getting injured, I would like primary sources."

"We have written ephemera," he says with a shrug, "stories of every little magical distraction, every twist and turn in this kingdom's magic, every fluctuation that has ever been recorded. The history of the land laid out in flows of magic. If that would interest you."

She turns her head and stares at him. "Yes. Yes, that would interest me."

"That'd be easy to arrange a delivery to the warded compound," he says, but he's staring out at the trees, hands on his hips. "Might help you understand all of this, why it's so critical."

She follows his gaze, and if she squints, there's almost a thread easing its way through the trees, into the thick grove, before the words he says crash down on her.

"Not at the compound," she blurts out, and both the dogs turn towards her at her tone, "not...not right now."

He shrugs one broad shoulder.

Confident, however, he reaches out, wrapping his hand around the thread like it's a physical thing, rolling it between his fingers, as if feeling for something.

"Tell me, Alette, what do you remember of being dead?"

Nobody had asked that.

Alette stills, and her fingertips throb in time with the pulse of energy around her.

"Not much," she says, cautious, "it was only for fourteen hours."

"More than most people who are alive can say," he says,

grinning at her, wide, with a strip of magic around his hand. "Did the necromancer tell you what would have changed?"

He gestures her forward, holding the strip of magic out to her.

"I'm not touching that unless you give me a detailed breakdown of how it's not going to hurt me," she says.

In her breast pocket, safely tucked next to her needle case, the glob of gold grows warm.

Not molten hot, not like it was the day before, but warm.

"People who were once dead have a different view of the world," he continues, his hand still out towards her, "even by mundane medical miracles, if they know how to look, they can see past what normal humans can perceive."

The only other person Alette knows that was raised by the dead was Lyra's own brother, and he never reported anything like this.

And Melekai. If he counts. He doesn't.

"And you," he pauses in the walking to hold out the fistful of magic towards her, "are actually educated in magic. From someone who had respect for this area, from someone who wasn't afraid to experiment."

"That's...certainly true," Alette says, still keeping her hands tucked into her pocket. "Probably a bit too much."

He nods at that, giving her the point. "But you're the only one who can help here, and I would not risk that by handing you something dangerous."

"What about Lyra?" At his blank look, she elaborates. "The necromancer? With Melekai, you know him."

"I do not keep track of many human names," he says, conversationally, but drops the hand holding the magic strip out to her, instead following it deeper into the grove. "Part of our deal with Melekai was to not embroil her in our business, and that he would bargain with any demons that would come in on our behalf."

Alette follows him, and the sand of the beach fades into the soft loam of the island proper. Despite the time of year, the trees are still green, and vivid moss carpets every surface.

Holly berries twinkle under half-melted ice, glinting in the setting sun.

Melekai hadn't told them the details of the deal, and no matter how much Alette has pried, Lyra refuses to press him on that, so this kernel of information is at least something.

"How could he, if he's human now?" Alette asks, finally, after taking in the crisp scent of the moss and the spruce and the berries.

It's not even a quarter mile away from the parking lot, yet it's like she's been transported somewhere entirely different. Somewhere outside of the bleak winter, outside of the tension of the beach. Somewhere magic glimmers off of each surface, like a haze in the very air.

Spot races past them, deeper into the grove of trees, and Grey streaks after him, a blur of shadow and darkness.

"He has his ways, I'm not going to divulge them," Zoel says, and it pulls her attention back, away from all the magic and everything, though the magic is still gathered in his hand, wrapped around like a rope. "This"—he gestures with the rope, and suddenly, like his movement illuminates it, the rope spreads out from him, glimpses of magic racing away, spreading through the grove—"is a Ley Line."

The stupid part of Alette's brain immediately compares it to an LED light suddenly plugging in.

It's twisted between each tree, each branch, knotted around leaves and twigs and stones and mired into the moss, like a ball of yarn batted around by a kitten until it covers every little part of a room.

"Oh," Alette says, intelligent, and there are strands twisted beneath her boots, trampled where they had walked. "Terese really did this?"

"Hold out your hand," he says, then shakes his head. "No, your injured hand."

8

A t first, Alette thinks she misheard him, but he still stands there, fist full of magic, his dogs racing everywhere between the trees.

Second, she thinks he's mocking her, and it settles poorly in her gut, below everything she tries to squash down.

Then, her brain actually kicks in.

"Why?" she asks, then shakes her head, as if she could clear the uncharitable thoughts from her brain. "I mean, I'm willing to do it, with a clear reason."

"You really are a scholar type, aren't you?" he says, bemused. "Because it's the hand already touched by a knot, and you'll have the scars to prove it. Because like draws to like, and it'll work better."

"Like draws to like, right," Alette repeats, and flexes her bandaged hand. It throbs. "I can assume that's a universal rule with this?"

"As much as there can be one," he says, then dumps one end of the rope into her hand.

Immediately, her hand spikes with sensation.

Not necessarily bad, not necessarily pain, but intense nonetheless. Like every little nerve in her fingertips connects with it, seeping through it.

It's soft, like a rope made from velvet, plush, though it pulsates with something so strongly akin to power that the hairs on her arm raise.

"This is what your aunt thought humans couldn't affect," he says, and there's smugness in his tone, a smugness that a less entranced Alette would have serious issue with. "This is what Terese tried to pull together to save herself, and now this is what's causing all those issues on that beach."

"Right," Alette says, and the Line throbs in time with the thudding of her heart.

It's beautiful, and it chases a shiver down her spine. It's tender, in all the ways the electricity at Buggees was not, and the glob of gold in her pocket is a soothing warmth.

Tentative, she ducks, unlooping it from a nearby branch, straightening it, and it almost snaps tighter in her hand. Like by unraveling that little piece of the puzzle, it pulls stronger to where it's supposed to be.

"This is beyond strange," she says, crouching down next to a dead brush it's completely tangled in, and she takes a moment, observing the pattern of the rope in the twigs. "Wouldn't it be possible to just find both edges of the Line and...pull really hard?"

"Only if you wanted this island wiped off the face of the ocean," he replies, quick, but a small smile plays over his lips. "Humans are always so strange, with their ideas of how to solve problems."

"I believe that," Alette says, and her ankle wobbles with the crouch, despite her boots. Careful, she tugs the rope free of a branch, and the twigs snap at her touch.

It's not unlike unravelling a mess in her sewing machine, if all her thread was warm and shifting in her hands.

Spot the shadow heeler sprints close to her, just long enough to thrust his snout in her injured hand, before dashing away.

Keeping her injured hand on the Line—the actual Ley Line, she's touching the very nature of magic itself—she unties the strip of linen from her braid. She doesn't have a free hand to stitch thread into the linen, to actually weave a spell to do some readings, but she rests the linen against it, and the golden threads she wove in long ago shine bright.

"I'm curious," she says, at his questioning look, "I've never been able to study something like this, and I can't thread a normal needle right now, so I'm checking to see what I can preserve and do readings later."

The corner of his mouth tugs up, before he turns from her, gently untangling the rope from around an ancient spruce.

The sun finally dips below the horizon, darkening the grey skies above them, and the Line glows anew.

There are a thousand questions she wants to ask, and a thousand thoughts racing through her brain.

"My aunt came here?" she asks, finally, as the strip of linen glows just as bright as the Line itself, until she ties it back into her hair.

It glimmers, ever so slight, catching the corner of her eye as she turns her head.

"Several times," Zoel calls, almost on the other side of the grove, propping himself up on a tree to get a loop of the line. "She had no idea we were watching."

"Knowing her, she probably had some idea," Alette responds, then she looks back over her shoulder.

The tide is licking in already, and only the rocks from the strip are sticking above the water.

"Don't worry," he says, as if he could read her mind, which is a wholly unwelcome idea, "you'll be able to get home safe and dry."

And she's had to trust him so many times this day, it almost stretches her temper, but she tamps that down.

"Could she see these?" Alette asks, holding a bit of the magic in her hand. Spot wiggles between two trees to get close to her, pressing his snout against where he bit her to drag her out, then sprints away.

"See, no. Sense, I think so." Zoel says, and he's braced himself between a stump and a giant spruce, pulling down a tangle. "She never spoke aloud, and her eyes didn't focus on them, but she followed them along by touch. Couldn't change them, just felt."

This is another aspect of her aunt she never knew. Another thing kept secret from her.

"She was smart, for a human, but couldn't truly affect the magic around her," he continues, and it pangs something inside of her. "We mourned her, and her effect on the world."

"Me too," Alette murmurs, almost too soft for him to hear, but he nods all the same.

It's so dark she can barely see the two dogs as they sprint around, only visible when they pass in front of a piece of magic that's currently alight. At one point, Alette swears she sees Grey, the bigger of the two, sitting and panting in a corner, but when she blinks the glint of his eyes are gone.

They work in silence as the sun fully sets, lit only by the strange glow of the Lines, and an hour must've passed before he speaks again.

"Don't be surprised if you see...more...now," he says, his

accent rounding out the vowels, sanding them down. "Humans are still relatively unknown to us, when it comes to this level of magic."

"More of this"—Alette gestures with the Ley Line—"or more people like you?"

"Well, yes," he says, and she can hear the humor in his voice, "more Wights will want to investigate, want to see who you are, with your break-touched fingertips and the Ley Line aura around you, but I mostly meant more Lines. More magic beneath the surface of things, more than you could see before."

He tugs loose another loop, and Alette can feel it sing in her bones. They're almost done, somehow, with just a few more tangles in the far edge of the trees.

The Line in her hand tightens, like it can tell it's almost done as well.

"It's easier, with a human here," he mutters, almost to himself, as they tromp in the dark to the far side of the tidal island.

Alette wants to ask why but keeps it to herself. For now.

She's compiling a list. Things to ask, things to investigate, things to research, but in the dark on an island isn't quite the time.

With the two dogs at his side and lit from the strange glow, he looks less of a human than he ever has before, in the times Alette has seen him since she was raised.

The tangle leads them to another soft sand beach, facing the wide ocean, and wind tussles the strands of hair that have fallen free from her braid.

The rope lies on the damp sand in front of them, glowing with something akin to bioluminescence, with the far end disappearing off across the sea, perfectly straight, knee high on the beach.

Which adds another question, with what do they do with the curvature of the earth, but for a split second the beauty takes away her breath.

Without speaking, Zoel sits on the sand next to the tangle, and she folds herself on the other side of it, her ankle grateful for the chance to rest. The two dogs settle in near them, their eyes glinting.

This bit isn't tied onto any of the trees or seashells or rock outcroppings, instead knotted deep on itself, laying limp.

"This is where the demon that was Terese stood," Zoel says, as if that clears up things, "after she tried to pull everything together, after she tried to get rid of everything that had happened to her." He gives her a sidelong look. "She stood here, and screamed, until she cried."

"I'm not going to feel sorry for her," Alette says. "She killed my Aunt. She hurt my best friend. She—briefly —killed me."

"You don't have to forgive her to acknowledge that she was in pain," he says, resting a hand on the knot. "It can be tragic and still never justify her actions." Slowly, he begins to pick apart the knot, and Alette watches. "It was odd, having two demons in our area for so long. They're always so solitary, and both of these had so much to do with the humans."

The moon rises over the horizon, lighting up the sand and paling the light from the Ley Line.

"And now, they want me to track her down," Alette says, and he gives her a sharp look, "see how much of a danger she is. Whatever's left of her."

He raises an eyebrow, then hands her a section of the Line, as he untangles a bit, tugging on the mess. "I doubt she'd be a danger to you, now," he says, and his voice is so carefully neutral that the hair on her arms raise.

"So you know her," Alette says, gripping tight on the Line in her hand. "Where is she, what is she—"

He shakes his head, resolute. "No."

"No, you don't know her? Do you know where she is? Is she just human now? What—"

His face pinches off, and both dogs rise to standing, so Alette falls silent.

"When she spoke to herself, your aunt mentioned a lot of 'theys', and it was never a good thing," he says, finally. "Is this the 'they' that's messing with your magic past the gates where we cannot go?"

"Yes," Alette says, crisp, tugging on one of the bits of knot with more force than is probably necessary. It squelches in her hand, a wholly unpleasant feeling.

"They should stop," he says darkly, and Alette agrees with him, privately. "They should stop and leave our shores for wherever they came from."

He climbs to his feet, the one final small bit of the knot in his hand, and Alette follows him up, her ankle protesting, her head thudding.

"This'll be bright," he warns her, and she takes a grip on the other side of the knot.

All that remains of it is a little slipknot, barely something that would stop her from sewing or knitting.

"Stand over there, and when I say so, pull," he instructs, almost formal. "Close your eyes if you need to."

After all that work, Alette wouldn't close her eyes if you paid her.

She stands where directed, loosely holding her edge of the slipknot, and to anyone looking on, she must look close to insane. Close to utterly batshit, standing alone on a beach in the moonlight, holding nothing with a heavily bandaged hand.

Even in the dim light from the moon peeking through the clouds, she can see him grin from across the sand, see the flex of his hand on the glowing Ley Line. See Grey and Spot at his side, vibrant and real and still cloaked in shadow.

In all her magical education, in everything she ever did or learned or studied, despite being raised from the dead, despite all of Axel's alchemy and her aunt's mysteries and Lyra's healing and the faces of demons she can now see, nothing quite compares to the raw power she's seeing. Raw power she's feeling, with a hand on a very foundation of magic in the area, that she helped untangle, that she helped affect.

It's exhilarating.

The power reflects in his eyes, glints off the dog's teeth.

"Pull," he says, and she does, throwing her weight into it.

For a long moment, it doesn't budge, and she can see him dig into the sand, pulling as well, and glimmers of light spiral up his arms.

Then with a pop so loud her ears ring, the knot comes loose, and the entire island is lit from the release.

Light, brilliant light, spikes up towards the sky, arching high above the trees and disappearing into the night clouds. Like a beacon to the entire world, like something shining for everything to see.

The Line rips itself loose from her fingertips, taking her bandages with it, and she stumbles back, falling on her butt onto the sand.

Zoel braces himself, releasing the Line like it's a string on a balloon, his entire face awash in the light.

She watches as the light streams upwards, a brilliant declaration, and somewhere inside of herself she can feel the inherent rightness of it. That this is how it should be, how it should always be.

Both the dogs dash forward, nipping at the light, but playful. Like they're nothing more than normal animals, playing with something familiar.

"That," Zoel starts, "is how this is supposed to feel."

He half stumbles towards her, taking a seat on the damp sand next to her, and there's a faint sheen of sweat visible on his face despite the chill, lit from the light.

"How are people not seeing this?" Alette asks, dumb, gesturing towards the giant fucking beacon only a few feet away. "Wouldn't the American coast guard have an issue with it?"

He laughs, and it's an honest sound, undignified, like it's pulled from him.

"What, they might?" Alette says.

"If they're particularly sensitive, they might see some-thing briefly shining in the sky but"—he gestures again at the shining beacon—"I'd be surprised if any non-magician even recognized this, and even then, they'd have to be here to feel it, and…" He smiles, wide, and it's a good look. A look of competency, a look of satisfaction at doing his job. "But this is a good thing."

Alette looks back towards the beacon and has to agree.

9

S uddenly, her phone beeps, breaking the moment, and she flinches. It beeps again, and again, multiple texts all at once.

"Ah yes, technology," he says, leaning back and staring at the light. "That probably got tangled up in all of this, too."

"So people will have cell phone signal here now?" Alette asks, pulling her phone out.

AXEL (4:28 PM): Asshole is being demanding again. Said you blew him off.

AXEL (4:43 PM): Hope the tourist trap is safe?

AXEL (6:01 PM): You good?

LYRA (6:19 PM): Axel is being neurotic at me, can you respond so he stops doing this?

LYRA (6:26 PM): Srsly.

Then, as she holds the phone in her hand, it beeps again.

LYRA (7:10 PM): Did you just do something? Mel just about jumped out of his skin.

GURLIEN (7:10 PM): Did you see that, where are you

and the other one, you need to come back to Dr. Frisse's Compound now.

"I think people saw it," Alette says, showing the phone to Zoel, who leans away from it while making a face, "at least, Melekai felt something."

"Any other demon within a few hundred kilometers probably did," he says. "And there's enough of a demon inside him that it probably felt very strange."

The dogs circle her, but it's not nearly as terrifying as before.

"And the other..." He glances sideways at her, still illuminated from the beacon. "Is that your 'they' who is giving you orders?"

"Yes," Alette says, careful, staring at her phone.

"Hmm."

When he doesn't say anything more, Alette taps out a few messages.

ALETTE (7:12 PM): I'm safe, sorry cell signal was bad, tell Lyra and Mel that I'll fill them in later.

AXEL (7:12 PM): Goddamn what did you do? They said it's impressive.

ALETTE (7:13 PM): Long story.

"Is that the hurt one?" Zoel says, leaning over her shoulder just enough to see.

"Yes," she responds, still looking down at her phone.

"I've never seen that before," Zoel says, and it's almost soft, "someone who had power and then had none. It must be terrifying for him."

It is, but that feels like some sort of betrayal of Axel's business, so Alette doesn't respond to that.

ALETTE (7:15 PM): Felt something strange, what was that? Didn't look out the window.

"Interesting," he comments, and Alette refuses to react

to that, "you seem like someone who would always tell the truth."

"Not when it doesn't suit me," she says, sharp, but he huffs out another laugh. "Now, in the interest of no other demons coming and finding us while we sit on a beach under a beacon of literal magic light, how are we getting back?"

The light clearly illuminates the sea, no land bridge to be seen, and white caps don the waves.

"Melekai's the closest," he says, conversational, "and I doubt anyone else would want to necessarily get closer."

While it doesn't answer her question, he stands, brushing the sand off his hands in a brisk motion, before holding a hand out to her to help her up, pulling with an ease of someone who's used to lifting much heavier things than her.

"This way," he says, nodding down the edge of the beach, and they skirt around the trees of the tidal island, staying in the soft sand.

The light doesn't dim necessarily, but it feels a bit less intense. Less of a brilliant shock against her senses.

"Now that you've seen some interesting magic," he starts, almost boasting, "done work with a Ley Line, actually affected the state of magic that'll be felt for miles, do you want to see some Wight magic?"

It means that none of this so far has been, so she raises an eyebrow at him. "Only if you tell me exactly what I'm dealing with."

He grins, as if that is a predictable response. "I can't spoil all my secrets," he says, and it's almost like he's teasing her. "I need you to come back to help me more, the entire area is covered in these knots, and I don't want them to spread."

Gurlien's words echo back at her, and, with a flip to her

stomach, she realizes what his sanitation would entail, if all of this would go away.

She takes a breath, then another.

People don't think of her as hot-headed, not really. They always see the mild-mannered young woman with her hair in her braid and glasses on her face, and don't generally think about what's going on underneath it all.

But her entire life she's had to hold back her initial gut reactions. Make herself wait, make herself find out more information.

And this is one of those cases. Because while Gurlien might be infuriating, and his words might suggest it, the small idealist part of her can't really comprehend the idea that the College would actually advocate for some sort of magical extinction of the spirits in the area.

She needs more information.

Zoel's watching her, eyes sharp, so she gives him one of her practiced smiles. "I expect some of those written ephemera before the next one, I won't do this for free," she says.

"Of course," he says, easy. "You'll get it by tomorrow."

Then, he holds a finger to his lips, before letting his other hand drift to his side, hovering near his hip, so she hangs back.

He hums, something on the bare edge of her hearing, like a piece of electronics being turned on close to her. Something she's not meant to hear, not designed to hear, but by some trick of her biology she now can.

And before her eyes, the sand around him stirs, swirling up together, like a bad special effect in an outdated movie. It forms a vague structure, like a skeleton of a canoe.

Before it actually coalesces, it disappears, the sand settling back down.

Clearly waiting for her to be startled, he rests a hand where the boat had briefly formed, like the air is solid. Even though it looks like nothing is there, Alette knows that something is now.

"I've seen enough alchemy to not be impressed," Alette says, but drifts closer, reaching out with her injured fingertips until they graze a cool, metallic edge. "Invisible is new, though."

The metal warms against the injuries on her hand, soothing.

"It's not alchemy," he protests, but pushes the invisible canoe closer to the water's edge. "Climb in, this'll carry both of us."

She's seen crazier things that day, so she does, and he pushes the canoe into the water before jumping in himself.

Without paddles, the canoe cuts cleanly across the water, unaffected by the white caps on the waves.

The dogs streak across the shallow water, blurs of shadows and bursts of motion, splashing around the now submerged land bridge and racing towards the shore.

Alette watches them, then looks down, where she's sitting in an invisible boat, but the water is too dark to see through.

"I want to come back here," she says suddenly, surprising herself with the words. "I want to see what this"—she points to the bottom of the boat, where her boots are completely dry—"would look like when I can actually see through the water."

"That can be arranged," he says, amused, "it's a fairly easy trick."

"Good," she declares, and he smiles at her.

The light from the beacon is lesser now as the boat glides the quarter mile back to the shore. If she looks back, looks over her shoulder, she can still see it, but it no longer casts shadows, no longer illuminates Zoel's expressions.

"May I take you to the main Line? At some point, not right now," Zoel asks, formal, and Alette eyes him.

"You mean this isn't it?" she asks, gesturing from the boat to the brilliant beam in the sky.

"Not even in the least," he murmurs, and the boat glides smooth across the black water. "It runs through the Birmingham harbor, spiraling out on the rivers and actuaries. This is just one small part of it."

"What happens if that one gets tangled?" Alette asks, still looking at the glowing magic of the island.

He falls silent, and for a few brief moments there's no noise but the gentle surruisisions of the ocean against the boat.

"Tangled, people—people like me—will starve, and slowly. Magicians will find their magic waning, until the spells that used to come as easy as breathing exhaust them, and they won't know why." His face is grim in the beautiful light. "If it breaks...if it fragments, if it disappears in any way, it'll kill."

She lets her hand rest against the side of the boat, dipping into the cool Pacific water. "I take it you're keeping a strict watch on it?"

He nods again. "It's stable, for now." Which is not the answer Alette would like. "If breaks fizzle back to it, it'd detonate, but"—he gives her a smile, and there's something heartbreakingly bashful in the smile—"but untangling messes like this stop the likelihood of it breaking. So that's why...that's why I'm doing this."

Before she can think of how to word any of her follow-up questions, the boat is at the shore, and he helps her out, gingerly, so she doesn't need to even get her feet wet. It's mistier on shore than it was just that short distance on the island, and the moon no longer peeks through the clouds.

The Cabin and convenience store are long closed, and Axel's Mustang is the only thing left in the parking lot, but he walks her across the pavement to it.

Spot dashes towards her, and, tentatively, she holds her palm out to the smaller dog.

He stops in his tracks, before giving Zoel an obvious look.

"He's worried you're mad about the bite," Zoel says, standing under the streetlamp. "I told you, he didn't like doing that."

Alette tucks her hand back into her pocket, and the dog bounds away. "They won't hurt me?" she asks, firming something up inside of her.

"Not unless they need to," Zoel answers.

"Them running next to my car, will that affect me?"

"Most likely not," he says with a shrug. "I don't know what they'll do if the car hits them, but they know how to avoid vehicles."

Then, he turns towards her, and even after the Ley Lines and the beacon and the invisible canoe, she's struck with his intensity.

"In two days, meet me at the eighteenth kilometer up Sunshine Coast," he says, almost formal. "There's a small marker with a cross, where someone died. Fifty feet away, there's another knot like this."

She'll have to find a way to get away, to skirt Gurlien's awareness and such, but she nods.

"It'll be best to be done at noon," he continues. "I'll have one of the dogs bring you the books."

And without another word, he turns, walking away into the thick mist.

10

Alette makes it two miles away before she lets Axel's car coast to a stop by the edge of the road, throwing on her emergency blinkers, and buries her face in her hands.

Her fingertips throb, her head thuds, and her ankle is sore in her stabilizing boot.

She breathes out harshly into her hands, the way she used to do when she was a teen and overwhelmed, but it doesn't help. It doesn't help, and she doesn't know what to do.

GURLIEN (7:52 PM): Tracking has the car near the light show when it happened, and I have trouble believing that the regular had anything to do with it. What happened.

Alette glances at the text on her phone, before disregarding it and continuing to drive towards her apartment.

She should probably go, see what Gurlien is demanding now. Read that email that's resting comfortably in her inbox, but she just drives on.

Two thirds of the way home, Grey streaks by the car, bounding along with her, then Spot joins on the other side. Even after the day they've had, they're just as fast as before, just as energetic.

AXEL (8:10 PM): I'm at your place, I don't want to bring your car back there, it's a goddamn miracle he didn't mark it for tracking last time.

As her car idles up to a stoplight, she wishes he wasn't. Wishes she could just go home, be alone for hours. Not have to deal with anything.

Wishes, stronger, that she could go to the Headquarters without any of the changes. Wishes it could just be like it was before, when the magic hadn't started to decay, and the technology still worked.

Outside her window, still obscured by shadow, Spot turns his head to her, teeth shining in a grin under the sodium street light. It's not nearly as terrifying as before.

"Right," Alette whispers, as if the dog could hear her through the glass windows and the aluminum doors. Because she doesn't know if the dog is tracking her, is protecting her, or is just...playing.

If dogs made from shadow and nightmares could play.

Too soon, her solitude ends, and she pulls up to her apartment, and both the dogs peel away to circle, then sprint back into the misty darkness.

She watches them until they disappear, before accepting her fate and unlocking her door.

"Good, I was this close to calling the cops on you," Axel says, laying upside down on her couch, head barely touching the floor, with a screwdriver in an old radio. The radio, Alette realizes, that he had once magicked into hearing demons. "I think Melekai would punch you if he saw you right now—I've never seen him that jumpy."

"That's an exaggeration," Alette says, and Axel nods, still upside down. "Did Gurlien call you back as well?"

"No, but he asked me why I lent my car, so..." Axel waves his hand, equivocating. "He thinks I'm insanely stupid. I'm not gonna dissuade that."

"Smart," Alette says, swinging off her coat, smoothing over her needle case in the breast pocket.

"Why'd you take the bandage off?" Axel asks, ever observant. "That's gotta hurt."

It's such a long story that she doesn't even want to start.

"I'm not going back there tonight," she says instead. "I'll deal with him in the morning, after I've actually slept and after I've had food."

"Yeah you had like one good night of rest and then concussion," Axel says, not budging from the couch. "Lyra thinks I shouldn't have let you drive."

She chucks off her boots, now fully encrusted in sand, and points at him. "There is so much to that sentence I don't know where to start," she says, then, still covered in grime, flops onto her armchair as Axel watches her, expectant.

The magic in her house swirls up, warming the chair ever so slightly, and the muscles in her back unwind. She rolls her ankle experimentally, and the bites pull and sting, but no new pain.

"Axel, do you believe in ghosts?" Alette asks, and gets a blank face in return. "Or spirits in the world, things that aren't human?"

"A, you died and came back, if someone told me that there were fucking vampires out there that only ate chickens I'd believe them at this point," he says, drumming his hand on the underside of her couch arm. "One of our friends used to be an actual demon, which suggests angels, which suggests a religion I'm not prepared to believe in, and your aunt's soul seemed to be the only thing keeping my home in functional condition. I watched a tape where a broken woman woke up from a coma and crawled out a four-story window and then was never seen again. I used to do magic." He stares at her, still sitting upside down on her couch. "Sure, ghosts could be real. Why not."

Alette exhales, then thuds her head against the back of her armchair.

"Wait, did you see a ghost? Like, an actual ghost?" This gets him to sit back up, properly so, eyebrows raised in his overly excited face. "Was it Frisse to tell us how to fix this?"

"No, no, I would have led with that," Alette says, shutting her eyes, then popping them open again. When her eyes are closed, her head thuds more. "I swear I'm not crazy, but...I've been introduced to a collection of otherworldly spirits in the area who think I can help them."

"Not like you have enough on your plate," he quips, popping up to standing. "Can you?"

It's not exactly the response she expected.

"I don't have a fucking clue," she says, and swearing feels nice. Like she hasn't been doing it enough and should swear more. "One took me to see a Ley Line—those apparently exist and aren't just myth—and untangle it from where Terese royally messed it up. I've been touching raw magic all day and my head hurts."

He nods, like her explanation actually makes sense, but he's always had a lower bar for accepting something as reality than her.

"Two days in a row, then," he says, and he's bouncing on his feet. "Whatever was in that electricity storm, and then this." He crosses into her kitchen, and her magic trails after him, like it's relearning who he is after she recoded her locks, then reappears only to chuck a granola bar at her. "Eat food."

"Yes, mother," she snips back at him.

"Let me guess, telling College Asshole would be bad," he calls back to her, "and you don't want to look crazy."

"I don't want to feel crazy," she says, for emphasis. "I feel...very crazy."

"Eh, you're not the worst," he says with a shrug, then returns with his own collection of granola bars. "All you have in your kitchen is power bars and vegan cheese."

"I have a lot on my plate," she quips, before trying to shut her eyes again, and her head immediately throbs.

It's a little better, knowing that her best friend doesn't think she's lost her mind, but the relief is stolen away, replaced with a bone deep exhaustion. The sort of exhaustion that comes when she does way too much magic, when she's expended herself past what's smart.

It's different from her normal exhaustion that comes from her insomnia. Insomnia creeps along her skin, buzzing against her senses and clawing at her brain. This is more like she's having the will to move pressed out of her by a weighted blanket, to where all she can do is just sit.

"I'm not leaving until you eat that," Axel says, almost sharp. Which makes sense, they've had to do that for each other for most of their lives at this point. "And if you don't, I'm calling Lyra."

"She's not my boss," Alette grumps, but opens the bar nonetheless. "All she'll do is be sad at me."

"Exactly," Axel says, then crosses his arms until she takes an obnoxiously large bite. "Tell me how you did it tomorrow."

"It was literally a string," she says around a mouthful of bar, "like a cat got into a ball of yarn. But magic."

"Weird."

"Very."

She sits there, determinedly chewing through the bar, as he gives her his best impression of being disappointed, even though they both know that he is far more likely to be the one to make foolish life choices.

"Do you need me to make sure you don't fall asleep again?" he asks. She just wants to rest. "That's only the first night, right?"

"Please leave," she says, and he tosses her another granola bar and filches his car keys from her entry, before opening the door.

She waits for the familiar click of her locks shutting, but it never comes.

"Uh, Alette?" he asks, and she makes herself stand out of the chair, as much as her ankle prohibits it. "There's a dog here. With a bag."

She lets herself have a brief moment of not wanting to explain anything further, before she joins him in the entryway.

Sure enough, Spot sits on her doorstep, prim, but actually solid, like an actual dog, instead of terrifying and cloaked in shadows.

And from his jaw hangs an honest-to-god book bag.

And his tail wags the moment Alette comes into view.

"I'll explain later," Alette says, as Spot drops the book bag and preens to Axel, who is more than happy to give pets as she grabs the bag.

Inside are scrolls.

"If your ghosts use dogs to deliver bags of books to you, I think they're trying to impress you," Axel says, and Spot sticks his nose in Axel's hand before sprinting away into darkness.

Axel blinks, then points out.

"That dog just disappeared," he says, then, at her unimpressed look, goes—"oh, magic dog."

"Magic dog."

Past his car, however, she sees Spot sit on his haunches, eyes glittering red, once more enveloped in shadow.

"But you're okay?" Axel asks, eyes sliding over to her. "I don't need to charge off and punch any ghosts or spirits or anything?"

"Please don't," Alette says, and he cracks a smile. "I'll tell you...I'll tell you if I'm in over my head. Promise."

"I'll hold you on that."

Spot sits, so obviously waiting, and Alette inclines her head as Axel climbs into his car, tires squealing down her driveway.

The moment the car disappears beyond the corner, Spot slinks back up.

"Yes, that was an impressive trick," Alette says, and Spot sits, primly, almost on her feet.

On his collar—because somehow the shadow dog has a collar—is a slip of paper.

"Right," Alette says, tugging it out and unfolding it, "don't want to be too suspicious, do you."

The note is simple, written in an elegant hand.

DO NOT LOSE THESE, BUT FEEL FREE TO PUT THEM IN YOUR COMPUTERS.

"That's good," Alette says, because digitizing ancient records is her jam, and she tucks the slip of paper into her pocket.

Then, tentatively, she extends her hand and pats Spot on his head.

There's fur, real fur, like most dogs would have, soft and

a little messy, and her hand tingles when it passes through the shadows sitting near his skin.

Spot stills, and she carefully scratches behind his ears, like most animals she's encountered seem to love.

"Do I need to write a follow-up note?" Alette asks, and Spot thumps his tail against the concrete. "Right—"

She ducks inside, just long enough to grab her favorite fountain pen and a piece of parchment—because of course she has that easily available, rather than a notepad like a normal person—and sketches out a quick reply.

THANK YOU, I WILL ABSOLUTELY DIGITIZE THEM. NEAT TRICK WITH SPOT LOOKING REAL, AXEL COULD SEE HIM FOR A BIT.

The moment she tucks it back under Spot's collar, Spot takes off, dashing off into the darkness.

Leaving Alette with a bag full of scrolls, an empty apartment, and too many thoughts in her brain.

11

After a night of puzzling through ancient scrolls that are definitely not written in modern English, she chooses her outfit with care. Picks her slacks that she made herself, that she herself stitched magic inside for secret keeping, for keeping her temper even, for appearing to know more than she actually knows.

On the inside hem of her shirt, she has linen stitched in around her cuffs, so that anything she touches gives her an impression she can read the next day, so she can get a glimpse into anyone's motivations.

They're not exactly her most ethical clothing choices, but she doesn't want to meet with Gurlien without something on her side. Especially if he can tell she did something she wasn't technically supposed to do.

She refuses to feel like a scolded child.

This time, she knows well enough to go straight to the grand ballroom, to grit her teeth against the sterile lack of magic.

Gurlien's righted the table that she once laid dead on, and bank papers and records of accounts are spread over the entire thing. On one side, he has set up a series of complicated instruments that look more like an ancient barometer than anything useful.

It's a delicate balance of glass tubes, colorful liquid, and bright golden cogs.

The conference room still stinks, still reeks of his cleaning spells and the magic that he's erased, but the equipment all but glitters.

Axel's trying real hard to not look interested, but techy equipment is exactly his jam.

It chimes softly, the glass tinkling against itself.

The tip of the glass hangs, pendulum style, over a pen and paper calendar, and it swings idly over a date a few weeks away.

Gurlien watches her, like he's expecting her to ask, so she doesn't. "Near as I can tell, it's when the main Line is going to go," he says, and Alette's stomach flips. "Whatever prevention or sanitation we do, it has to be before that."

"How does it work?" Alette asks.

"I'm monitoring the stability of the magic," Gurlien says, as if it's obvious. "It'll give us a warning, if something critical goes before we think it will." He cracks his knuckles. "Or the Necromancer might tell us. They know of these things."

"How much did my aunt tell you of the Necromancer?" Alette starts, instead of letting him question her first, and he looks up to her with a start.

"We know that you had contact, proof of abilities, and that she helped bring down the Demon that was Terese," Gurlien says, listing off from memory. "She did not divulge the age, location, or power level of the Necromancer, how they've survived the obvious demon threat, or what the proof of abilities is."

And that, she realizes, means he doesn't know that Alette had died.

"Any information would be appreciated," he says finally, leaning back and looking at her expectantly. "I don't know why you aren't divulging it."

Alette shrugs gracelessly instead, sitting down at the table, though her skin crawls at the idea of touching it. "What bank accounts do you have for me?"

Gurlien pauses, then looks, deliberately, at Axel, and doesn't say anything.

The moment stretches on, with just Axel drumming his fingers against the table.

"Axel, you need to leave," Gurlien says, voice as calm as if he's remarking on the weather.

"No, he doesn't," Alette snaps out.

Axel's eyebrows don't raise, which means at some level he was expecting this, which is just worse. "What are you going to say to Alette"—he gestures at her—"that you couldn't say to me?"

Alette recognizes that tone. It's his pseudo over-protective tone, one he only got after his magic went away.

Like he doesn't fully believe that Alette still has hers.

Gurlien just gives him a one-shoulder shrug. "Important things."

The ugly sentence just hangs in the air, until Axel sighs, explosive, shoving his chair away from the table, shaking the glass instrument, before striding off.

Gurlien sets his pencil down on the table, on top of the papers spread all over. "Tell me where you were yesterday," he says.

"No," Alette says. "I do not need to report my movements to you." Especially after that display to Axel.

His lips thin, and she sees his eyes drift over to the different spots in the room, to the different places that Alette knows they practiced magic, to what must be incredibly obvious to someone who's deliberately trying to find it.

"I don't expect this to be news to you," he starts, like he's picking and choosing his words, "but someone did something spectacular to the magic off the coast of Washington yesterday."

"I gathered," Alette says.

"Your...magic-less friend's car was there, or close enough," he continues, as if Axel hadn't just been in the room. "I don't believe he could have done anything like that."

"From what my aunt told me, no human could," she replies, and he raises an eyebrow, just enough to catch her attention, "that such displays are solely in the realm of other spirits."

"And demons," he says, sharp, "and people who cross between the world of the dead and the living. Like," he pauses, "a Necromancer."

Alette just remains silent.

"A necromancer, untrained, could wreak even more havoc on the state of magic," he finally continues, "they could wander in somewhere, decide to raise a random creature, and then the next thing you know there's a horde of demons on top of them, messing with the breaks in the Ley Lines and making everything worse."

Lyra would find that description hilarious, Alette's sure of it.

"And I don't want to think that you're aiding and abetting someone like that, now, do I?"

Alette blinks. "Being a Necromancer would hardly be illegal," she says, "it's not like people can choose how they're magical."

"But messing with the state of magic, especially when it's as fragmented as this, is." He looks back down to the papers, and very visibly changes tactics. "Do you want your friend Axel to be cured?"

She stills.

"I assume you both very much want him returned to how he was before Terese," he continues. "The faster this is wrapped up, the faster we could get to work on restoring his power."

"You can just...do that?" Alette asks, her heart in her throat.

"Yes," Gurlien says, easily. "But I won't, unless I get your full cooperation."

He pushes a packet of papers over to Alette, who's frozen in place.

"What do these bank records tell you?"

Alette can't look, she can't, she can't even blink. "You could fix him, you could do it, and you're not?"

"Not yet." Gurlien smiles, grim, with no joy in it. "Now either look at these papers or tell me where you were last night."

A pit of anger, hot, opens up in Alette's stomach, and she pulls the paper to her.

It's merely the bank account Aunt Frisse had set up for her mystery daughter that no one knew about, Alette and Axel found it while going through her will the first time, but the rage bleeds into Alette's eyes until she can hardly focus.

"It's her daughter, she had a kid, this is a college fund," Alette says, tossing it aside, none of the magic she put in the outfit to keep her temper in check even remotely working. "How do you fix him?"

"And this?" He pushes another set of bank statements at her, ones that Alette hasn't fully decoded yet.

"I don't know," she says, and her hand shakes as she looks at them, "we couldn't find anything that it correlates to."

"It's paying the mortgage of a property, not too far away from here, in the forest," he says, and he was just testing her, he wasn't actually trying to get information from her. "Did she ever bring you there?"

It's yet another secret, yet another discretion her aunt kept from them, and her stomach is just falling, falling outside of her control.

"No," Alette says, as crisp as she can. "We also found a condo in Toronto."

"We knew about that," he says, business-like, then passes her another piece of paper, his fingers grazing against hers, and he stills.

Alette just stares him down, completely not in the mood for any of it.

His lips thin and, quickly, he throws a small diagnostic reading spell at her, with just a twist of his wrist.

Alette flinches back, but he's fast. Faster than her aunt, faster than her, faster than even Axel was at his best with his small tricks.

Her hand glows, starting from her palm where she had gripped the Ley Line, spiraling up her veins and illuminating the wounds on her fingertips.

It's not a spell Alette recognizes, and she thought she knew all the ones of that type.

He sits back, eyes narrowed and bank statements forgotten, crossing his arms.

"What is that?" he asks, as the glow starts to fade from her hand, almost as quick as it appeared.

"I am unfamiliar with this spell," Alette says automatically, turning her hand over and over again.

The wounds throb, just a bit.

"That's not what I meant," he says, and his eyes bore into hers. "That's not human magic."

And this is where Alette wishes Axel was in the room, with his fast thinking up lies and his ease of delivery.

"Probably that static cloud," Alette says, after too long, though her hand looks normal now.

"You must think me interminably stupid," Gurlien drawls, and it's the most personality he's had so far. "I investigated that spot, it looked nothing like that." Still, he leans forward, his eyes narrow. "What did Joyanne teach you about the other spirits of the world?"

"Not much," Alette answers, truthfully. "We were preoccupied with demons."

"And you didn't know of ghosts," he supplies, and his demeanor changes, like she suddenly has become a puzzle to be solved, instead of a problem. "Wights leave humans alone, Shadow Walkers can only be seen by the dying, and Sprites generally can't touch a human—they go right through."

"Can you provide definitions?" Alette asks crisply, though her heart thuds. "I did research, but these creatures aren't mentioned."

"And one of them seems to be touching you," he continues, as if she's not even there. "Were you...conscious last night? During the event?"

Alette blinks at him. "What?"

"Were you conscious? Did you wake up in any strange places? Did your body move without your knowledge?"

"No?" Alette says, her mind racing, concerned that he jumped to that conclusion. "I mean, yes, I was conscious, I don't think I was unconscious, I looked out the window and saw the flash, but—"

He's silent, for a bit too long for Alette's comfort, but maybe, just maybe, he has given her a way out of the scrutiny.

"If a spirit is using you," he starts slowly, "then you could be in danger."

"That sounds logical," Alette says, then remembers that she's supposed to be an esteemed magician with an excellent control of herself and her magic, and well accomplished in theory and application. "I need more information."

"Information for information," he says, and she wants nothing more than to smack him, "Where is the Necromancer?"

"The United States," she says, which is true. "Define those beings."

"Be more specific," he replies.

"The Pacific Northwest. She...moves around a lot." Again, technically not a lie, as Alette is under the distinct impression that Lyra hopped around the country as a child quite a bit.

"So it's a she," he says smartly, and Alette can't see why that's anything important, but hates that she gave that information all the same. "Ghosts are dead spirits who didn't go where they're supposed to go."

"I gathered," Alette says, when it becomes clear that he wasn't going to elaborate any more.

"How did 'she' live to adulthood?" he asks, steepling his hands and leaning back, and Alette gets the sudden rush that he's enjoying this. Enjoying this as banter, instead of withholding crucial information from her.

"I don't know," Alette answers, because that's again, relatively the truth. "I know her mother forbade her from using any powers as a young child."

"Shadow Walkers are mostly animals, almost only able to be seen or touched by the severely critically ill"—he ticks off on his hand—"some have tricks to appear like normal animals for a small amount of time, to those who aren't actively dying, but according to lore it drains them."

She hopes Spot wasn't too drained by getting pets from Axel, then wants to kick herself, because she should probably be more concerned with the actively dying part.

"And Terese, any update?"

Alette wants to curse him, because that's one thing they'd absolutely share with him, without any hesitation, but instead she just smiles and shakes her head.

"Did Joyanne teach the Necromancer how to bind demons?" he follows up, which is a practical question.

"Yes?" Alette says, squeezing her eyes shut and telling herself that it's because she's already technically been dead that she can see the dogs. "That, along with the perfectly functional gold binding spell, is how we stopped Terese the first time."

"Wights," he starts, ticking off another finger, "are creatures of the land. Some humanoids, some animals, they act as pseudo guardians of an area. They cannot leave, but if they are wiped out, within a few generations they are back. They ignore humans, with the exception of intense and sudden pollution or decay of the land. What was the proof of abilities?"

Alette lets herself think, to lift that definition of Wights up to what she knows of Zoel, knows of the other Wights who chatted with her, and it seems...accurate.

But he's watching her, and she can't ignore his gaze for forever.

"I didn't see it," she answers, once again technically truthful, "but I saw her blow up a tree and resurrect a moth, after the fact."

"Sprites are a subset of demons, technically, and they cannot interact with humans unless the humans have been otherwise altered," he says, then leans forward. "Alette Jyoshti, which one of these touched you?"

She stares at him, then looks away.

He sits back again. "Well," he starts, "if this is your idea of full cooperation, I'd be surprised if your friend ever gets healed."

"That's cruel," Alette bursts out, "that's cruel."

"The cruelty's all on you," he says, and she pushes up from the table to stand, to do something. "All you would have to do is stop these half answers, stop holding things back, and Work. With. Me."

She looks away, standing, awkward, a knot in her stomach.

"Did you get those sanitation spells I emailed?" he asks. "That'll be the fastest way to get through this."

AFTER AN ENTIRELY FRUSTRATING session of going through her aunt's myriad of bank accounts, she begs off for a few hours on behalf of the still relatively recent head trauma and hunts Axel down through the Headquarters.

She finds him elbow deep in what might've been an old

TV monitor unit once upon a time, deep in the secondary basement.

The entire air stinks of the decaying magic of the place, even though it's brightly lit and well ventilated.

"Is it safe for you to be in here?" Alette asks, instead of saying hello.

"That much of an asshole, huh?" Axel says, barely glancing up at her, instead grasping around at something. "I know I changed the receiver in this—it still works, but I want it to perceive demon energy now, and that's a hell of a lot more difficult to do without actual magic."

Alette folds herself on the ground next to the wall. "Demon energy?"

He barely glances up at her. "Mel says Terese still might have traces. I thought we could run some CCTV through this, pick up some things."

"He had more questions about Lyra," she says, not quite able to bring herself to talk to him about what Gurlien's holding over her head. "I answered them the best I could, but..."

"We should decide what we're telling him and stick to it," Axel says, sticking his other hand in the TV tube as well. "It still connects to power, but it shouldn't. I made it charge-free, but it charges anyway."

"Axel, I have no earthly idea what you're talking about," Alette says, and shuts her eyes, leaning her head against the wall.

It gnaws at her, the guilt, of telling more of Lyra than Lyra would want, of not immediately telling Axel about the promise. Of the very idea of sanitation spells, and what they might do to the Wights—and ghosts and Sprites, apparently —in the area.

Axel immediately launches into a description of the

inner workings of a television, and she just squeezes her eyes shut, more and more guilt welling up inside of her.

"He doesn't know I've been raised from the dead," she bursts out, after a long lull in Axel's description. "He doesn't know and keeps on asking me things about Lyra and any answer would just reveal way too much and I'm tired of it."

Axel finally sits back, away from the unit, and looks at her. "But you're fine, now."

Tears well up in her eyes, so she just squeezes them shut further.

"Is this about the ghost thing?" he asks, after a long moment. "That's something to do with you dying?"

"Wights, apparently, they're somehow different from ghosts, and yes," Alette says, weariness seeping into her bones. "I don't..."

"You don't want him to know," he continues, and she nods. "Have you asked your...Wight, you said? Maybe he has opinions on the goon knowing about him."

He's probably right, but outside of the dogs showing up at her house again, Alette has to wait until the next day, with the next knot to unravel, and—

"I need you to keep him busy," Alette starts, and Axel's eyebrows raise up. "Tomorrow, near noon. Keep him indoors, keep him away from investigating. In here, if you can help it."

"Vague, but okay," Axel says, suspicious. "How on Earth would I do that?"

"Oh, I don't know, show him where Lyra blew up all those bugs, that should keep him interested," Alette says, things solidifying in her mind. "I'm going to meet with... with the Wight...and I'll ask him."

"Will you be safe?"

"Probably," Alette says, which isn't as comforting as she means it to be.

ALETTE TAKES herself down past the border, to the Bellingham harbor. She's been there before, many years ago, when she had just begun to study under her aunt's tutelage and her aunt had wanted to check out a library.

They had stopped for donuts at a small shop.

This time, however, she lets herself drive by instinct, until she finds herself on a secluded cove made from mostly rocks and pebbles, and steps out of her car.

She breathes in, and, somehow, almost as tantalizing as the Line at Shaman's point, there's magic in the air. Little glimpses of reflections dancing on the pale January light, thrumming in her veins, pounding in her heart.

She can't see any line, not truly, but there's so much power trilling down her veins that it could be nothing but.

"Ah, you found it," Zoel says, and she jumps.

Of course he'd keep an eye on her, trail her to this place. She hadn't seen his dogs, but that doesn't mean they're not there.

"You can't expect me to not investigate something for myself," she says, instead of snapping or anything ruder.

He has the temerity to give her a grin. "It's healthy, don't worry."

"I'm not," Alette says, looking out towards the water, letting the salty wind rustle through her hair.

When she looks back, he's disappeared again.

12

ALETTE (9:01 AM): Hand your phone to Mel, I have some questions for him.

LYRA (9:02 AM): Rude, but okay.

LYRA (9:02 AM): What.

ALETTE (9:03 AM): It's shadow dogs, and since I was raised from the dead.

LYRA (9:04 AM): Meet me at that diner.

ALETTE ONLY HAS time for this if Melekai is quick, so when he brushes his way into the diner with nary a look to the waitress, she flags him down.

"You're not currently dying," Melekai says instead of a greeting, and Alette barely has time to activate her old silencing spell before he says more things like that. "You shouldn't be able to see them, and one shouldn't be able to bite you like that."

"I think they're pets of the Wight," Alette says, and

Melekai squints at her. "They seem to always be around him, and they're...affectionate."

The waitress swings by, dropping off water and coffee, and Melekai scowls at her as she hands out the menus.

"Wights don't keep pets," he says, once the waitress walks away. "Is this one of the locals?"

"Zoel," Alette says, and Melekai's eyebrows raise slightly, before his face smooths over. "That's what was the...beacon in the sky."

He gives her such a flatly unamused look that it's only because of years of training that Alette doesn't squirm.

"He asked for my help," Alette says, taking a sip from her water just for something to do, "said the magic of the area was affected. Goals aligned and all that."

Melekai crosses his arms and leans back, and it's so foreboding that she is immediately reminded of his...unlikely background. "So he's using you to untwist all the damage of Terese?" he asks, almost more of a statement. "That's an interesting tactic from him."

"Care to explain why?" Alette asks, matching his tone, and he bares his teeth at her in a grin. "I'm tired of people not giving me answers."

He regards her, and she's not sure if he's weighing his words or weighing her worth.

"It'll...cause difficulties with other Wights, I believe," he starts, deliberate in his word choice. "Some liked the fact the area had such a Grand Magician like your Aunt"—he spits that out like he's cussing—"but some found her troublesome, and involving her niece isn't going to help."

"He said it's because I have...technically died," Alette says, forcing past the awkward knot in her chest that always comes when she says things like that, "that I can help."

"I'm sure he thinks that," Melekai says, bullish.

"And I haven't seen any other of the Wights I used to," Alette pushes on, and Melekai's eyebrows raise. "When this first started...I saw many. Now it's just Zoel and his dogs."

"You should ask him," he says, and he looks profoundly uncomfortable, like discussing this is betraying something about himself that she isn't aware of. "Most Wights are...hunkering down. If I had to guess. Avoiding humans."

The sanitation spell sitting in her email sends another pang of guilt down her back.

"Introducing humans into the mix of a local magic is always a risk, humans are by nature...more chaotic than not," he says. "If he isn't careful, it could backfire and make things worse, or fundamentally change who you are as a person."

That's...grim, so Alette looks around the tiny diner, to everyone she can't hear because of her silencing spell.

"Well, his dogs like me now," she says. "One dragged me from the—thing—when I couldn't move, and then he used them to give me books."

"Give you books," he states, then rubs his forehead, which is such a breathtakingly human action that it almost startles a laugh out of Alette. "Just...be careful. Don't become so entwined that you forget who you are. Lyra actually likes you, and she'd be sad if something happened."

With that, he pushes himself up, never actually ordering food for himself and leaving her with the water and a menu and a rather awkward waitress.

ALETTE (10:21 AM): Make sure Melekai eats, he didn't while at the diner and I think he forgot.

LYRA (10:22 AM): I still have her phone.

LYRA (10:22 AM): Asshole.

ALETTE (10:23 AM): You should really consider getting your own phone.

LYRA (10:23 AM): No.

෴

THE EIGHTEENTH KILOMETER up Sunshine Coast is a breathtaking drive, and Alette's in too poor of a mood to enjoy it. Only the larger dog, Grey, runs next to her car, and he's a blur of shadow, sprinting in the pale light of the late winter.

This time, instead of all her magical protection, she wears hearty hiking clothes. Waterproofed fabrics that don't restrict movement, a warm base layer, and sturdy mountain climbing boots.

Still, her needle case and the chunk of gold sit in the breast pocket of her favorite jacket. She didn't need them last time, but she's not...going to be caught off guard when she might.

She parks her car, and Grey circles her, sniffing at her shoes and her jacket, before hanging close to her.

The blackberry brambles are barren of leaves, just thorny vines, and grey ice slushes underneath her shoes, despite the sun peeking through the clouds.

Zoel's nowhere in sight, but she locks her car, grabbing her survival backpack, and looks around for the marker.

This part of the Vancouver coast is dotted with them. Too many people take it too fast, with ice on the road and gravel beneath their tires and end up crashing into trees or the giant stone cliffs. She saw four on the drive up, and she had to stop herself from stopping at each one, until she knew she had come to the correct distance.

Grey dashes out, then dashes back, crashing through the thorny bramble.

"So you're doing the herding thing again?" Alette asks, and gets rewarded with Grey thundering over to her and spiraling around her in fast, chaotic movements.

"You'll have to forgive him, he's used to keeping people together in a group," Zoel says, once again walking out of nowhere and once again startling her. "Do you enjoy the books?"

She gives him a glance, like she can read something from his face, and he smiles at her, warm.

"I can't exactly read them," she says, after almost too long of a pause, "but I am scanning them in, and I'm sure I'll find a translation."

He nods idly, looking out to the bramble of dead blackberry bushes, and when he's facing half away, she can see fine lines around his eyes and brackets around his mouth, like he's suppressing some stress.

"So this"—Alette gestures to the cross marker—"is this another Ley Line?"

"Smaller," he says, still looking out at the bramble. "More like a creek, instead of a raging river." He nods at her to follow, then starts to tromp over the blackberries, without a trail.

Alette takes a deep breath and fates herself to getting many scratches.

Out of the woods dashes Spot, who sticks his nose in her palm before running off, joining Gray in the thicket.

This time, following Zoel doesn't seem so much of a leap of faith.

"Do you always see magic as a liquid?" she asks, stepping delicately over a particularly thorny branch. "Or is it just a metaphor?"

He raises an eyebrow at her step, then, as if conjuring it out of nowhere, hands her a pair of rough leather gloves, the type that gardeners or builders use.

She shoves them on, and they're much warmer than she would have expected. Softer, too, like they're lined with the finest of wool.

She's seen enough magically generated things that it doesn't quite shock her. It's nice, however.

"A little of both," he says easily, holding a particularly nasty looking vine out of her way so she can step up next to him. "It flows like water, but is less...capricious. See—"

He holds his hand out, and it's empty, until his fingers twitch and a thin strip of the magic appears, twisting off into the distance.

Alette peers at it, not too full of herself that she won't examine something new when presented so prettily in front of her.

It's similar to the Ley Line they untangled before, to the beacon but, like he said, much smaller. More of a thin ribbon, less of a rope. It glimmers in the pale light, almost like a prism, a flash of rainbow among the January gray.

"So much smaller in scale," she says, running her gloved fingers over the edge that trails off his hand, and it's the same soft warmth as the other, even through the thick leather.

But somehow weaker. Like it pulses less than it should, like it's been sick for longer.

"But not less important," he says, then shakes his hand out, leaving the thin ribbon in her hand only. "This one connects to a community of wayward spirits past the cliffs, and without it, they'd die."

Which only brings to focus the direness of this entire situation.

"How many...knots are there?" Alette asks, keeping the ribbon in her hand as they start to walk. "Are they all because of Terese?"

"Knots happen naturally, and...we untangle them. Naturally." His face tightens, again, like he's holding something back. "Terese just caused them everywhere she went, and the humanness of her destruction kept us from being able to fix it, and your aunt had kept so many in line just by existing."

She can no longer see the dogs but can hear them crashing in the forest.

She's not sure when their motions became audible. She doesn't remember them being so before.

"Then I know where another would be," Alette says suddenly, and he gives her the barest of glances. "I...we clashed with her many times."

"That could be useful," he says, ducking under a low hanging branch, then holding it up for her. "I'm only finding them when someone reports an issue, or that people are dying out, or when I stumble upon them."

She thinks about asking him if it's something he's doing alone, or if it's something that falls upon his shoulders, or if he took it upon himself, but keeps those questions in.

"I can get you a list," she says. "Is it best to send by dog or do you have a cell phone?"

"Technology doesn't work well for me," he says, flashing her a smile, which sits well on his face, "but Spot was incredibly happy that you wrote a note."

"Axel was happy to see an actual dog, didn't know that Spot could appear to him," she says conversationally. "Cool trick."

"Spot's a sucker for affection," he replies. "It won't be the last time, if your friend responded well."

"Can you do that?"

The question seems to stump him for a second, like he hadn't actually ever thought of it. "Of course?" he says, puzzled. "It's not easy, it's not sustainable, but we'd be pretty ineffectual caring for the area if we couldn't interact with the dominant species."

Alette smiles at him, almost reflexively, and his eyebrows raise.

"It's not something fun," he continues, still sounding bemused, "it's not something I'd do just every day."

He brushes aside a snow laden branch, revealing a small clearing.

And one of Terese's bright spots of death.

Alette stops short, even though the ribbon of magic in her hand pulses.

It's unmistakable. There's some snow gathered on top, where Terese's power had expanded out, had kept everything how it was the moment she did it. The sapling is still summer green, the grass is untrampled by the damp ice, and frost glitters in a perfect circle around its base. The ribbon of magic swirls around it, haphazard.

Lyra had called it a death bubble, and here, so well preserved with the ice around it, it just seems apt.

"I died in one of those," Alette says, words falling from her lips before she can stop them. She drops the ribbon of magic, and it flutters, listless, to the forest floor.

Even her gut is cold.

She hadn't gone back to the ones she knew about after. Lyra had told her she destroyed one of them, broke it apart, but Alette...didn't go check. Didn't want to go check, didn't want to face that again.

"Is that how it happened?" Zoel murmurs, and his words

are almost lost in the din of her ears. "We had wondered, but it seemed rude to ask."

He moves around it, like he's examining it clinically. Like it brings no fear for him to do so.

"I took down one, but it was much simpler than this, back barely in Oregon," he continues. "After a certain amount of time, as she got used to the human body, they became more complex, and beyond what I could do."

"You could touch them?" Alette asks, and her words come out small. Small, instead of confident. Instead of intellectual. Instead of someone who's dealt with magic her entire life.

His eyes flicker back to her once, then again, and his brows furrow.

"Well, yes," he says, casually laying a hand on the surface of the bubble, and Alette's breath hitches. "Can you—"

"No," Alette blurts out, then squeezes her eyes shut, pressing her forehead to stop herself from fragmenting apart on the edges. "That is, only our Necromancer friend could walk freely in it."

"Hmm," he says, noncommittal, and she opens her eyes again to find him watching her intently, like he could read her. "It won't harm you now."

She doubts that.

"What can I do without touching it?" Alette asks, clearing her throat to get her entire reaction under control. "I apologize if I'm not going to be much help—"

Spot creeps up to her, close to the ground, then noses at her leg until she reaches down and pats him on the top of his head.

Zoel watches, a hand still casually on the death bubble, and his face is kind, cruelly so. Like he can see inside of her, all the anger and things she's keeping hidden, deep down to where her fear resides.

He remains silent, for a long moment, as Alette breathes hard out of her nose and pats Spot on his head.

"Here," he says, and he holds his other hand out to her, palm up, "let me show you."

"I'm not touching it," Alette says, not moving towards him.

"I'm not going to make you," he says, and his voice is soft, a balm to her anxieties. "I'll be a buffer, but I'll demonstrate its..." he flounders for a moment, voice deepening in its accent, before, "sûreté. Safety."

She looks at his hand, still outstretched. There are calluses on his hand, like working with magic could do that.

"I understand French," she says, which is so beyond the point, but lets herself take one step closer.

Spot matches her step, huddled close to her.

"Are your dogs scared?" she asks, stilling again.

He shakes his head before his lips twitch up into the smallest of smiles. "When we first found them, yes, but not since. He's more concerned that you'll get angry."

"I'm not angry," Alette says, which is almost certainly a lie.

"Fear and anger often look very similar in humans," Zoel says. "Whatever power you think is still here, it won't transfer through me to you, I can guarantee that."

And she had seen him conjure up a canoe, had ridden it across the water without being able to see it.

So she takes another step, and, still keeping the gloves on, lightly rests her hand on top of his.

He folds his fingers around hers and gives them a gentle squeeze. She doesn't die, but swallows down a little bit of extra fear.

Hesitant, she draws in a breath, and it's normal and even. Not even a squeezing of her chest with a press of magic.

"This might be bright, but it won't be anything like the Shaman's Point," he warns. "Just unexpected."

She nods, and he squeezes her fingers once more, until the world blooms gold around her.

The bubble that he's touching is full of golden threads, warping and coarse, ever moving. The ribbon of magic is twisted inside, entwined, like the chains of her necklaces if she just tosses them in the box together.

It's also a wholly new way of looking at magic, and she scowls at it.

"Was this...intentional?" Alette asks, peering at the ribbon twisted in it. "That looks too chaotic to be intentional."

"Almost nothing the demon that was Terese did was intentional," he says, and he studies the bubble as well, "but she knew these would kill on impact, that's for certain."

"Understood," Alette says, then drops his hand.

Immediately, the gold thread vanishes, and she blinks away the black dots that come from looking into a bright light that suddenly gets turned off.

"Ah," Zoel mutters, "so that's not transferable."

Alette shakes out her hand. It doesn't sting, it doesn't feel any different than normal, but still, the impulse persists.

"I saw Melekai show the Necromancer that way, and she could see it even after they broke contact," he says, then gives her a rueful grin. "Demons are stronger than Wights."

"Demons are stronger than most things," Alette says, to give herself space to process what she saw. "So the thing that killed me, killed my aunt, looked like that?"

"We can go check?" he offers, which is a hard no for her.

"I'd like to finish this one, but we could always go there next, unless something else comes up."

"I don't ever want to go there again," Alette says, as declaratively as she can, and his eyebrows raise. "I'll tell you how to get there, but...no."

He regards her, and she hates it, before he very visibly moves on. "This one still has to come down," he says, and relief pools in her gut. "The spirits past the cliffs will die off in a few weeks if it continues to be like this."

"That fast?" Alette asks, and when he holds out his hand again, she takes it.

The world blooms gold once more, and a small part of her wonders if Lyra still sees like this, or if that went away when Melekai became human.

"Pull—lightly—on the ribbon," he instructs, placing it in her free hand. "I want to see how it's twisted, and where."

She does, and the glimmer of multi-colored rainbow shimmers in her grasp but pulls taut to the point where it meets the bubble.

"If all magic...went away..." Alette starts, which hurts to even say, "how long would these spirits live?"

"Not long," he says, still concentrating on the hinge point where the bubble grasps the strip of magic, prodding at it with his other hand. "Some smaller ones, a few hours. Wights, maybe a few days." He twists his fingers inside the threads and they fray apart easily. "But that doesn't happen, not...not without something catastrophic."

Like those sanitation spells.

He tugs on one of the threads and it unravels, freeing up a section of the ribbon, and a small chunk of ice drips into the hole. It's fussy work, and the frayed threads drop to the ground, listless.

Suddenly, Alette wonders what would happen if she threaded one of those through her needles.

"Is it safe for me to pick it up, once you have dropped it?" Alette asks.

"It's safe for you to touch it regardless," he says, almost disgruntled. "I would not needlessly endanger the one human who can help me."

Which is fair and logical and something that should convince Alette, but still, she hesitates.

She hates it, the irrational part of her, the fear born out of someone else's actions. That someone could do something to her, and she'll remain frozen there, blocked from moving past it.

She's a woman of study, a woman of scholarship, and here she is, unwilling to touch something that has been assured as safe to her, from someone who hasn't lied to her yet.

Her aunt would be ashamed.

"You know how to contact Lyra, right?" she asks, and Zoel nods idly, still focused on untangling the bubble.

"Melekai was insistent that she knows who I am, though I get the feeling she does not know my name, nor is she particularly observant when I am around," he murmurs, not taking his eyes away from his task. "She continues to astound in how much of her world she does not notice."

"She's untrained," Alette says, feeling pushed to defend her friend, "and for what she doesn't know, she's remarkably effective."

The threads on the bubble warp around Zoel's fingers, ever shifting, and it's fascinating in its own right. That Terese's magic could have such a visible aspect, hidden away from all humans.

"I saw her sense a dead bug within a few seconds of it

dying, while two Wights and a Sprite were just feet away, and she had no idea," he says, and that does sound about right. "I half think Melekai must find it amusing, to put up with her." He glances at her, quick, like he's gauging her reaction. "She's very kind."

"Obsessively so," Alette agrees, and his face relaxes, like he really cared that much about her opinion of him. "She had met me all of three times before she brought me back."

"She befriended a demon, obsessively kind is an understatement." He rests his hand against the bubble. It fluctuates and twists near the contact, then he tries to yank the ribbon out of a particularly rough spot.

It doesn't budge, and the rest of it pulls taut against Alette's hand. Like it's actually fighting Zoel, instead of coming loose.

Taking a deep breath, she reaches out her fingertips in the gloves, still keeping the grip on the ribbon, and lets them graze against the bubble, near where the tangle is.

A quick race of magic sparks up her wrist, and she flinches, but doesn't move away.

It spirals to where her arm had been broken, then to where her shoulder had been injured, and settles near her lungs.

Lyra had said those had been crushed.

It sends tingles down to her still scabbed ankle, then back up, to her still burned fingertips, a spark moving to her breast pocket, where the lump of gold still sits.

And she doesn't die.

Slowly, she exhales, not letting herself have any reaction besides that.

"It's a little like the maelstrom," she says, and her voice is a whisper, "back at the store, but...less."

"She had tasted Necromancer at the store," he says, but

his face is soft as he looks at her. "Look, it can tell you've felt it before."

The threads of the bubble twine around her fingertips, coarse, shifting, like it's trying to figure her out. Like it has its own personality, left behind by whatever burst of anger and desperation that Terese had expelled.

The ribbon falls free from the tangle Zoel had been working on, the Line going slack in her hand.

"It can't be that easy," Alette says, and Zoel drops her hand to move to the next tangle, and her vision of the gold threads disappear.

But they remain warm on her fingertips.

"Human's perspective of easy is so strange," he says. "It's not easy to find a trained magician who has come back from the dead who has been killed by the person making the knots and who has enough sympathy to work with me." He takes a deep breath, then offers her an embarrassed smile. "And who happens to know the last Grand Magician in the area so she has insight into how she controlled so much."

"Guess not," Alette says, focusing all of her attention on her hand, as one thread twists its way up to her wrist, to the spot it had been broken by Terese, curling around it. "Why would the magic care so deeply about those things?"

"Because so much changed with Terese," he says, eyes flickering to her wrist. "What happened there?"

"She broke it," Alette says, "with her blast."

The warm thread circles her wrist and worms its way under her bespelled glove, coarse like burlap twine, not restricting, but moving softly against her skin.

It's terrifying, to feel something against your skin but not be able to see it.

Alette starts to move, to pull away, but the thread tightens just enough that she freezes again.

"It can get possessive," Zoel says, and she can only see the ribbon of magic, as he pulls it out of more and more tangles, crouching next to the base of the bubble, "but it won't hurt you."

"Magic doesn't have feelings," Alette says, and he only gives her a blandly unamused face. "It's...it's a force of nature, it's like the wind. Wind doesn't care."

"Wind absolutely cares, just not in any way you would think," he says, then stands. "I know Lyra tried collecting some strands from the bubble she took down, but she's not a spell weaver."

And Alette is.

13

Alette breathes out, lets the magic curl against her wrist, warm and pulsing.

She's not quite sure how she feels about Terese's magic being possessive of her, but she's still alive, so she lets it prod at her skin.

"I wonder what it would do to Axel," she muses, as another bit of the ribbon falls loose. "Am I just...distracting it, then?"

"That's simplistic," he says, but he flashes her a grin. "We could try with your friend, if he would want to."

Alette doesn't know if he would trust it, or if he'd jump head first into it. Both options are about equally possible, if she had to guess.

Slowly, telegraphing her movements, she reaches her hand with the magic entwined to her breast pocket, and withdraws the lump of gold, laying it in her palm.

Zoel looks up, then stands up, cradling her hand, his fingers gentle.

The thread of magic releases her wrist to probe at the lump of gold, slithering down her palm.

The gold grows warm. Not molten, but warm. Like it's been out in the summer sun for a few hours, basking in its rays.

Zoel swipes the pad of his fingers gently across the lump of gold, like it's just as fragile as the ice on the trees. "How'd you manage this?" he murmurs.

It still looks like a lump of gold to her. "Charging into the maelstrom with it in my hand," she replies. "It's why my fingers are still messed up."

Zoel's fingertips brush against the scabbed over blisters, safely under their Band-Aids and gloves. "I thought it was from the magic itself, not gold," he says softly. "No wonder everything's working so well."

He glances up at her face, asking for permission.

"All my needles are gold," Alette says, as if he would need the lecture.

"Let me..." he trails off, still lightly touching her fingertips, just small pinpricks of contact. "Do you want a better tool?"

"Always," Alette says, and he flashes his grin at her, "but, explanation first."

"You're not an alchemist," he says, which is obvious, "but when the magic hit this, it changed it, fundamentally. It's still gold, if you looked at it under a microscope it'd still appear like gold, but now it's...attuned. To the area, to the magic."

"So I should forge something new from it?" Alette asks, and he plucks the lump out of her hand.

The magic stretches out towards it, before plopping back down on Alette's wrist and curling around her former break.

"May I?" he asks, holding it up between his fingers. It glints in the pale January sunlight.

And Alette's curious.

It might not be her best idea, to let a magical being play with a piece of her gold, but beyond fairytales she hasn't heard of any specific warnings against it. Just that all Spell Weavers' tools are personalized, and one does not generally go about lending them out to anyone who asks.

Her aunt had helped her make her first few needles, before teaching Alette to do them herself, and Axel has handled them a few times in an emergency, but other than that...she can't really think of another person who's actively held anything so personal to her.

But there's something different about this moment, standing so close and so entwined in magic.

So she nods, the threads warm and familiar against her wrist.

He loops the ribbon of the Ley Line around her hand for safekeeping and the threads stir near it but stay against her wrist.

Then, carefully, he places the golden lump on top of it in her palm so it rests against the ribbon.

"This will grow warm, but it will not burn you," he warns, which she appreciates. "But don't flinch away, even if it's startling."

Alette wouldn't dream of it.

In front of her, his eyes flutter shut, and he fits his hand over hers. Over the ribbon, over the lump of gold.

And for a moment, there's nothing, and Alette feels briefly, irrationally, foolish.

Both of the dogs skid back to them, crashing through the blackberry brambles in a blur of overactive shadows, stopping abruptly at Zoel's side, red eyes glinting in the sunlight. Spot's tongue lolls out at her, and if her hands weren't so busy, she'd try to pet him again.

Then, somewhere between one moment and the next,

Zoel disappears, and Alette barely bites back a gasp. Still, it sits there in her throat, her heart pounding.

She can still feel his hand against hers, a firm pressure, and the dogs still sit there, watching her, so she forces herself to still. To observe.

The threads of magic against her wrist stir, briefly warm up, and the ribbon shifts in her palm.

Her palm she can see, despite the pressure on it. It's a wholly odd experience, feeling something without seeing it, and she's used to dealing with magic.

The gold in her palm starts to shake, then vibrates, like a hummingbird beating its wings. It doesn't hurt, but it's something akin to grabbing a piece of shaking machinery, or Axel's car when he didn't realize he had done some alchemy wrong.

There's a tug, deep behind Alette's stomach, and Zoel blinks back into appearance in front of her, his hand still on hers.

"There," he says, seemingly unruffled that he had literally vanished. "Look."

He lifts his hand and in her palm lays a perfectly curved upholstery needle, sharp and delicate.

It's not nearly as aggressive as her net needle, much smaller, but the shape is perfect and smooth.

The threads of magic around her wrist prod back up her hand, as if reaching for it.

So she pulls at one, twisting it in her wounded fingertips —which don't ache, not like they've been aching all week— and threads the needle with it.

It's like the world shudders to a stop. Like everything else in her awareness ceases to be, so the world is just made up of her and her magic.

Her blood pounds in her ears as she turns the needle over and over in her hand, the thread of magic bright, warm, and pleased.

Zoel whistles lowly and the rest of the world comes back into focus. He's still standing there, the dogs lean against him, and the ribbon of the Ley Line is still in her hand.

Something's sparkling in his eyes, at the sight of her, and she can't bring herself to feel embarrassed.

"Would I be able to thread a proper Ley Line?" she asks, her voice rough.

"I wouldn't, but it would theoretically be possible," Zoel says, and his face is bemused, like he has no idea what he just handed her, how strong and powerful she just felt in that one instant moment. "But everything, all local magic, will react to that needle."

Alette holds it up to the light of the pale sun, as if that could illuminate it any more, and Zoel gently tugs the ribbon of the Ley Line away from her hand, working on untangling it once more.

"Did I thread this with demon energy?" Alette asks, giving him a glance. "Because that has startling implications—"

"You threaded it with magic that had once been from a demon, but has existed for so long here that it meshed with the natural world," he says, and the ribbon's falling free, much easier than before. "The demon who was Terese was not wholly playing with demon magic, and therefore it does not decay like demon magic."

Suddenly, Alette can't wait to go back to the Headquarters. To go to the rift where the building meets nature and see what she can do.

"There's a break in the magic at the Headquarters—how

can I get you in there to help fix it?" she gushes, and he straightens. "I know Aunt Frisse had protections, I can find and lower them, and—"

"I'm not going in there while you have that guest," he says, sharply. "I have seen people like him before, and they do not mean well to any Wights."

It stings, especially knowing the spells in her email—the spells she cannot imagine ever using, not on any massive scale, not after this, not after him—but she nods.

"Then how can I help here? With this?"

It takes another hour of untangling before the ribbon springs free and goes taut, stretching into the woods, and Zoel sits back with a sigh.

"That was, by far, the easiest time I've had taking care of one of those," he says, wiping his hands off on his jeans.

Which is another question, about where Wights get their clothes, but Alette's still too preoccupied thrumming from the amount of magic at her fingertips to be truly obsessed with the answer.

"Can I save some of this?" she asks, trailing her fingers in the now invisible bubble, where the threads still warp and twist around her hand. "If I sew it into my linen, it should save itself until I can use it." She sits down on the icy ground next to him, pulling out her pack, where her test muslin lays in neatly folded strips, "I know it's illogical, but—"

"No harm in trying," he says, and the same sheen of sweat is on his forehead, but he's grinning, the self-satisfied grin from something going well. "I've never made one of those before for a human."

Alette unfolds her test strips, picking one that is wider than most. More space to store the magic.

"Are there Spell Weavers among the Wights?" she asks, smoothing out the creases in the strip.

"Not how humans define them, but yes," he says, then leans in close to see what she's doing, so close she can feel the warmth from his body in the cool air.

Still keeping the needle threaded, she weaves it along the cloth, going with the bias of the linen. It's harder to do with a curved needle than it would be one of her ballpoints, but it's sharp enough that she's able to prick through the weft of the cloth.

He hmmms, then delicately touches the edge of the linen strip.

"Human magic is bizarre," he says, voice rounding out into the accent, "though having some magic that's so protective of you could be useful."

She shifts so she's leaning back against him ever so slightly, easing the strain on her back as she sews. "I still don't know how the magic that killed me would feel protective," she says, the meditative and quick motions of her sewing freeing up her mind to think, "but it is, in fact, interesting."

"Like calls to like," he says again, and his fingertips graze the curved edge of the needle, gentle enough that it doesn't throw off her stitches. "You've now been touched by this in many ways—it's going to respond."

"I wish my aunt was here," she blurts out, then briefly shuts her eyes in horror at saying something like that to a Wight who she still barely knows. "I mean, she'd be fascinated. She'd take so many notes and be insanely jealous of this."

He doesn't say anything, which almost makes the statement worse.

"She always wanted to learn new things, to figure out more parts of the world," Alette continues, outside of her control. "I mean, I know she was bad, I know she did things she shouldn't have, I still don't know what she did to Terese before this all started and what she knew ahead of time that she kept from us. If she had told me any of this I could have helped much sooner, but—"

"But she was your aunt," he finishes, still holding the edge of the linen. "Family bonds are important, even when the family member is indefensible."

"Yeah," Alette says, muted. "Yeah, and I miss her."

She comes to the edge of the linen, and the entire piece glows warm in her hands, casting a soft golden light on the little clearing as she ties off the thread, gently unlooping her new needle.

"If my observations of her were correct," Zoel continues, and it pangs Alette, because he knew her too, even in a limited way, "she'd immediately give you pounds of gold and have you try to duplicate the experiment."

Alette laughs, just a bit, just a torn sound wrenched from somewhere deep in her gut. She hooks the needle into the empty place in her case, before tucking it back in her breast pocket.

"Or she'd try to get the alchemist in here, to see if he could change it further," he continues, "and then she'd find another strip of Ley Line, and try to do the same, and she would absolutely try to get you to thread it with that needle."

He climbs to his feet, then extends a hand to help her up.

"Do you want to see who you just helped?"

"What?" Alette asks, and her mind is still reeling from the conversation.

"You did this, do you want to see the lives you just saved?"

Dumbly, Alette nods.

14

They follow the ribbon of magic through the woods, further and further away from her car, over bramble and vines and twisted trees, until it disappears into a cliff face of black stone and wispy moss.

Zoel pauses there, a hand on the stone, before giving her a sideways glance.

"How are your rock-climbing skills?" he asks.

"Non-existent," Alette answers, curving an eyebrow at the steep face. It's far beyond what she would consider an amateur cliff face to climb, and she isn't even on that level.

"Are you...what's the word...claustrophobic?" he asks, his voice lilting up into uncertainty, like he's not sure if he picked the correct phrase. "Can you walk through a small area and not panic?"

Alette hasn't had much need to do that in the past, but she shrugs. "I believe so; is it rough terrain?"

He shakes his head, then gestures for her to follow him,

and they trail along the cliff face before he leads her to what looks, for all intents and purposes, like a crack in the rocks.

"This is short," he says, though she would have no way of measuring what he would call short. "It's used mostly by the children who are not able to climb yet."

Children. There are children where they're going.

Alette steels herself, and he ducks inside the crack in front of her, shimmying sideways to fit with his broad shoulders.

Both the dogs whimper in unison, and Zoel pauses to throw them a look.

"Go run around," he says, waving them away. "You know how to get there."

Spot sits on his haunches, throwing a mournful look over at Alette.

But Zoel doesn't get stuck, and he's far bigger than she is, so she turns herself sideways to fit as well.

The rock presses against her, heavy, and for a second, it's like she's being suffocated, before the crack opens up into a small hallway, rough-hewn stairs cut into the rock.

Zoel has to crane his neck, but Alette's head doesn't quite touch the ceiling, so she stands up straight.

"They don't like caves," he says, slightly disgruntled. "They know how to run to the top, they're fine, they're just being babies."

It's musty in there, musty with the scent of still water and too much dust, of air that doesn't circulate as much as it should, but light leaks through the crack in the cliff face, casting long shadows on the stairs.

She pulls out one of her needles—not her new one, it's still too unpredictable—tracing a small light spell on the palm of her glove. It glows, a tiny little ball of light that's more akin to a nightlight than a flashlight, but enough to cast the cave in a low warm glow.

"Impressive," Zoel says, even though it's really not. "I take it you can't see in total dark?"

"Can you?" She squints at him.

"Mostly," he replies, a bit smug, before gesturing her up the stairs in front of him.

Her ankle protests just from looking at them, as she tries to avoid stairs on principle even when completely healthy, but she takes another deep breath of the musty cool air, and steps onto them.

They're almost too small for her foot, and the stone corridor is thin, so her shoulders brush each edge, but she can breathe, she's not dying, so she continues upward. Her ball of light casts deep spirals up the stairs, and there's dust playing in the beam.

Zoel is behind her, hunching his shoulders in, a hand near the small of her back, ready in case she falls. Or, at least, she thinks that's what he's doing, and she doesn't hate the idea of it, with how narrow the staircase is, how small each step is, how precise she has to be with each fall of her foot.

"These spirits haven't been seen by a human in generations," he murmurs behind her, as the staircase spirals upwards. "They might be curious."

She throws him a look over her shoulder, but it's difficult to see his face in the light.

"They won't attack," he says, as if sensing her question. "They observe humans all the time, but none can see them."

"Still ominous," she says, forcing lightness into her words. "Still quite some pressure to be an ambassador for the human race."

"It's not that dire," he says, though she can hear the

smile in his voice, "you're coming with me, they're the ones that petitioned me to fix their magic." He falls silent as they climb the uneven stairs. "They mostly will be puzzled that I brought a human, when they don't think humans can help."

"Let me guess, because most humans haven't died," Alette says, sarcastic.

A crack of bright sunlight appears ahead as they turn around a spiral rock, and a puff of fresh air hits her face.

"You're not wrong," he says, and steadies her when her foot slips on one of the steps, strong and immediately there, "just be aware they might prod."

They turn the spiral, and the light shines in, with tree branches and ice glinting in the sun. The mouth of the cave is little more than a hole, jagged in a boulder, and Alette has to heave herself out.

The strip of linen, now folded in a pocket of her coat, pulses against her awareness as she does, as she puts pressure on the wrist that was broken.

Interesting. If it's doing this, then it should absolutely be interested in Axel.

And Lyra, when she thinks of it. Maybe Melekai.

She scoots herself out of Zoel's way and he hauls himself up, biceps bulging. Which is another interesting thing — demons don't react to the environment around them in such ways—but Wights obviously do.

"Zoel," she starts, climbing to her feet on the boulder, "are Wights strictly physical?"

He gives her a sidelong look, blue eyes wary.

"Demons aren't, as you know, until they take a body," she continues, reaching a hand to him to help him to his feet. "But you seem to exist very much in the physical world, just invisible to most humans." He takes her hand, and he sure feels physical.

"You need to read those scrolls," he says, but in good humor. "We hide ourselves from humans, but if a human hit us with a car, we'd definitely feel it." He dusts off his hands, rubbing them briskly against the cold, "More of a survival mechanism than anything else."

"Because humans are dangerous," she says, and he nods, absentmindedly, "and we're not great at respecting boundaries."

"And tend to think that you're the only type of people who matter," he says, but there's no anger or malice in his tone. "That's why we liked your Aunt. For all of the things she shouldn't have done, she was at least conscious of us, encouraged us, made everything so that we could flourish."

"And then never told anyone else," Alette finishes. Put like that, at least, it made sense, if a bit bittersweet.

"We've talked with Lyra a few times, she didn't know who we were," he says, looking out in the trees, as if scanning for something. "Back before you two found her. A few of us would pretend to shop at her store, just for some contact."

She cranes her neck behind them and looks.

The cliff drops off, majestic, so she can only see the ocean beyond it, waves white capping along the rocks. It stretches on for forever, no islands visible, just never-ending ocean.

"Hell of a view," she says, and he gives her another soft smile, like he doesn't even notice the vista in front of them.

He tilts his head at her, a silent request for her to follow him towards a trail only he can see. It's rougher going, up on whatever cliff they climbed, and she's not looking forward to going back down those stairs after.

But her curiosity pushes her along, despite the throb

starting to come back to her fingertips under the gloves, and her ankle protesting at the scabs.

After a few minutes of tromping over brambles and patches of snow turned into ice, Spot and Grey streak past them, shadows trailing behind them.

"Did they just climb the cliff?" Alette asks, and he throws her a smile.

"I don't think they have the ability to do that," he says, "or, you know, opposable thumbs. They ran around to the other side of the cliff."

And she's seen them keep up with her car for extended amounts of time at freeway speeds, but it still boggles her mind.

Grey crashes back into view, and Spot skids to a stop behind him, pushing his snout into Zoel's hand.

"And to think I was scared of them," Alette marvels.

To which he gives her a double take, eyebrows raised.

"They're clearly made from shadows and they first started appearing when I rose from the dead, of course they scared me," she says, before he can say something witty. "I thought I was going insane."

Instead he just rolls his ice blue eyes, pushes aside some trailing moss, and lifts his finger to his lips, so she falls silent.

In front of them, in a tiny clearing, is a...village. Settlement. Something.

There's a ring of stones around the edges, obviously nestled in the base of every tree, and the thin ribbon of magic weaves its way around every branch and vine.

Instead of the haphazard twist and tangle of the bubble, this is precise. Intentional. Almost like a woven fence.

Inside the ring of stones and magic, still hazy to her view, are buildings of some sort, half invisible unless she squints. Like the suggestion of a building, of a shack, appearing in and out of her peripheral vision.

Lights twinkle in the half-formed windows, and dim on the wind, she can hear chatter. Children laughing, as if playing.

She stills herself, listening further, feeling further.

With each breath, the idea of the buildings grows more real, grows more distinct. There's a plan to them, four or five neatly tucked in this tiny clearing, facing inwards. A small community, hidden up on a cliff face, only visible from the air, and even then probably only the stones surrounding the clearing.

Zoel's watching her, she can feel his eyes on her, and she doesn't know how she became so aware of his gaze so quickly, but it's there. Like she can tell the moment he gazes in her direction, like something clicking into place.

"I can barely see anything," she whispers, and he nods, as if that's expected, "but—"

"But you do not need to," another voice says in front of them, and she jumps.

Suddenly, appearing much like she's used to demons appearing, there's a woman, her age completely indistinct. Her hair is more of a suggestion of a rich brown color, and her face has creases but not wrinkles, and she's clothed entirely in fine wool clothing.

Zoel nods at her, and she nods back.

"I assume you're the one that fixed it?" she says to Zoel, her voice warm. "We could tell immediately."

Alette looks back to the community, to the buildings that exist only in a haze to her.

This is something her aunt would have dreamed about. Yearned for.

They slip into French, as easy as it is to breathe, and

Alette lets them, not bothering to listen closely enough to understand them. Lets her mind wander, away from the words and their meanings, and to the sight in front of her.

Proof, actual, tangible proof, of other spirits. The sort of proof that's not supposed to exist outside of storybooks and legends.

And Gurlien and the College want her to wipe it out.

All for some nebulous threat that he's only claiming, a threat that seems nigh impossible, for all of the progress they've made.

Alette takes a deep, shuddering breath, and both of the people in front of her snap their attention to her.

"You're really related to the Grand Magician who died?" the woman asks, skepticism behind her voice, skepticism that Alette doesn't really blame her for. Dr. Frisse was a tall, statuesque white woman with gray in her hair, and Alette is...not.

"By marriage," Alette clarifies. "She was married to my uncle."

The woman shoots a glance at Zoel, so small that Alette almost misses it.

"She was trained by her, and brought up by her," he clarifies, as if Alette had missed some of the context to the question, "and given the reins to all her studies."

She doesn't bother to correct him, that Alette knows about maybe a third of her studies and research, but the woman in front of them nods thoughtfully, then extends her hand to Alette.

"Thank you, Death Touched," she says formally, and the hair on the back of Alette's neck rises. "I know that humans do not need to help us, so thank you."

"You're welcome," Alette says, taking her hand. The

woman's hand is rough against her glove, like she worked with her hands.

"The Grand Magician did many things she shouldn't have," the woman continues, which Alette knew, of course, "but she would help those whenever she could find them, and for that, we respect her."

"I'm glad," Alette says, unsure of what to say. "I'm...I'm glad."

The woman gives a deliberate glance to Zoel, one that Alette can't interpret. "Do you need food?"

"No—" Zoel interrupts, before Alette can answer, and he gives her a sideways smile in apology, "it would probably upset your digestive system."

"Then this," the woman says, and all but vanishes, becoming more of a blur of motion Alette can barely see, tracking to the nearest house, the edge of the door opening and swinging shut, before the woman appears again, mid stride, walking back towards them. "We don't have much in the way of things humans would consider precious, but here."

She grips Alette's hand, and carefully places a perfectly round, perfectly clear stone, right in the center of her glove. It's small, about half the size of a normal marble, and it glistens like water.

"It's not worth any of your money, it's not usable in any of your magics, but keep it with you, and others like us will know you have helped." The woman's face creases into a smile, and she looks immediately younger. "I would show you our children, but they're afraid, a human's never come up here before."

Zoel shoots her an apologetic look, like it's his fault for telling her.

"Thank you," Alette says, because accepting gifts from

other spirits should at least probably be received with gratitude. She tucks it into the same breast pocket as her needle case, and it fits there perfectly. "I hope...I hope I can help more. Again."

Her stomach sinks, though, further and further, at the thought of what the College wants her to do.

15

After that brief conversation, Zoel leads her back down to the staircase to the cave, and the moment they step out of view of the light, he turns on the stairs, looking at her.

"I'm sorry for that reception," he says, almost painfully earnest. "I did not know they would be so skeptical of you."

"You realize I have no frame of reference," Alette says, strangely touched. "I thought it was fine."

"Nah, they were fairly rude by their standards," he says, and there's a hint of a grin on his face in the dim light of the spell Alette lit on her hand again. "It might take a few encounters before they trust you, that you won't bring more humans to their village."

"Of course," Alette says, then gives him her best approximation of a polite smile. "That's perfectly understandable."

She's not exactly what she'd call trustworthy in this situation either.

"Still," Zoel says again, and he's being so perfectly earnest it almost hurts, "I apologize. I should have given them a warning and given you more background."

She gestures for him to start down the stairs again, and he does, the shadows from her light flickering.

"I always appreciate more information," she starts, and he huffs out a laugh, "but I'm not taking this personally. If anything...Aunt Frisse would've killed for this experience. For this concrete proof before her eyes."

And for that, even with all the complicated emotions and the grief in her heart, she's a bit thankful.

He's silent for a few more steps, still hunching down so he doesn't hit his head, until they emerge from the crack in the cliff face, and despite the ice on the ground Alette is sweaty.

Halfway back to where the bubble is, her phone beeps in her pocket, and Zoel gives her a sideways look as she pulls it out.

AXEL (3:21 PM): I have heard three hours of real estate law and magic amendments to it, please tell me you are almost done.

ALETTE (3:23 PM): I believe so.

"You should do your best to get rid of the man inside your headquarters," Zoel says, and he's in no place where he could read over her shoulder, but still, she gets the feeling that he did. "I don't know how, but you should."

"I would love suggestions," Alette says, frowning at her phone. "He's...awful."

Zoel tilts his head, and they're walking side by side together, and it's just enough that she can see something cunning flash over his face. Something playful.

"I won't reach him in there," he says, a grin in his voice, "but if you could bring him outside, we might be able to...do some things."

"Ominous, but possibly fun," Alette says, and gets rewarded by a proper smile that time, with a dimple in his cheek. "You'd get along great with Axel, he lives for those sorts of things."

"What I have observed of him is that he is rather preoccupied with his appearance," Zoel says, and he's really not wrong, "but that when he was an alchemist, he was very adept."

"Yes," Alette says. "He's also a pain in my ass about being too uptight."

Zoel gives her another sideways look. "Is he your...cousin?" He waves his hand, as if that explains things. "We all saw both of you arrive at the same time, and you're always together." There's something tentative in his voice, something probing, like he's gathering information.

"No, no relation," she says, raising an eyebrow at him, "practically a brother. I know him better than my own brothers."

Zoel's lips twitch ever so slightly at that.

"I've known him since we were kids," she continues, pushed to clarify by something even she doesn't quite understand. "I haven't seen my actual brothers since I was twelve. We've seen each other through breakups, through upsets, through...through my aunt, and now this. I'd call him my brother if people didn't think it was weird."

His eyebrows raise, but something in his face eases, something she's not sure she knew to look out for.

"Do you track all magicians in and out of your...territory?" Alette asks, the back of her neck prickling at how suddenly weighty the conversation got, and for no reason. "So you knew when we arrived?"

"Yes," he says, almost immediately visibly relieved, which is again strange. "Always better to know who the people of power are than be taken by surprise. We knew whenever Melekai would come and visit, like clockwork every thirteen months, and when Terese..." he trails off, like he's searching for words, "when she happened, we knew almost immediately. Couldn't stop it, couldn't do anything to save her, but we knew."

"We tried, too, at first," Alette says, as the mostly deconstructed bubble comes into view, now almost a physical thing she can see, "but I didn't even know she was a demon until after...after she killed me."

It's still weird to say that. Still feels wrong.

"The Grand Magician definitely should have divulged that," he says, drawing to a stop at the bubble, staring thoughtfully at it. "You and your friend did well then, with what you had."

"Thanks?" she says, and it feels odd to say that. "I guess."

She usually likes to project more confidence than this, project being more in control, but some part of that broke down with the bubble, with the needle in her pocket, and the cloth sitting next to it.

It sure didn't feel like they did well. The only thing they did well was find Lyra and turn the tides of the battle.

"You said you knew of many of these," Zoel says, still thoughtfully. "I know of some, where people are in danger, but we should work on fixing all of them. Can I...can I call on you? I need to evaluate what should be done next."

"I'll work on the list," she says, "and flag down Spot or Grey when I have it."

"Any places you know of your aunt's magic breaking as well," he warns. "That is more dangerous to the humans than the Ley Line, if I had to guess."

"Good to know," Alette says, and she's not sure when it turned awkward, but now it is and it's horrible. "Thank you for the needle?"

He grins, sudden and sharp. "Practice with it," he says,

voice low and round, and her stomach flops. "I want to see what Wight magic does in human hands."

She raises an eyebrow at him, but it does nothing to stop his grin as they head towards her parked car. "I assume it's safe?"

"Of course," he says, and there's now some bravado there, bravado she doesn't quite know how to read. "Some spells might react unpredictably, but it will never double back on you."

She peers at him, and he's smug, of all things. Like this is a point of pride in him, that she's missing a giant context with it, context that's going to require some study.

"Can you provide a translation key?" she asks, instead of any of the theories buzzing around her brain. "I'd love to get started with the scrolls when I'm not coordinating with the College or helping detangling magic or hunting Terese or researching how to fix Axel."

"Lot on your plate," he says, then his face twists. "You won't be able to. Fix your friend."

Her heart thuds to a stop.

"I don't know if that will ever be possible," he says, face sympathetic, "but it wouldn't be by your hand. That sort of thing...would require something else."

"Something else," Alette repeats, hollow. "The College says they can do it."

He tilts his head, sweeping a bramble out of her way. "I do not know all of their resources, but I wouldn't trust them."

It hurts, such a quick dismissal of it, but she's never one to turn down free information. "My aunt didn't either."

Her sensible sedan comes into view between the trees, still perfectly parked on the side of the highway.

"If you know so much," she starts, then pauses herself,

as to not react in anger immediately, "what do you think could fix him?"

He remains silent for a long moment, looking at her car. "Something you don't have access to," he says finally, continuing the trend of speaking in riddles and not giving concrete information. "I'll see you soon?"

It's nice that he's asking, but the hurt still bubbles in Alette's stomach, so she nods instead of snapping at him. It wouldn't be fair, not quite, for her to snap at him, and he has so much information that she can't alienate an ally in all of this, and—

He settles his hand on her arm, right where her glove meets her coat, and she about jumps out of her skin.

People don't just...casually touch her. Even Axel doesn't, even her aunt was stingy with her affection.

"Thank you, for today," he whispers. "Most humans would not be so invested in protecting the magical wilds, and I, for one, truly appreciate it."

She freezes, his hand warm on the thin strip of skin, and he doesn't move, doesn't drop the point of connection.

He had helped her up, they've grazed contact several times in the day, but this feels startling, undeniably different. As if there's magic in his touch, when he wants to.

Melekai once said he could tell when a magician grabbed Lyra without her permission, and, suddenly and irrationally, she wonders if Zoel could do the same.

Another thing she's going to have to research.

Maintaining careful eye contact, he raises her hand to his lips, pressing a formal kiss to the back of her gloved hand. "Thank you," he says, and it's too stilted for her to think anything more.

"You're welcome," she breathes, after an embarrassingly long pause of just staring up at him and trying to guess at obscure Wight and spirit magic, "I...I want to help."

He nods, and with a swipe of his thumb against her arm, he disappears, leaving her at her car and wondering what the hell just happened.

SHE DRIVES DIRECTLY to the Headquarters, the dogs joining her a few kilometers down the highway, running with glee next to her car the entire time, before peeling off the moment she reaches the Headquarters' gates.

After being out in the forest with the clear air, after fixing the magic ribbon of the area, the entire Headquarters stinks, like the magical malaise permeates through her nose now.

It's gross. Like the entire place is rotting, and she wrinkles her nose as she steps out of her car, still in her hiking gear.

The runes along the parking garage column waver as she strides past, and she pauses, then backtracks.

They waver again as she draws closer, then still when she's further away.

Which is...interesting. They've never done that before.

She lingers next to the runes, staring hard at them.

The pillars aren't quite load bearing, but if they get brought down it would do substantial damage to the building as a whole, and she's not willing to do that for the sake of scientific experimentation.

Her hand flutters to her needle case, to the strip of muslin neatly folded next to it, and it's warm.

Nice little magic detector, if that's what it is. Nice little tool.

As she walks through the corridor in the oft familiar hallways of the building she was practically raised in, new magic seems to rise up from the carpet. An old spell, one she thought her aunt scrubbed away years ago, one that makes the walls glisten, shines through.

Like her very nature is bringing things back.

The hair raises on the back of her neck, and she wonders just what she brought back with her.

16

Her footsteps bring her to her aunt's solarium, where she kept her magical components and favorite houseplants, and sure enough, she finds a very bored Axel and a rather energetic Gurlien. Axel's hands are in his hair, like he wants to pull it out but is somehow holding himself back, and his eyes flicker to her the moment she hovers at the doorway.

"It only crosses over when both the underwriter and the receiver both have education from—" Gurlien cuts himself off and he twists in his chair, following Axel's gaze. "Where were you?"

"Hiking trip with friends," Alette says, having prepared that lie ahead of time. "Sorry, I didn't have time to clean up before getting Axel's text."

The Solarium is glass covered, warmed by electricity instead of magic, and the same weak January sun shines through. The plants are fed by a drip system, so hoses wind their way through every pathway.

Despite her aunt's death, most of the plants are still alive, though her prized spell orchids look brown around the edges, and Alette's not sure she wants to spend the effort to keep them alive.

But the basil and the rose bushes are flourishing and the citrus trees in the large pots are blooming, filling the area with their cloying scent.

Gurlien gives her a second look, and she can see the calculating look fit back over his face like a mask. "Welcome back, I was just working on convincing Axel to take some courses in law."

Behind him, Axel shakes his head vigorously.

"He would be at an advantage, due to his ability to dedicate time to his studies and it would help take care of this place's legal status, that's for sure," Gurlien continues, though he narrows his eyes at her. "Hiking?"

"Hiking," she confirms. "Up at a pretty cliff on the Sunshine Coast. What did you need me for?"

"Practice," Gurlien says easily, and even that feels grimy. "It's far past time you learned the spells I sent you. There's a dangerous instability on an old highway on the way to the old southern library."

Alette and Axel briefly lock eyes. Of course there is. Another place where Terese caused damage.

"And it cannot be...resolved otherwise?" Alette asks, and Axel's eyebrows furrow. "I'm sure some can be, given enough time."

"Remember, collapse of magic for a generation," Gurlien warns her, like that's something she could forget. "This isn't something we can let unravel with enough time."

And she had heard children up on the cliff.

She purses her lips, staring off at the flourishing plants around them.

"The sanitation spells won't kill any humans," Gurlien continues, like this isn't a rehash of their first conversation.

"You and any magician can relocate for a few years until the magic recovers enough."

Axel's eyes flicker between the two of them, and she's known him for enough time to know that he's putting things together.

"I dunno, I want to hear Alette's idea?" Axel blurts out, like he's unable to keep himself from doing so, and if he's had to sit still and listen to a lecture for so long he's probably bursting from restlessness. "Shouldn't it be worth a try?"

Gurlien hesitates, eyebrows drawing up.

"How many breaks are there?" Alette pushes, at his momentary speechlessness. "I know there's many, but if we track down everywhere we know Terese used magic—"

"Impossible to do," Gurlien interrupts. "She was active for months, there is no way that we could find—"

"And solve them individually, until they become not a problem." Alette finishes, despite his very good point. "Less interruption to the magic of the area, no mass killing of the spirits, and—"

"And the ever-looming threat that this will spread and kill thousands." Gurlien finishes for her, but his brows are furrowed. "Is this about your Necromancer friend? Is she refusing to move?"

She absolutely would, but that's almost beside the point.

"We could convince her, though she might wish to lose her powers, if the rumors of necromancy are true." His gaze sharpens, like he thinks he's close to the issue. "If she wants a normal life, that is."

"I don't know what she would prefer," Alette says, sitting primly on the bench near them, "but I don't think sanitation—"

"The College doesn't care what you think," he interrupts. "The College is only concerned with saving the world."

Alette looks away, unable to put into words all the retorts swirling around in her brain.

"Where were you this afternoon?" He switches subjects, turning his back on Axel and focuses all of his attention on her, like Axel is a thing to be dropped. "Don't think I buy that you just have a regular hiking group."

"She does," Axel drawls, "they're miserable to hike with." He's examining his nails, leaning back, though she can see the muscle in his jaw clench at the snubbing.

Alette owes him.

"Don't think I don't notice that you're conveniently missing when two magical events have happened," Gurlien warns.

"What magical event?" Alette asks. "I didn't feel anything dramatic."

Gurlien purses his lips at her, then he stands, sweeping out, as if that small conversation had hurt his feelings.

Alette watches him go and resists the temptation to throw a plant at his retreating back.

"Guess your practice can wait," Axel says, leaning back on the bench and crossing his arms. "Asshole."

"Sorry you had to deal with him," Alette says, scowling at the door.

"Seriously, sanitation? That's what he's going with?" Axel turns to her, intense. "Alette, you can't do that."

She knows he means it because he uses her full name and not just the nickname of the week.

"Did you...did you meet up with your friend?" he asks, after the moment stretches on. "The Wight? Not a ghost?"

"Wight," Alette says, and he shrugs. "But yes. We...found one of the death bubbles and broke it down."

Axel's eyebrows do the weird thing where he looks like he's going to raise them skeptically but doesn't want to give that much away.

So she reaches into her breast pocket, pulling out her needle case and laying it on the bench, pulling out her new gold needle.

In the setting sun of the solarium, it still thrums with power.

"He gave you a needle, huh?" Axel says, leaning over it but not touching, "First books, now a fancy new—"

"He made it," she says, and his eyebrows do the thing again, "from the gold that melted in the maelstrom."

Axel gives her a deeply skeptical look.

"Right in front of me, with it in my hand. Just...remade it." She picks it up from the bench, and it sings in her hand. "I've done nothing with it except for taking down the bubble but it...it's fantastic." She unfolds the linen next to her needle case, with the vivid bright bit of magic still woven in its strands.

Even this far away from its source, the magic still shines bright, perfectly preserved.

"A, that's just a bit of cloth," he says, but in good humor. An old joke between them, from before they were ever in such dire situations. Back when he could very well sense magic himself, just in a different way than her.

"I took some of the magic from the death bubble," she says, laying her hand on it, and it grows warm to her touch. "Apparently that magic likes me now."

He leans back, eyebrows still raised, and evaluates her.

"I brought it to do experiments, to see what could be done with it, but today I was literally distracting the magic just so Zoel could untangle some that a village of spirits needed to survive and then we got to see them and—"

Axel holds up a hand, in the age-old signal to slow the heck down, so Alette falls silent.

"Zoel?"

"That's...that's the Wight's name," she says, almost prickly. "He's been the main contact for this project."

"Project," he repeats after her, but his eyebrows steadily rise. "And now Terese's old magic likes you."

"It didn't kill me, that's for sure," Alette jokes, but it falls flat.

His face twists into his thinking expression, like he's weighing his words. "I have a few things," he starts, which is absolutely to prevent her from interrupting him, because they both know that she will. "One: using someone else's magic like that is pretty damn risky." She nods along. "Two: using a magical item created by a non-human entity is...probably damn risky. We're gonna have to ask Melekai if there's any risks to using it 'cause only stupid people pick up other people's implements and expect them to work the same—"

"It's not another person's, it's mine, he made it for me right in front of me," Alette interrupts, and he waves his hand at her to stop interrupting.

"Three, what the heck does this guy want if he's trying to woo you so badly?" At this he grins at her, suddenly mischievous. "Seriously, books, now a gold needle, it's like an entire course on how to impress you."

Alette pauses long enough to give him a flatly unamused look, at which he just gleefully smiles at her.

"Do you need your answers in order?" she asks loftily, which does nothing to stop his grinning. "Fine. One, I know, the magic was literally crawling up my arm, but it got it to behave and I was not going to not run experiments on that."

He nods, giving her the point. "Two, you're probably right, I'll run diagnostics on it—"

"—I'm still texting Mel," Axel interrupts.

"Three," she raises her voice to speak over him, "literally he wants my help. Literally there was a community that would have died in a few weeks if we didn't untangle it. I'm fairly certain these are bribes to make me come back. No wooing involved."

"Hell of a bribe," he says, and he's not inherently wrong. "What are you going to tell Gurlien?"

"Nothing," Alette says immediately.

"You think he's going to let you run around for forever while putting off those spells that he says will save the world?" he asks, which is another good point that she hates giving him. "I say we bring him in and show him actual progress is being made—maybe he'll back off."

Alette bites back her initial gut reaction to that sentence and lets herself think.

He's not entirely wrong, though the prideful part of her wants to keep Gurlien as far away as possible.

"I'm not convinced that he is telling the whole truth about the world ending—yeah, he told me that too, to 'try to get your cooperation,'" Axel uses air quotes on that. "But I'm also not convinced that he's not. Especially with how this place looks, and the store."

"Me neither," Alette says, though her brain spins off, beyond her control, until she is caught up in her own thoughts and Axel turns back to a piece of surveillance equipment he's tinkering with, well used to her thinking face. "But we can't...just wipe everything out."

"That'd include your Wight, wouldn't it?" Axel says, confident. "Then we don't do that. Easy decision. I'm on Team No Genocide."

Alette's gut sinks, because he wouldn't say that if he knew what else Gurlien is holding over her...and she can't quite make herself tell him.

Not yet, at least. Not while they're like this, still trying to figure things out.

THE NEXT DAY, Spot's sitting neatly outside her door when she opens it, a paper bag in his mouth, and his tail thumps when he sees her.

"Hello, boy." Alette waves the pieces of paper she already prepped, everywhere they clashed with Terese categorized by severity and by GPS location, and folds it up neatly. "Everything's all prepped."

It's printed out neatly from the spreadsheet onto three pages.

Carefully, like he's carrying something fragile, Spot sets the paper bag down, then bows his head, letting her fix the pages onto his collar, before he nudges the paper bag towards her.

"Okay—" Alette starts, but as she bends down to pick up the bag, Spot sprints away, shadows trailing after him. "Right."

Alette takes a moment to stare after the shadow dog, before opening the bag.

Inside, are daffodils. A fair amount, all tied together with a stem of another plant, vivid in their colors.

It's far too early for daffodils, and Alette hasn't seen them in any stores nearby, and there's still bits of dirt clinging to their stems. Like they were picked that very day, as impossible as it is in this stage of winter.

Alette touches one of her fingers to the petals, but it

bends, exactly like a normal flower, soft and tender. It stirs no vague idea of magic, no taste of the unreal.

Just some flowers.

Despite herself, a smile tugs at her lips, and she sweeps back inside to tuck them into a vase.

17

A XEL (8:01 AM): Are you up? Got a lead.

Alette, having woken up three hours earlier and spent the entire time in a feverish haze of decoding the scrolls, briefly considers throwing her phone against the wall.

ALETTE (8:02 AM): You're going to need to be more specific. We need leads on many things.

AXEL (8:03 AM): The demony asshole herself. Terese.

Slowly folding her hands over the scrolls, Alette lets her heart pound for a few seconds.

AXEL (8:04 AM): I'm on my way.

BY THE TIME he picks her up, she's put on all her armor and fine clothing and oiled her hair back into its braid, but her heart still hasn't stopped pounding.

"Where is she?" Alette asks when the door opens, instead of a greeting. "Where is she and who found her?"

"Sandwich is in the car," he says, jerking his thumb at

his Mustang, and she grabs her knapsack and throws it over her shoulder, swinging her coat over it. "I texted Mel and Lyra, they're available for a rescue if we need it."

"Excellent," Alette says, and her hands don't shake only by force of will, as she pushes past him towards the car.

It's been too long since they've had any leads, and she had forgotten the sheer fear that comes along with it, the sheer fear and uncertainty.

Because she could still be dangerous. She could still be insane.

Spot circles Axel's Mustang, sniffing strongly, all shadows and glinting eyes, though he thumps his tail when she comes into view.

And Zoel had said that Terese wasn't a danger to them.

Alette's going to have to press him more on that. See what he means. See what he knows, see what he can tell her, instead of these half statements and unclear messages.

"Remember the magic dogs?" Alette says, as she pats Spot on the head before getting into the car.

"Are they here?" Axel asks, a bit too eagerly. His fingers drum on the steering wheel, and two empty 5-hour Energy drinks are in the cup holders. "Can they help?"

"I have no earthly idea if they can help, but if I pet the air, that's why," Alette says.

Axel starts the car with a rumble. "Your life is weird."

He peels out and, immediately, Spot sprints along the edge of the car, eyes glinting red.

And they're still on their way to possibly confront Terese.

Alette presses her hand against her breast pocket, against the needle case, feeling its familiar weight. It's a small motion, one she tries to not do, because showing where your weaponry resides is never a smart decision, but she could swear she could feel the warmth of the new golden needle through her coat.

"Where is she?" she asks finally, as the suburban streets turn to freeway.

"Weird little town of Skykomish, Washington," he says, as Spot bounds next to them. "Remember Luis the Scholar? He drove through on his way to some skiing, said there was a rumor of a half-demon, half-human woman with short blond hair living in the abandoned railway maintenance tunnels."

"Oh, we're going underground," Alette says, because that would have been good information to have.

"They're structurally sound," he says, almost defensive, and out the window she catches the barest glimpse of Zoel, watching as the Mustang speeds down the highway. "Apparently the locals have been avoiding it lately, saying it feels, and I quote, 'super haunted'."

Alette snorts, unladylike. "I can't imagine a world where an abandoned railway tunnel isn't super haunted," she says, as lofty as she can, and gets a grin from Axel.

"Got this, too." Without looking, he hands her his phone, where a grainy black and white video is paused. "Told you I could fix up that TV—I got the security footage from a nearby carpark, ran it through the receiver."

She presses play and it's just a CCTV video of a pathway near a parking lot before a figure with short hair and a leather jacket, cautious, looking both ways, crosses the screen.

"Here, pause it when she looks." He taps on the phone and the video freezes, with the figure turned towards the camera.

The eyes reflect the light back.

Chills run down Alette's spine. It's close, it's so close to how demons look, but still too blurry for confirmation.

"What are you thinking? We confirm she's there then blast some sort of stunning spell?" Alette says, putting the phone down.

"I'd say stun first then ask questions later," he says, but jerks his thumb towards the back of his car. "If we don't report back by end of day, Lyra's gonna come find our bodies."

"Dark," Alette says, having no wish to go through that entire process again, "but I guess a nice backup."

The road turns more rural, to high reaching trees and black stone boulders jutting out of the ground. Less snow, more of a grim and depressing dampness everywhere she can see.

Rain mists onto his windshield, and she could swear Spot is dancing in between the drops.

"I mostly want confirmation," Axel says after a while of comfortable silence, muted. They must be growing close to the location, by Alette's amorphous grasp on where this town is.

She waits for him to continue as they drive through the dreary landscape of northern Washington.

"Some confirmation that she's out there, some confirmation that we did something before, some confirmation that we aren't insane or crazy, some confirmation that this isn't a wild goose chase, that there is an end possibly in sight." It's more maudlin than what she usually hears from Axel, so she gives him his space, looking out the window onto the rain-streaked roads.

At some point in the last hour of driving, Spot had peeled away, and she's not sure entirely when. Still, the lack of his joyful bounding casts a dimmer light on the conversation.

"That if we find her, maybe everything will stop breaking apart," he continues, which isn't better, and she knows, she just knows where this is veering towards, "that everything could be fixed."

It's something Alette has thought of, too, of course. That by finding Terese, they could have every aspect of their lives back.

"I know," Alette says, more to the window, as he clicks his turn signal on to exit the freeway, to cross an old railway bridge onto a gravel road, towards a small cluster of buildings.

And then she spots it.

Floating through the middle of town, lackadaisical, is a strip of magic. Not quite as big as a full Ley Line, but larger than the ribbon, and healthy, unencumbered.

She inhales, eyes tracking it, but it doesn't tangle through the trees, doesn't catch on anything.

So this is what a normal one looks like.

It glimmers with the promise of health, which isn't something she knew could happen but apparently it does. It flutters around the few people striding around, ebbing and flowing around them, reacting in real time to its environment. It disappears off on a gravel path, merrily trailing away until the end is out of her view.

It's beautiful in its simplicity.

"Luis says it's fairly easy to hike to the tunnel—it's well marked. Used to be a popular hangout place until the last few weeks," Axel says, pushing onwards with forceful cheerfulness, before he pulls out a gun from his glove compartment and fits the holster on his belt.

"Did we cross the border with that?" Alette asks, and he just nods. "Axel…"

He tucks a Taser into his pocket. "What, they're Americans, they're not gonna mind some extra guns in their country," he says, clipping a knife on. "You have your magic, I don't right now, I want to defend myself."

She doesn't have an answer to that, so she steps out of the Mustang and onto the gravel parking lot.

The town itself is little more than a few official looking buildings and spread out tiny houses, run down with the sort of poverty that comes with these small abandoned railway towns. Blackberry brambles cover the fences leading away from the town, edging into the gravel pathway, like one good summer is all it would take for the blackberries to take over, to consume everything.

The mist settles lightly in her hair, too light to be called rain, too damp to be just fog. The strip of magic glitters with it, like it too can collect water.

As if sensing her presence, the strip flutters close to her, as if exploring her own sense of magic. As if it could recognize someone new and go investigate.

Alette holds perfectly still as Axel rummages in his trunk for his go-bag and lets the strip explore.

It bumps against her hip, whisper soft, barely a touch, before flickering away, fluttering back on the course she saw it.

Consider herself examined.

A smile tugs on Alette's lips.

"Did Luis say anything about the magic in the area?" she asks, finally turning away from the now completely disinterested bit of magic.

Axel gives her a sidelong look. "What are you on about, is this another break?"

"Not at all, I'm just..." Because how does one explain this? "Wondering."

"No, but he's not the most attuned, he just studies shit," Axel says, swinging his go-bag over his shoulder, before starting to stride towards the thin gravel path to the forest, the thin gravel path that the same strip of magic trails along. "If you keep this up, you're gonna take the creepy mantle away from Lyra."

"Impossible," Alette says, following him.

The magic flutters against her again as she walks alongside it, and, tentatively, she rests a hand on it.

Just like the first Ley Line, it surges with power, thrumming through her veins and pounding with her heart, so she drops the connection quickly.

No need to give Terese—if she can still sense magic—any warning.

They walk in comfortable silence, the magic bumping against her every once in a while, as if checking to see if she's still there.

They draw closer to the hill, and the sense of dread grows in Alette's stomach, and Axel's hand rests on the butt of the gun, fingers nervously tapping. It's densely wooded, and the gravel trail narrows several times, until they can no longer walk side by side.

"Should have brought a machete," Alette says, as Axel has to bat away a trailing vine of blackberries.

At that, the strip of magic bumps against her harder, almost knocking her back a few steps, as if it could tell what she's saying.

Which is another question she's gonna have to ask Zoel, and, for the first time that day, her heart thumps with something resembling hope, instead of nerves and terror.

"I wish..." Axel starts, then falls silent, his profile tense.

"I wish, instead of a bureaucrat, they had sent a combat mage."

"Now, that'd be actually useful," Alette agrees. Because while she knows combat magic, while she has limited combat training, it's not her strongest suit, and—

Suddenly, something trickles down the back of her spine. Something between a ward and a premonition.

She stills on the gravel path.

Her instincts aren't the best—how could they be, if she had been so easily fooled by her own aunt so many times— but something, somewhere pokes at her awareness.

Axel stops after a few steps, turning back to look at her. "You okay?"

"Yes," Alette says, precise, then focuses.

There are no obvious wards, nothing she can see or sense, nothing tied between the trees, nothing physically stopping her. No written runes, no demon magic sticking out like a sore thumb, and the strip of magic is still happily fluttering along the path.

Alette shakes her head, but the sensation doesn't come loose.

"I hate this," Axel says, an unhappy tilt to his mouth. "You're sensing something, aren't you, and I can't do anything."

"I know," Alette says, and the creeping drips down the back of her neck. "It's not anything distinct, just...the heebie jeebies."

He gives her a flat look. "Heebie jeebies," he repeats.

She takes a breath, as if to ready an answer, but nothing's coming easily, so she takes another, letting her eyes wander.

"There's no rune, there's nothing demonic," she says, scrunching her face up, "just...a sense I shouldn't be here?"

The flat look doesn't go away.

"Nothing concrete, nothing I can really define, just..." She hugs her arms to herself. "I'm sorry, it's just weird."

Axel takes a moment, and she can see him bite back his anger at the situation, at his own powerlessness, before he nods, curt.

"Well, we've done weird before," he says, with a forced cheerfulness that seems wronger than anything else. "Shall we?"

Alette nods and makes herself take another step forward.

The feeling doesn't go away, but stays there, pressing down on her, making every little motion a little bit more difficult, a little bit more treacherous.

It's not exactly a difficult hike, but by the time they draw close to the mountain and the barren ruins start to appear, sweat trickles underneath Alette's collar, and they both hang back.

The entrance to the underground tunnel is...fine. Identical to all the other railway ruins and forgotten mine entrances that dot the Pacific Northwest. Rotting planks frame above the tunnel, and what might've been tracks to a handcart still rust on the ground.

But the blackberry brambles have reclaimed large pipes, and metal tools crumble against the mountainside, like they've been forgotten by time. Graffiti, all normal vandalism sprayed by bored teenagers, decorates the rock wall, quick little scratches that prove that people were once here.

"I'm not getting haunted vibes, are you?" Axel asks, and he hasn't lost that flat look from his face, like even being around Alette and her abilities is causing him upset.

Alette has to look real hard at her surroundings to avoid feeling bad.

"I'm still getting fuck-off vibes," she says, which is about the least scientific she's ever been, "but no, no magical abnormalities."

In contrast, the strip of magic remains healthy and, to the best of her knowledge, happy, and it twists and flutters directly into the heart of the tunnel.

She wishes she knew more about it to know what it could be leading her to. If healthy magic always means good things or if it's just a neutral state of being.

Carefully, she stows her water bottle to pull out her needle case and selects the new curved golden needle, her blood thrumming in time with whatever magic it's imbued with.

The leaves still clinging to the trees and the needles on the spruce rustle, turning towards her direction like iron to a magnet.

The strip of magic pulls taut, as if it could tell she had armed herself, before ruffling and resuming the lazy meander.

Axel whistles lowly as the leaves calm down. "Was that on purpose?"

"No," Alette says, but lets her finger dance over the curve of the gold, "it just feels pretty strong."

Axel looks up to the rotted wood over the entrance, then huffs out a breath. "A, I don't want to doubt you," he starts, "but should you use unpredictable magic when we're about to confront someone who's dangerous? It could, quite literally, blow up in your face."

"I know," Alette says, but doesn't put away the needle, keeping it lightly between her fingertips.

The creeping sensation down her neck stops, then recedes, in time with the dripping of the condensation from the tunnel.

At her motions, Axel rests the palm of his hand on his gun, unbuckling whatever holster strap keeps it in place. She knows he knows how to use it, having been raised mostly on a farm in America, but it's still beyond strange, seeing him rely on weaponry like that.

But Terese had taken so much from him, she doesn't blame him for wanting to protect himself however he can.

They look at each other, then nod, neither one of them really wanting to speak out, and it's only years of knowing each other that stops them both from chickening out.

It seems too easy, it most likely is too easy, but they've done so many of these searches now, in godforsaken places, that Alette forces herself to exhale.

"Well," she says, and this close to the entrance, her voice echoes, "let's make sure this place is empty, then we can get some truly disgusting fast food on the way home."

"See, you say that, now you've jinxed it," Axel says, flicking on his flashlight.

The inside of the tunnel is as damp as outside, and what Alette hopes is a mouse skitters away from the beam.

"How long is the tunnel?" Alette asks, and takes a step inside.

Immediately, all sound drops away and she can see Axel's mouth moving, but hears nothing.

Alette holds up a hand, and he abruptly stops, before she steps back out.

"Silencing spell," she says, and they exchange another grim look, "right across the entrance."

"Aaaand I'm texting Mel and Lyra," Axel says, quickly typing on his phone. "Can you let your ghost person know where we are? He'd come rescue you, right?"

"He doesn't have a phone," Alette says, but casts her eyes around for any hint of the shadow dogs.

Nothing.

Still, she uses the needle to pull a bit of power from the world, a little gossamer thread, and hooks it on the edge of the rotting planks over the entrance. A sign for if someone comes looking.

She rests her finger on the thread and lets her eyes shut. Tries to think of Zoel's face, of the set of his jaw, of the pep in his shoulders, of the strange, shuddering feel of his wholly inhuman magic when she walks next to him.

It's far too easy to draw the picture in her mind.

Then, on her exhale, she imbues some strange earnestness to see Zoel, that if something happens, the thread would reach him. That if the danger reaches a certain point —she's never figured out how it measures the danger, but it does—that it would find him.

Axel watches with a raised eyebrow. "A phone would be easier."

"I agree," Alette says, lifting her finger away from the thread, and it quivers against the rotted wood, ready for any signal from her or any major hurt. "But there. Rescue magic at the ready, if we need it. No clue where he is, so it might take him a bit—"

"—Can he teleport?" Axel interrupts.

"I haven't gotten the faintest idea," Alette snips back. "Disappear and reappear, yes, teleport, who knows."

"I'm honestly surprised you haven't badgered him for an answer," Axel says, bouncing on his toes, before he looks back in the tunnel. "Let's...let's try this."

With a curt nod, Alette steps back in with Axel right behind her.

"Weird," Axel whispers, and his voice falls away but she can hear him inside.

Outside, she can see the spruce needles rustling, but

can't hear them. Just the drip of condensation and her own thudding heartbeat.

"Might not be her," Alette whispers back, "but it's something."

He lifts up his hand, idly examining it. "Different," he remarks, dryly. "Silencing spells still feel weird even when you don't have magic."

She eyes him—even without his magic it seems like he can still sense it. And...maybe, just maybe, not everything is lost.

It'll require testing, when he doesn't know it's coming. Randomized, so she can see what he can feel, what is still there.

Her mind spirals off, making plans on top of plans, tests she can run and things she can check, both at the Headquarters and out, spells she can write and spells she can try.

In the last month, he had shown no ability to feel anything before. So what changed now, and how can she duplicate it, how can she ensure reliability, ensure replication at needed times, and—

Deep in the tunnel, something moves, whisper fast, and both of them snap the flashlights over.

Nothing.

Alette exhales. "I've been in caves too much recently," she says, though the joke falls as flat as the noise in the tunnel.

"Zoel take you in one?" Axel asks, but he, too, is focused down the tunnel.

The walls look like they were once cleanly hewn, but disuse and humidity have taken their toll, and boulders and reinforcement beams dot their view, leaving lots of places for something—or someone—to hide.

"As a shortcut," Alette answers, rolling the needle

between her fingers as subtly as she can, threading it just enough that if something happens, she won't have to think about it.

Eyes wary, Axel pulls out the gun, holding it loosely in his hand.

They take a few extra steps silently in the tunnel.

"How long is the tunnel?" she whispers, the gold still singing in her hand.

"Less than a quarter mile," Axel answers, "just long enough to be good for a hideaway."

Deep down the tunnel, there's a tinkle of a falling pebble, like someone kicked it, audible even through the muting spell.

Alette swallows past the fear as the tunnel winds around a corner in front of them.

If she was going to ambush someone, it'd be there.

Axel knows it too, and he inhales, shooting her a look before bringing up the gun, aiming it down the hallway.

He's a good shot—he's practiced too much the last month.

There's a thin sheen of anticipation inside of her, that this might actually be a place where they can check off this grim task, deal with this problem.

Actually be effective for once.

"Protect your eyes?" Alette murmurs, barely audible, and Axel nods, sharp.

With the power already threaded through her needle— resisting the temptation to thread with the healthy and flowing strip of magic, she lashes out.

It's a spell she's done hundreds of times, both in the carefully controlled practice room with its foam walls and in the wild, and it's far flashier than it is destructive.

But flashy it is.

Even through her squeezed shut eyes, the magic sparks and then ignites, blasting the entire area in a blaze of vivid white light, snapping around the corner and surging down the tunnel.

It crashes, loud, so loud it used to make Alette's ears ring, so loud it punches through the silencing spell and barrels down the tunnel in a cacophonous din.

All other sound blooms around them as the silence spell shatters apart. Tinkling pebbles, Axel's harsh breathing, her own heartbeat thudding against her brain.

And running footsteps, skidding towards them.

In between one moment and the next, mere yards down the tunnel, Terese is in front of them.

And the seconds slow down and Alette pulls more magic into her needle.

Terese's hair is longer, much longer than the harsh shorn cut it was before, her skin pallid and her pale eyes rimmed with dark circles. Her leather jacket hangs loose on her shoulders, and she's hunched in on herself.

She locks eyes with Alette as Alette threads the magic through the gold and there's no demon. No double vision of a monstrous face, no red/black glow.

Terese reels back at the sight of them, before she slams her hand down onto the ribbon of magic next to her, yanking it towards her, brilliant against the darkness.

Alette has just enough time to reach her hand up to her face before the power whips over to her, bashing her into the rock wall and knocking her glasses askew, and—

Shaken, Alette pushes against the magic but it slams her hand against the rock of the tunnel wall, holding her needle immobile.

Axel shoots, the gunshot echoing too close in the tunnel. Her ears ring, it's too close—

Terese's head snaps back, blood blossoming on her forehead, but—

She staggers, feet digging in on the gravel tunnel, but not falling.

She rights herself, her eyes blinking blankly at them, a gory hole in her skull, blood running in rivulets down her nose and her blond-white eyebrows.

Axel's hands shake, but he doesn't drop the gun.

"Who are you?" Terese asks him, able to speak despite the literal bullet in her brain, and her singsong voice has the temerity to be puzzled. "I know her"—she nods at Alette, blood dripping down her chin and onto the dust of the floor—"but who are you?"

Axel's finger tightens around the trigger again and this time a bloody hole punches itself through Terese's chest, through her dirty white shirt, and she staggers a few steps back.

But her grasp on the magic doesn't let up, no matter how much Alette struggles against it, grip like a vise on her wrist.

Terese's eyes slide over to her, and Alette can see part of her ribcage and bits of her skull. Deliberately, Terese stills, and despite there being no demon inside of her that Alette can sense, power thrums in her gaze.

Confidence replaces the panic Alette saw on first glance, as Terese's eyes slide to the needle in her hand, to the little gold curve.

"Fuck," Terese says, eloquent, then, just as suddenly as they first saw her, disappears.

18

Without Terese's strange magic pinning her against the wall, Alette sags to the ground before jerking upright, grabbing the ribbon of magic in front of her.

It pulses against her hand, warm, but entirely harmless.

"What," Axel breathes out, and he's still holding the gun out, his hand shaking like a leaf, "the hell."

Alette releases the strip of magic and it flutters merrily onward, down the curve of the tunnel.

There's still blood and bits of bone and brain matter on the gravel pathway.

"I'm okay," she says, stowing her needle, but Axel doesn't even look at her, "it was just immobilizing, I'm okay." Her head rings, her back will be sore, but she's okay.

Probably.

When Axel doesn't move, she strides over, pulling the pistol out of his hands with no resistance. She flicks back on the safety, then tucks it into her bag.

There's a small collection of items, things, tucked against the wall, and Alette's heart is pounding too heavily to comprehend what happened, what they're going to do, so she inspects instead. Tosses her brain into investigation mode, lets herself lose herself in logical thoughts, into concrete information in front of them, so it doesn't spiral out into desperation and despair.

She nudges the small pile with the toe of her boot as Axel remains frozen on the spot. The pile does nothing, just tumbles over.

There's an extra jacket—another leather one—and a spare shirt, a battered notebook with a pen, a single can of unopened dog food, and...

And a perfectly clear stone, half the size of a marble, that glistens like water.

Alette raises an eyebrow at it, resisting the urge to pull out the identical one from her breast pocket.

So Terese had dealt with the spirits. Maybe the same ones she had.

Not touching anything with her bare skin, Alette loads the few items into her bag, magical cross-contamination be damned, before she crouches with a small Ziplock baggie and scoops some of the bloody dust into it.

"I don't know, something might help," she says preemptively.

But Axel's still. And there's no magic, nothing keeping him in place.

"Did she hurt you?" Alette asks, because she didn't see anything, no magic, nothing visible, but—

"How'd she not know who I was?" Axel blurts out, spinning towards her, eyes manic. "I've hunted her, we've seen her so many times, she did this to me, and she didn't know who I was—"

Alette stands and he abruptly falls silent, like the words are torn away from him.

"I don't know," she says, but Axel starts pacing. The tunnel isn't wide enough, just two strides long.

"She did this"—he jabs at his chest and Alette knows exactly what he's talking about—"to me, and she didn't even remember me?"

Alette's stomach sinks. "Axel," she starts, but he doesn't stop the pacing, "Axel, you look different."

That pulls him up short and his face falls then shutters closed as her words register, before he ducks his head and looks away.

Alette lets him, pulling another sample of what might be a bit of bone from the ground and sealing it into a bag.

He doesn't speak as she hoists her bag up onto her aching shoulder and gestures for him to follow her.

"We don't have any leads," Alette starts, but he's still silent, "but maybe, just maybe, we can get a tracker on this."

He nods, curt, but follows her anyways.

OUTSIDE THE TUNNEL, the sprinkling has turned into steady rain, mixing a mud out of the dust and grime coating Alette. Axel's shoulders drop from around his ears when they make it out, but the grim set of his jaw doesn't go away.

Between one breath and the next, Zoel appears, walking next to her, knee deep in the blackberry bramble.

At Alette's quick intake of breath, Axel turns around. "What?"

It's the first word's he's spoken since—

"What are you doing here?" Zoel asks, and they're both talking to her at once so she squeezes her eyes shut, lets herself breathe, for just a moment, until her pounding heart is under her control and she can open her eyes again without feeling like she's about to have a panic attack.

"Axel, the Wight I told you about is here, I'm going to be talking to empty air," she warns, and Axel nods. "Hi."

Zoel gives her a half-amused look, the dimple appearing, before the expression vanishes. "What are you doing here?"

"Should I be introduced?" Axel asks loudly, shifting back and forth on his feet and looking wildly around the forest. Which really, after Melekai, he should be used to someone having conversations without him being able to see or hear. "I'm Axel, she likes the books, how are you?" She recognizes the mask, the sudden change in demeanor—he's grabbing onto the distraction with both hands and running with it.

Zoel's eyes track over to Axel, then flicker back to Alette.

"I think you're fine," Alette says to Axel, who gives her a shrug, before Zoel sighs and—

Everything about him flickers, before stabilizing again, and Axel takes a step back.

Ah. Did whatever Spot did that one time, made himself visible.

Looks exactly the same to Alette.

"Hello," Zoel says, a thin layer of irritation on his voice, and he's gritting his teeth, like this takes effort out of him. "I'm Zoel, what are you two doing here?"

There's Terese's stuff in her bag, blood samples and everything.

"Did you get my alarm?" Alette asks, too exhausted to pretend otherwise, now with mud and possibly blood splatter on her front, "Sorry—"

Zoel glances between the two of them, before his brow furrows and softness makes its way back to his face.

"Are you hurt?" he asks, dipping his voice down low towards her, like he needs to check. "Did she hurt you?"

Axel's eyes flicker between the two of them.

So Zoel knew who was in this tunnel. Or can sense it.

"No, I'm...I'm unharmed," Alette says, and she feels like she's about to shake apart, from all the scares and the adrenaline and everything.

"She got bashed into a wall," Axel says. "Terese left."

It's such a wholly incomplete summary of what happened that Alette has to shut her eyes to stop from reacting.

"I gathered," Zoel says, disgruntled, "or else you'd either be in there trying to continue whatever you did, or she'd be out here running."

Despite his rough words, however, he reaches out a hand, touching the edge of her sleeve, where rain water mixes with the grime, and there's specks of blood.

"It's not mine," Alette says, and the lines around his eyes soften. "I'm okay, I was immobilized, not bashed."

"She was bashed," Axel says, crossing his arms over his chest. "How'd you know who it was?"

Zoel's blue eyes flicker to hers and he curves an eyebrow at her, like he's checking in, checking to see what she's said, but Alette can't answer, too close to falling apart.

His hand gentles on her elbow, a support, and Alette wants to lean into it, lean against him, beyond all logic.

They're in the rain, and it's not far to the car and she's absolutely gross.

"Her magic is obvious," he says instead, but his tone promises words later. "I can go bring medical help."

Axel relaxes, but his brows draw together, and she doesn't like the look on his face. It's the look of sizing someone up, of the big brother trying to determine some-one's worth or something.

She's seen it far too many times, and she's far too tired to deal with it.

"I don't need medical help, I need a night of rest and some good food and a shower," Alette says, and starts walking again.

She doesn't need to look behind herself to know that both men exchange glances, but they follow her anyways.

"This is a lot of head trauma over not terribly many days," Axel says loudly.

Alette ignores him. If he gets to fall apart and have a breakdown back there, then she can have a miniature one on the trail.

"I can arrange for food at the end of the trail," Zoel continues, in the same tone of voice as Axel, which is really not helping things, "if that is the sort of thing that is needed."

"Any idea why I could literally shoot Terese and it does nothing?" Axel asks, and Alette has to close her eyes briefly, then pushes forward again.

"Did you think that a mundane weapon would stop her?" Zoel asks, but it's not combative, it's the honest curiosity that she almost expects from him.

"Ouch," Axel quips back.

"I don't think a gun would do much to Melekai, either," Zoel continues, which is again interesting information, "and there is far more to Terese than there is to him."

The strip of magic flutters against her and Alette lays her hand against it, and Zoel cuts his words off, going suddenly silent.

She casts a glance behind her, but both of them are still walking behind her. Zoel's eyes bore into hers, like he can feel her touch through the magic instead of through the physical.

Axel raises an eyebrow at her, almost amused, like the distractions have been good for him, like he's recovered whatever part of himself he got tied up with back there.

Which is good. Means that he can help Alette figure out ways to track Terese, even if he can't execute the magic himself.

The blood and the items weigh heavy on her back, so she releases the magic. It flutters against her again, a gentle lean.

"Like I said, like calls to like," Zoel says, with a nod at the strip of magic.

"Wha—" Axel starts, before cutting himself short.

"Terese used this one, too," Alette says, and it's more bitter than she expected the words to come out.

He nods, like it's not a surprise to him, and they are going to have words when this is over, when Axel's gone.

"I'm glad you're okay," Zoel says, neutral, and she doesn't need to look at Axel to know that his brows are raised, "and I'm glad she didn't...injure you two further."

The path widens, and almost as one, both of the guys sidle up next to either side of her, and Alette knows when she's being ganged up on.

"I'm fine," she says, again. "She disappeared when she saw the needle." She gives Zoel a significant look at that, but he doesn't seem surprised.

"Yeah I have questions," Axel says, and it's like he's gaining more confidence with each step. "What should she avoid doing with that fancy tool?"

"I wouldn't give her something that wouldn't at least be all purpose," Zoel says, but he bumps his shoulder against hers, achingly gentle. "It'd be better at fixing things, rather than destructive."

Alette wants to speak up, say that Axel needs the babying more than her, that he was the one treated so casually, that he needs the emotional support, but as the adrenaline drains out of her, she can't make herself bring it up.

She can't believe they actually saw her. They actually found Terese, even if only for a few moments.

She's definitely alive, she's definitely still powerful.

But something in Alette has trouble figuring out if she's a threat or not.

Beyond the obvious. Beyond the absolute casual immobilizing of her, beyond the utter lack of care she showed to a gunshot to the head, beyond the easy grip of magic. Something in the encounter, something in the entire thing, wiggles in the back of her mind.

She stumbles, and Zoel immediately catches her by the elbow.

He shoots an apologetic look to Axel. "Sorry," he says, before everything about him flickers once more, before he stabilizes her, helping her with her balance.

Axel flinches, full body.

"He's still here, he's just invisible," Alette says, and Zoel winks at her for that, before he throws an arm around her, letting her lean against him.

"This is just like Melekai at first all over again," Axel grumbles, but gives her a nod. "I take it physical touch is difficult when he's actually appearing to the not-magical?"

"I wouldn't call you not magical," Zoel says, then sighs the moment he realizes Axel can't hear him.

"What do you mean by that?" Alette asks, her mind desperately searching for something to think about that's not the day they've had.

Zoel gives her a look, like she's supposed to know what he means.

"Why do I have a feeling you're going to be very sore?" Zoel says, which is unfair. "Any chance you can take it easier tomorrow?"

"Doubtful," Alette says, but she leans against him all the same.

Much faster than the hike in, the end of the trail with Axel's Mustang comes into view, and three perfect bags of takeout food rest on the trunk.

Alette cranks her head over to look at Zoel, who has the temerity to look smug.

"Did he..." Axel trails off, then sighs. "He absolutely got food for us, didn't he."

Zoel smirks, dimple appearing on his chin.

"Yup," Alette says.

"Been here the entire time?" Axel asks.

"Yup."

"Blame Spot and Grey," Zoel says, which again doesn't make any sense because she's seen no hint of the dogs on this walk. "They make getting out the message pretty damn easy."

He hangs back as Axel trots forward to examine the bags and, almost instinctively, Alette stands with Zoel.

The moment that Axel could be conceivably out of hearing, even though Zoel wouldn't be able to be heard by Axel anyways, Zoel turns to her, close, but pauses, like he's looking for what to say, like what he needs to say is delicate.

"Thanks for the food," Alette says, when a few moments of silence passes, too tired and too wound up to actually let things grow awkward.

"Of course," he says, and his hand is still light against her elbow. "Alette...you're okay?"

She takes a deep breath, then another, pushing past the initial gut reaction to deflect, giving herself a moment to figure out his answer, to figure out what she needs to say.

"This is the first time I've seen her since she killed my aunt, and we were an afterthought," Alette says finally, as the rain lightens to just a mist. Her hair is plastered to her forehead and detangling her braid is going to be a mess, but the mud is thankfully almost gone. "I could do nothing."

Tentatively, he reaches his hand to where her head hit the wall of the tunnel, but it barely hurts. "She is...far more powerful than you think," he says, which no shit, "but unless you come after her, she's not going to hurt you."

Alette swallows past her anger, swallows past the flash of rage at his words. "You know her now, don't you?" she asks, and it's only from years of practicing control that she knows how to keep her words even. "Are you...what are you doing with her?"

He ducks his head, still cradling her by the neck, and despite the rage she doesn't want him to stop.

"It's my...job...to keep people safe here, whenever I can," he says. "And I do not judge by who controlled them before."

"The College..." Alette trails off as his jaw tightens at the mention. "The College wants us to bring her in."

"You shouldn't," he says immediately. "They'll dissect her and hurt her and she, that human back there who's so scared she's hiding in tunnels, does not deserve that."

Alette looks back towards the tunnel, now obscured by trees and blackberry brambles.

"The demon, yes, she would have," Zoel continues, "but what is left, should not be under their thumb."

She doesn't know how to answer that, so she forces

herself to breathe out of her nose, forces herself to remain still.

"Zoel, she killed Aunt Frisse," she says, and her voice breaks halfway through, breaks in a way it hasn't in years, "Zoel..."

Slowly, as if telegraphing his motions, he leans close to her, until their foreheads meet, and it's far more tender than she has any right to feel.

"I know," he says gently. "Can you trust me on this?"

Alette blinks up at him, and his eyes are so blue so close, but he's earnest, of course he is. "I..."

"If she—the human—ever becomes a threat to you, or to any humans, or to the magical structure how it is right now, I will stop her," he says, so perfectly earnest, "but if you try to bring her in, it'll only result in you getting hurt or her suffering for something she didn't do."

It's hard to think about, so she looks anywhere but him.

The mist falls softly on the spruce needles, darkening the gravel path, and Axel sits on the trunk of his car, keeping an obvious eye on Alette but munching on a burger nonetheless.

"Can we...can we talk about this?" Alette forces herself to say. "Can we meet and discuss this, so I know...so I can know she won't..."

He nods, his forehead still against hers. "See if you can call off the College."

Alette snorts and he smiles.

"I'll try," she says, leaning back, but gripping his hand and giving it a squeeze. "They're not great at listening to me."

His blue eyes flicker down to her hand, so she drops his, wondering if she crossed some sort of line.

He leans back as well, and it's awkward, it's all of a

sudden very awkward. "You should go eat," he says with a nod to where Axel's watching with a raised eyebrow. "I'll...I'll send the dogs with a message."

Then, without waiting for her to say anything, he disappears, and it's so close to when Melekai felt awkward that a smile tugs on her lips as she goes and rejoins Axel on the trunk of his car.

"That was interesting," he says, handing her a bag, which includes the exact veggie burger that she prefers, which she has absolutely never told Zoel. "Sure he's not trying to court you?"

"Shut it," Alette says, and Axel grins at her. "I think he's just..."

"Sure," Axel says, standing and stretching his legs before opening the car door, "he's just giving you books, needles, knows your fast food order, put his arm around you, showed up when you might be in trouble, didn't want you hurt"—he ticks them off on his fingers—"sure there's a reasonable explanation."

Alette sighs, then follows him into the car, because at least he's not in a spiral of despair.

"He thinks Terese isn't a threat, as long as we leave her alone," she says, after a few minutes of driving, until they're out of the town and onto the tree-lined highway.

"Sure seemed like a threat back there," he says, but he's relaxed enough that he's able to drive. "Did you tell him you got the tracking stuff?"

"No," Alette says, though a smidgen of guilt winds its way through her.

"Good."

19

Three days later, Gurlien demands her to come with him on a drive, and no matter how much she makes suggestions that Axel should come as well, he refuses.

One tensely silent drive later, they arrive at a barren stretch of land, the only thing visible is chaparral and rough stones.

And no matter how much Alette peers, no strips or fluttering magic. Nothing like the Ley Line on the beach, like the strip at the death bubble.

"Do you understand why I picked this place?" Gurlien asks, after sharply watching her pick her way across the broken boulders.

Alette hates saying she doesn't know something, so she just looks further, letting the wind tease out the strands of hair from her braid, inhaling the salty stink of rotten sea water.

It's off. Everything about it is off.

Alette toes her boot against a dried-out shrub. It shatters

easily, giving her no resistance, fragmenting as if it was never a cohesive, living plant.

Considering the entire area had a deluge slush and rain storm just a few days prior, it shouldn't be this bone dry.

The entire land is full of the skeletal husks of the plants that once lived.

"I have reason to believe Terese stripped the magic from this place," Gurlien continues, after it becomes clear she isn't answering, "broke it so much that nothing can exist."

She scuffs against the dirt of the boulder. It brushes away, barely more than crumpling dust.

"That she enacted her plan, that she wanted to take all of the magic, twist it to her own use, until she alone controlled it," he says, bending over to pick up a sun-bleached hollow of a branch. It seems like it belongs more in the Southwest deserts than in the Pacific Northwest. "The only reason this didn't spread further is how remote it is. No communities of others, no connecting magical Ley Lines, nothing."

It almost sounds like Terese had been testing her limits, but Alette knows better than to voice something like that.

"I believe," and Gurlien pauses, intensely gauging her reaction, like she'll reveal more than even she knows. There's a thin sheer of sweat along his foppish blond hair, and it irritates her that she notices. "I believe that this is back when she was still in communication with Joyanne."

Ah.

That's why he brought her here.

She schools her face. "I told you, we weren't let into that at all," she murmurs, like speaking too loud on such a landscape would disrupt whatever dead that lurked. "She only told me and Axel once Terese went rogue."

"Pity," Gurlien says, voice similarly soft. "You might have actually been useful."

Alette holds her expression still only by strength of will. "Or Terese might never have gone rogue," she points out, eyes stinging from the wind and the dust, "or we might've been marked for her vengeance as well."

"Or your common sense might've stopped your aunt," Gurlien says, and it might be the closest to a compliment she's heard from him. "Electric storm not-withstanding, you at least seem to have a bit more caution than Joyanne."

"And Axel's good for getting people out of problems," she says, scanning the land for something, anything to resemble life.

There's a lump of dead fur to one side. Unmoving.

It would be hell to a Necromancer, with how Lyra describes her magic. Just death everywhere.

"I brought you here to show you what could happen if we don't fix the magic," Gurlien says, squinting his eyes in the dusty wind. "This would be over the entire world."

She raises an eyebrow at him.

"This much death, and this little magic." He regards her solemnly. "This is why we shouldn't delay much longer."

BEFORE SHE GOES HOME, she detours to the grocery store, and both dogs peel away as she hits the parking lot. Makes sense that they'd leave. Grocery stores feel more modern than they are. Like, if she were them, she would not know what to do if she saw someone so embedded in the magical nature of the area in someplace as mundane as a grocery store.

But still, she needs food and she can't exactly hunt or

forage or...or whatever Zoel does, and her head still hurts a bit from being bashed into the stone wall the few days prior.

She meanders through the store, picking up whatever food hits her fancy, whatever vegetarian meal she thinks she could easily make, until there's a familiar noise, right on the edge of her hearing.

She stills, setting down the bag of lentils back on the shelf, but doesn't look around, letting her eyes stare at the shelf.

It's a sound she can't immediately place, a sound that isn't quite concrete, but something that doesn't sit well with her instincts. Like it doesn't belong.

So she breathes, stilling herself, and if anyone observes her, it'd just seem like she's absorbed in reading the bag of lentils.

There it is, the sound again, almost imperceptible.

She's not one to act natural very well, so she jerks her head up to look around.

Far on the other end of the grocery aisle, stands Terese.

Terese the human, no trace of demon inside of her.

She faces Alette, full on barring the aisle if someone needs to move past her, but she's dressed in a clean white tank top, a different leather jacket, and a skirt, of all things. With comfortable boots and a purse slung over her shoulder.

No hint of the bloody mark from Axel's shot, no blood spackle from before, but the same dark circles under her eyes and unkempt hair.

And there are people everywhere. A business man passes behind her, completely oblivious to the stare down happening in the rice and grains aisle. There are cans that could be disrupted and things that could go flying, damage to be had.

And it's hundreds of miles away from the tunnel in Oregon.

Terese's eyes shift, like she's counting the exits but is unwilling to move.

Telegraphing her motions and very much not wanting to be bashed into the shelving unit, Alette picks up the lentils, placing them calmly in her basket.

Terese watches her every movement in small jerking motions.

Zoel had said she wasn't a danger to her. Had asked her to trust him.

"I'm just shopping," Alette says softly, but knows somehow deep inside that Terese can hear her, "I'm not here to attack you."

Terese lifts her chin.

Unwilling to move away from the display in front of her, Alette adds a small bag of rice to her cart, making deliberate motions of normalcy.

Soothing wild animals has never been her strong point, and this feels astoundingly like trying to trick a deer to come closer.

Or trying to trick a bear not to attack.

"How did you find me?" Terese asks, her melodic voice barely audible over the grocery store panache of music.

"Tip from a traveler," Alette lies. "Friend heard of a haunted tunnel."

There's little response except for rapid, too fast blinking.

Alette carefully sets a can of tomatoes in her cart, something she could fling if needed. A weapon that would be mundane, instead of magical.

"Did I hurt you? Three days ago?" There's a careful precision in Terese's words, one found in people who are desperate to show they aren't in any way impaired. Like she has to put effort into sounding normal.

And Alette has a feeling she wouldn't appreciate being lied to about this.

"I'm banged up," Alette says, turning from the shelf and finally facing her full on.

Terese flinches, but doesn't disappear, just gives a cautious look over her shoulder.

"You're...better," Alette says cautiously, not moving any closer.

Terese gives her a blank look before her eyes clear and she nods. "Bullets won't kill me."

"I gathered," Alette replies. "We've been..." and she trails off, suddenly at a loss for how to convey what she needs to convey without scaring her off, without causing her to rabbit away. "Look, we need to talk—"

"Who was with you?" Terese blurts out, completely ignoring her. "With the weapon, who was that? Did I know him? Did he know me?"

"...Yes," Alette says, brow furrowing. "Yes, he...you struck him, in the fight with Lyra and you..." The words leave Alette, because how the heck does she describe what happened? "Yes."

"But..." Her face screws up, and it's such a normal motion it's foreign on her pale face, before her colorless lips thin and she scowls.

It's the scowl that's haunted Alette's dreams, and she finds herself taking a step back, completely outside her control, and Terese vanishes.

Leaving Alette in a grocery store aisle with a cart full of food and a pounding heart.

Still moving like she's being watched, she pulls her phone from her purse.

ALETTE (7:02 PM): Saw T while grocery shopping. She asked questions then vanished. No attacking I'm fine.

AXEL (7:02 PM): What the fuk?

ALETTE (7:03 PM): I know!

ALETTE (7:04 PM): She asked if she hurt me, she asked if she knew you, then disappeared.

AXEL (7:05 PM): Of course she did.

AXEL (7:05 PM): Do you need backup?

ALETTE (7:06 PM): No, checking out now.

GUILT SITS sour in her stomach, as she drives away from the store. The two dogs race along with her, appearing between one moment and the next, racing and bouncing in front of her car like it's a toy.

It does nothing for the pit inside of her, but Spot dashes around her car, joyful, flashing his glinting teeth and his blood red eyes like he wants her to play as well.

They circle her car as she parks, and Spot pushes his snout in her hand once more...then at her front left wheel.

"Oh, what'd you find, boy?" Alette murmurs, crouching down next to her car. Her hiking clothes stick to her skin, the sweat now long cooled.

Spot prods at her front left wheel again, and Alette sighs, pulling out her needle case, but before she's even gotten the needle out, the rune is obvious.

Gurlien tracked her car, too.

"Oh, fuck you," Alette mutters, and Spot shies away from her. "No, not you, you're fine, good dog."

So she sits back on her heels and stares at the tracking rune.

There are a few things she can do. She can let him track

her—and all her activities, all her efforts with Zoel—but gain his trust, if that's something she wants to gain, to possibly sway him.

Spot whimpers again, then circles around the car, pushing his nose into her front right wheel as well. Because Gurlien didn't bother with just one, he needed multiple insurances.

Alette stands, dusting off her hands, and it's like she can feel the needle, the golden one, grow warm in her case.

Theoretically, there might be a way to keep it active, but turn it on and off, though that was far more her aunt's forte, doing the magical trickery like that, and Axel's mindset.

And she's sick of this.

With more force than necessary, she yanks the new golden needle out of her case and the entire world sings with her when she does. It takes next to no effort, to will the fabric of existence to thread her needle, and even less to knot it around the rune, prying it off the surface of her tire with barely a flick of her wrist.

Too easy.

Too easy, but her blood fizzes and power thrums around her, and she could do anything.

20

L ater, something wakes her from a deep sleep, the sort of sleep she hasn't had in months.

She keeps her eyes closed, keeps her breathing even, and listens to her apartment, feeling for the magic she wrote into it.

There's no one there, not even a creak in the wood floor, but something stirs at the edge of her awareness. Like something big is about to break, and something inside of her responds to the cracks beginning to show.

Slowly, she pushes herself up, and the magic written in the apartment gradually glows alight, giving her just enough so she can see that she's alone in her place, utterly alone.

Still in her (very tasteful) pajamas, she shoves her feet into her house slippers and stands. It's still dark outside, the deep dark of late midwinter midnight, and the one sodium light across the street shines in the freezing mist.

And the feeling of wrong, the sense that something horrid is going to happen, just grows, magnifying itself until it's doubled, tripled, until every fiber of her being drips with dread.

"Okay," she whispers to the soft glow of her apartment, "okay."

Grabbing her needle case, she swings her coat over her pajamas, and steps outside, into the mist.

It swirls around her, dancing along the hem of her coat, and the taste of ozone fills her nostrils with its impossibility.

She stills, right on her doorstep.

It's not quite like the breakage at Buggees, but it's close, which is just wrong. Terese never tracked down Alette to her apartment, never did any of her death bubbles outside on her lawn, nothing. There'd be no reason for something to go wrong, not here.

Suddenly, out of a glimpse of the corner of her eye, she sees a glimmer of magic. Like something winds its way past her, fluttering wrong.

"Hello," she whispers into the mist, and it swirls in front of her, like it's carried as much by her words as it is by the very air.

The glimmer of magic, barely more than a thread, trails back into the field behind her apartment complex, brushing against her apartment building. It's gnarled and frayed along the edges, like it's a few small motions away from fragmenting apart.

The dogs aren't near, she can't summon Zoel without them, so she takes a step towards the thread, following it into the field. Not quite touching it, but resting her hand near it, like it could guide her.

She had never known there was anything this close to her home before, and it feels glaringly out of place. Like it's lost, like something happened and it's unmoored, trying to return to where it's supposed to be.

"Where are you going?" she whispers to it, stepping into the half-frozen field with it. The ground squelches against her house slippers—she's going to need new ones—but she treads on.

It's not the smartest thing in the world, to walk into a misty field in the middle of the night, but she pushes onwards, propelled by some sense of urgency outside of her.

Alette's smart, but it doesn't take a genius to know that the urgency's coming from this little thread of magic, so close to being broken. That somehow, it fears.

"It's okay," Alette whispers, stepping deeper with it, and holds out her injured hand. The healing blisters throb in the cold, but the strip of magic flutters against her fingertips, tentative, like it's afraid she's going to hurt it as well.

There's something to be said about not anthropomorphizing things that should not be personified, but this late at night, she doesn't feel a wisp of regret at doing so. It's after midnight, let her be whimsical and illogical.

The field gives way to trees, and the thread grows thinner, like every motion and flutter in the wind brings it closer to snapping.

It shouldn't even be influenced by Aunt Frisse, as her aunt had made sure that every bit of magic in her apartment came from Alette only, and she certainly didn't go for a magic trip in the woods behind her place.

Alette herself hadn't really ever tread this way before.

The thread isn't caught between the trees, however, continuing to just flutter against her fingertips as her feet grow cold and wet, and she hadn't even grabbed her phone before stepping out of her door.

But the urgency pulls her forward, deeper and further away from her house, until—

With a sound she hears in her very bones, the thread snaps, shattering apart between one second and the next.

It hits her like a slap, not quite physical, but not quite

outside of the realm of the real, and she flinches back. Fast, too fast for her eyes to track, the edges of the thread spiral away, fraying apart in front of her, like the tension of it was the only thing keeping it together.

And before her, the entire woods fragments apart.

Bark flies off a spruce, shredding like it's nothing more than wet paper, before the wood itself splinters, spraying pine needles and shrapnel everywhere. Blackberry vines, dead in the heart of winter, twist back, blackening as if they were crumpled into a fire.

The ground beneath Alette's feet shudders, then drops. Just a few inches, like the supports holding up the ground break down.

Black grows, twisting and flashing out, killing everything in its path. Another tree, falling to pieces, more blackberry brambles crumbling to ash.

Alette's in the middle of it, and she recognizes three things.

One, there's something numbing her, against all the magic, like someone claps earmuffs over her ears at the last second. Her head rings, like it's been hit by a concussive force, but she can see, her heart is pounding, she's alive.

Two, this is growing far faster than it should. She doesn't know how she knows this, how she's able to tell these things, but it's racing far beyond what it should be.

Three, she's probably in danger.

"Shit," she whispers, and, almost blindly for the stars behind her eyes, she reaches out and grasps the edge of the magic that broke, right on the exposed wires.

It jolts against her fingertips and pain blooms anew, but she grabs on. Sparks fly from it, coursing through her, down her bloodstream and across her heart and through her other hand.

She opens her other palm, and the sparks arc through the air, to the other side of the rapidly fraying string of magic.

And. Somehow. It stops in place.

She gasps, but makes no sound she can hear, like the magic itself takes up all the volume she can perceive.

For a few breaths, a few ragged, electric breaths, nothing changes. The spot of black, with her in the middle, doesn't grow, and the pieces of magic stop falling apart, and it's just the sound of the sparks in the moonlight of midnight.

It's bad. She knows, deep inside, that it's bad, that this is happening. That she's here, that she's stuck in the middle of it, that it's happening at all.

With another deep breath where ozone fills her lungs, she pulls her uninjured palm back to her, and the black grows, blackberry plants crumbling to ash, and another tree pops and flies apart.

So she can't let go. Not yet.

She reaches the palm back out, and it doesn't bring the deadened part back, it doesn't repair the tree, but the growth stops again.

There's no one around. There's no one around, not a way to call for help, not a phone she can magic to her, not with both her hands taken up, not with everything still so broken around her.

The fraying deepens, until she can feel it in her lungs, like the magic's circling her lungs and making it hard to breathe and—

Out of the corner of her eyes, she sees the glint of red eyes and teeth in the shadows, ears flattened back.

"Zoel," she breathes out, and she can't hear her own words, as her own eyes darken and her head lightens. "Get Zoel."

And then she sees nothing.

21

S he doesn't so much wake up as she floats back to consciousness.

There's a dull thudding in her body, something that suggests that pain is nearby, but lurking outside her grasp. She's warm, she's wrapped in something soft, there's the far away smell of campfire, but—

She ventures her eyes open.

In front of her is an iron belly wood burning stove, with a fire flickering cheerily behind its grate, completely silent.

She doesn't have one of those in her apartment. She doesn't have one of those in the Headquarters.

She doesn't know anyone with one of those.

Without moving, she tries to determine how she is, how her body feels. She's against a cushion—a couch, she's on a couch, facing the fire—and there's a heavy blanket thrown over her, with another one over her feet.

Her coat is hung near the fire, clearly to dry, and her house slippers are next to the stove, mud-marked and dirty. Her glasses are folded up neatly next to them.

Everything still feels like it has the potential of pain, like if she moves at all it'll spark up around her, consume her, and—

Spark up.

The strip of magic.

She bolts upright, and the blanket slides down. She's still in her pajamas, she never changed out of them, but—

Tiny sparks of pain shiver over her body, like it's crackling by itself, like she's still touching the magic thread, even though she can't see it, she can't feel it.

"Don't panic," behind her, Zoel murmurs, and that almost causes her to jump off of the couch, "you're safe, don't panic, panicking will make it worse."

Twisting around, pain chilling up her back and crawling up her throat, she spots him, standing and leaning against the counter of a small kitchen, a towel thrown over his shoulder, like he had been doing dishes when she woke up.

They're in a cabin, a rough rag rug on the bare wooden floor. There's a table thrust against a wall, looking out a window, sun streaming through it.

It had been dark when she was outside.

There's a short hallway, leading down to another doorway, but she can't see past it. Grey lays out in the hallway, eyes closed, obviously asleep, and Spot splays out next to the couch, clearly for the warmth of the stove. The couch itself is plush, if a bit old fashioned, like the things she half remembers from her grandparents' house when she was a small child.

Tentatively, she reaches over, grabbing her glasses and fixing them on her nose.

Zoel's blue eyes watch her, and the edges of them crinkle up in something resembling concern.

She opens her mouth to speak, then stops, words failing her.

Her hands in front of her crackle with electricity, like she's still not out of the magical break, sparks flickering over the surface of her brown skin. Each one doesn't hurt, per se, being taken into the wider static of her pain, but—

Her breathing hitches.

With a sigh, Zoel puts down the towel and crosses the small room to her. "I said, don't panic," he says, but his voice is gentle as he sits on the couch next to her. "You're safe, you're going to be safe."

He holds out his hand to her, as if to take all the sparkling electricity from her, and she doesn't move.

"Where am I?" she asks, but hears nothing. She clears her throat, but no sound comes out, nothing.

She can breathe, she can inhale, but no sound.

"Here," Zoel murmurs, and takes her hand. Sparks shiver down her fingertips, but they don't seem to affect him, don't seem to hurt him. "You're in my house, you're safe, you're experiencing some side effects of the break, you've been asleep for two days—"

"Two days?" Alette blurts out, and she still can't hear herself, still can't moderate her volume, has no idea how loud she's being—"I need to go home, I need to call Axel, I need—"

Magic sparks off of her, an audible snap, and both the dogs lift their heads and stare at her. Spot looks like he barks, makes the motions to do so, but she hears nothing.

Zoel's just watching her, eyes soft, and she takes the moment, takes the second he has given her, to gulp down some breaths, gulp in some air and some confidence, until something like herself solidifies inside of her.

"Why can't I hear anything?" she asks, and his eyebrows raise. "I can hear you, I can hear the static, I can't hear anything else."

"Static," he says, still gentle, and rolls her wrist in his hand, like he's testing her mobility, and the electricity shivers down her skin. "That is what humans would equate it to, isn't it?" He traces his fingertips across her palm, and it doesn't stop the sparks, but it...helps. Like they aren't quite so sharp anymore, like they don't pierce into her skin with each motion. "That'll fade, you're still very much having side effects "—the magic snaps up, again, loud—"please stop panicking, it makes it much worse."

"Okay," she says, though it feels very much not okay and not what she can deal with. "I need to call Axel, or Lyra, or—"

"I let Melekai know," Zoel says. "I assume he told your other friends." He drops her hand, picks up her other one, resumes the soft motions there, until her blood doesn't prickle there anymore. "Your hearing will gradually come back over the next day, though your ears may ring for a bit longer."

That brings up more questions, more things she wants to know, but she just watches his fingers against her hand, soft against the pinpricks of the magic.

"You are," he starts, and for the first time there's something else beneath his voice besides gentleness, "so incredibly stupid."

She should sit back, she should pull back at that, but she doesn't really know how to argue against that.

"I don't know how you're still alive, when you were so close, but you should be dead, just like the spot of land where it broke, just like—"

"I didn't know it would break," she says, and it's bizarre not hearing her own words when she speaks. "It seemed distressed."

Spot rises from his spot next to the stove and splays out at Zoel's feet next to the couch.

His hands are still on hers, moving her wrist, soothing the sparks.

"Next time you feel that," he murmurs, "summon one of the dogs, send for me, don't go it alone."

"I wouldn't know how," she responds.

"My dogs thought you summoned them just fine," he says.

She flexes her fingers. They ache, deep and cold, but her skin is less raw, though the sparks still visibly race over her skin.

"Is my face like this?" she asks, pointing at herself, and he nods. "Do you have a mirror?"

"No," he says, bemused.

"Why can I hear you and not myself?"

He raises an eyebrow, then flicks up the sleeve to her pajamas, still making small circles, bringing something close to relief with every motion.

"My voice," he starts, then falls silent, like he's picking his words carefully, "is probably not heard through your ears."

That brings up all sorts of questions about directional hearing when it's someone magical, of how she could hear Melekai when he was a demon and Axel couldn't, until he modified the technology. Of how sound works when blended with magic, of whether or not it could be recorded or broadcasted over a phone or technology or—

"But the dogs are?" Alette asks. "I thought Spot barked but I didn't hear him."

He sighs, and she definitely hears that. "You really cannot put aside your curiosity, can you?" he asks, and underneath the gentleness, underneath the possible anger, there's something resembling fondness. "They're not the same magic as me, they just like me. Is that an answer?"

"Somewhat," she replies. "Can I go back home?"

His eyes flicker up to hers. "Of course," he says immediately. "Is your lock coded to your magic or to your genetic signature?" At her unamused stare, he shrugs. "Of course I know about the lock, it's intense."

"Magic," she says begrudgingly, because while she changed it for Axel she didn't think to change it for herself. "I take it this"—she lifts up her free hand, and it sparks, snapping loud against the silence of her words—"might interfere?"

"It might," Zoel says, though there's the faintest hint of a smile tugging at his lips. "I've never seen a human try to do what you tried to do, not at that scale, I don't know how it could have changed...you."

He lifts a hand and waits, a clear checking with her before he moves any further, and, unsure exactly what he's asking for, she nods.

He settles the hand behind her head, where her hair sits tangled, close to the base of her neck, and immediately the shivers racing down her body are less.

"Are you absorbing it like a sponge or something or are you changing how my skin is processing it?" Alette asks, then scrunches her face at the weirdness of her own question. "I mean—"

"Wights are creatures of the land," he says. "The magic that is foreign to you is natural to us." He lifts the hand away from her and there are sparks on his fingertips, but muted. "You absorbed it yourself, it's going to be a part of you, I'm just..." His face twists, again, like he's searching for words beyond what they have. "Reassuring the magic that everything is okay."

Alette would say it's ridiculous, but she tried to soothe some magic herself as it was distressed, so she can't really talk.

"I have many questions," she starts, and he surprises her with a grin. "I know, I know, but—"

"I don't have all the answers," he says, before pushing himself up to stand. "You probably need food, humans need a lot of food."

"Can you contact Melekai and tell him to bring me my phone, so I can let Axel know I'm actually okay?" she asks, as he strides to the kitchen. "He's like a brother, he's going to worry until he hears from me."

Zoel nods, before opening a fridge, which brings to mind questions on what he needs to eat and what electricity he needs and whether or not magic could be substituted in any way. Or whether or not Wights just forage, or if they shop, or—

He pulls out a jar of jam, then a loaf of bread that looks more handmade than not.

"I didn't anticipate having a human here," he says, apologetic, "or else I'd get more, but unless you want dog food are you okay with toast?"

"I'm fine with toast," Alette says, instead of any of her questions, and, tentatively, she pushes herself up to standing.

The magic races up and down her body, sparkling in her blood and pinpricking at her skin, but her legs hold and her body doesn't dump her on her butt again.

Zoel watches her from underneath his eyelashes as he cuts a chunk of bread, before fitting it in his toaster. "You won't sit still, will you?" he asks, but again, there's the fondness underneath his words. "The moment you can, you're going to race off into your next adventure, aren't you?"

And Alette went on the hiking trip with him the day after she was in the first break, so yes. Yes, she is.

"I try—" She sets her hand against the wall and it sparks, loud. There's nothing, not a sound from him, but he raises an eyebrow at her, as if she handed him all the evidence he might need with that small action.

Her knees still feel wobbly, so she keeps the hand on the wall, but it doesn't snap again.

"Just as you coded your place with your own magic, so did I," Zoel says, setting out a plate and some silverware. "It's not going to hurt you, but it reacted about the same as if I went into your apartment and discharged some magic into your wall."

Alette peers at the rough-hewn wood, but it still looks the same.

"How are your legs?" he asks, dragging her attention back over to him. "You were...crumpled...by the time I got to you."

She rolls her ankle, but other than shaky it seems fine. "I think I just fell over."

Carefully, using the wall as a guide, she takes another step, then another, towards the small kitchen table. Her skin still crackles, little pinpricks all up and down her spine, but she puts as much control as possible into her muscles, sitting down as careful as she possibly can.

"I don't mind eating on my couch," Zoel says, amused, "especially when someone's sick." Still, he strides over as the toaster works away and sits on the chair across from her.

It's awfully intimate, just the two of them sitting at the table in the small cabin, practically knee to knee, and it takes her breath away.

He holds his hand out to hers, and resumes soothing the pinpricks of pain away.

This may be more direct physical contact than she's had in years.

"Did I make it worse?" Alette asks in the deafening silence of not being able to hear her own voice, hear her own motions, her own footsteps.

He hesitates and it's the worst hesitation she's ever seen.

"I don't know," he says, finally. "I went back, and it hasn't spread, so that's good, but the...severity of the break is startling."

He swipes the pad of his thumb over her palm and a wave of soothing follows in its wake.

"I'm surprised you weren't dead," he says, and he's already said something similar, earlier, but it's different this time. Rawer. "I saw you on the forest floor, in the middle of all the black, your fist around the broken magic, and I thought you must've been killed instantly."

That would have been one hell of a way to be discovered. Right up there with getting hit with a death bubble while defending a small town.

"Instead, you were still breathing," he continues, and she can't help but stare at the crackles of electricity in her skin, at the motion of his hands, "and Spot was howling and the magic was dead all around you."

"I'm sorry," she says, and he shakes his head, but she continues. "No, I'm sorry, that's pretty terrifying. I'd be...not okay if I came across you that way."

"I've come across three other humans that way," he says, and the back of her neck prickles, and she's not sure if it's because of the magic or because of his words, "lying dead in the middle of a field, a break around them, clutching at the magic. I wonder if they tried to fix it as well."

He lifts his eyes to hers, in their eerie ice blue, before he startles and looks over his shoulder.

The toaster. The bread had popped up, and he heard it, but she couldn't.

He drops her hand and it's almost painful in its lack. "Do you need water?" he asks as he stands, whirling the plate in front of her. "I always forget, do humans need water every day?"

"Yes?" she says. "Yes, we need water. Fresh water, not salt," she clarifies, because who knows, that might be a thing she needs to specify. "I should be...far thirstier if I've been unconscious for two days."

He gives her an odd look before filling up a rustic mug from the tap, and the curious part of her brain runs off in the direction of wondering what the plumbing looks like for a Wight house, before he sets it down in front of her.

Now, with the toast and water in front of her, her stomach turns, as if the idea of food is a poor one.

"Thank you," she says, and the magic crackles over her knuckles as she grabs at the cup. Her hand brushes against his and another spark jumps, startling her.

It doesn't harm the cup, but...

He shrugs at her words, as if brushing off their importance. As if he probably hadn't saved her life.

"This is strange," she remarks, as conversationally as she can without revealing the deep anxiety inside of her. "But thank you, I mean it."

His face twitches, like he's just as uncomfortable as she is. "I did very little, except bring you back. Your body did the rest, healed the marks on your hand." She immediately looks at her hands, but sees no difference, but—

"Oh, the burns," she says, examining her fingertips.

With everything happening, with the craziness of actual visible magic all over her, she didn't even notice that the blister burns on her fingertips are gone, without even a callous remaining.

With a glance at him, she sticks her ankle out from underneath the table, and the Band-Aids are gone, revealing smooth, unmarked skin. Not even scabs.

She hikes up her pant leg to her knee, where she had a few nasty scars from falling as a child, but they're completely unmarked.

Throughout all of it, Zoel's watching her, and she doesn't know what he's watching for.

"Huh," Alette says, eloquent. "Huh."

22

H e leaves shortly after with the promise to contact Melekai, leaving her with the two silent dogs and an entirely too empty cabin.

She hadn't known she's so attuned to sound, so attuned to listening to everything around her, that the absence of it...just reminds her of being dead. Of being submerged somewhere, floating aimlessly, before waking up on the conference table.

Taking that thought, she flops back onto the couch next to the iron stove, watching the flames flicker inside, and desperately tries to ignore the instinct telling her to run, telling her to avoid everything that is going on, to go back home immediately and ignore that this ever happened.

That sort of thinking hasn't helped her before.

So, instead, she sits cross-legged on the couch and tries to feel. Not reaching out with her magic—she's not going to do something expansive without figuring more out—but without the ability to take notes she's going to just...observe.

First things first, everything is off balance, tilted strangely, like her very sense of self twisted somewhat and emerged off-kilter. She's had this before, when attempting too large of magic, when doing something so outside her depth, so she mentally moves on.

Second, the pinpricks of pain have largely receded, leaving behind a strange static, like a limb that has fallen asleep and is in process of being awoken. It's unpleasant, but...but manageable.

Third, she can tell where the dogs are without opening her eyes.

Without hearing them or seeing, she knows that Grey gets up, lumbering deeper into the house before flopping on a rug. Grey's paws hurt, like he stepped on something long ago and it never healed correctly.

Spot's still in front of the couch, but he's shifting slightly in his sleep, like he's chasing after something.

And Zoel's far away, a dim ghost of a smudge against her awareness, but distinct.

There are other smudges, traces of other figures, but her mind skips over them. She doesn't know them, she can't identify them, but they're there.

She pops her eyes open, and sure enough, Grey's further away, exactly where she thought.

"So that's new," she whispers, even though she can't hear herself at all. "Okay."

Spot lifts his head, blinking at her, then, with a burst of energy that she can't actually comprehend, jumps on the couch next to her, curling up as if it's his nest and laying his head in her lap.

He seems unaffected by the sparks, so she tentatively rests a hand on his head, feeling the short bristle fur underneath the shadows.

"Did I wake you?" she whispers at the dog, who thumps his tail at her. "I didn't mean to."

The dog closes his eyes in response, content.

She needs to talk to Melekai about this. She needs to talk to Axel, someone to tell her she's not crazy, Lyra to make sure her body is still working how it should be, someone—

Whisper light against her senses, she somehow knows that Zoel is on his way back to the little cabin, and she has no idea where it actually is. She's seen him as far north as almost reaching Whitehorse Pass, and as far south as Oregon, so it could be anywhere in there.

A shiver of excitement worms its way down her spine, completely at odds with what she should be feeling.

She should be more scared—and she is, she definitely is —but somehow, the predominant emotion fluttering to the surface is...excitement. This is new, this is all new, and...

Combined with the needle and the Ley Lines and the sparks across her palm, she feels powerful.

She's used to feeling powerful, she's a magician and a damn fine one at that, but this...this has the possibilities of being life changing. Of being so uniquely hers that no one could dictate what she does, that no one could force her to do anything she doesn't want to.

A spark of magic cracks and she flinches back. Spot lifts his head in a jerk, like she startled him.

"Sorry," she says.

First things first, she's going to have to learn to control it. Which will require study, which is awesome, and more information, and -

The door to the cabin swings open, but she doesn't need to look to know that it's Zoel. He's warm against her aware-ness, broad shouldered and handsome, even without her eyes on him.

"That's interesting," he drawls, setting aside a bag on the table next to the door, and she twists to look at him. His eyes crinkle up at the corners, but still, his face remains serious. "I am fairly certain humans can't generally do that."

"I don't think so," she replies, eager, and his dimple appears even without grinning at her.

"I let Melekai know you're awake, he says I am, and I repeat, 'a total asshole'," he continues, and pulls out her phone from the bag. "He had Axel go in and get this, and Axel looked like he wanted to punch something."

"Did you actually speak to him?" Alette asks, and Zoel just shakes his head. "Wait, you said I'll be fine, why did Mel call you an asshole?"

Zoel then gives her a look, and it's halfway between stern and seeing right through her, but she's faced down tougher people without even flinching, so she just gives him her best smile.

Still, he sweeps over to the couch, sitting next to her, and the sparks of magic calm down with just his knee pressed against hers.

"Melekai's sole motivation in this world is to make sure his Necromancer is happy," Zoel says, but his voice is soft, "and you getting hurt upsets her. And your friend Axel seems to be...overprotective."

"He's been that way since we were kids," Alette says and presses her leg against his for more contact. Even through her pajama pants and his rough jeans, the prickles soften.

He hands her the phone and, of course, there are tons of messages, but the moment the magic of the sparks hits it, it abruptly turns off.

Zoel sighs, before picking up her hand. "I thought that might happen," he says, and each little touch of him is like a balm. "You might need to wait a bit before technology works for you."

"Inconvenient," she says, and he cracks a smile. "So what, exactly, am I doing?"

He presses his leg against her as well, and she knows herself well enough that there's nothing quite platonic about this, and her heart jumps.

And, of course, a spark cracks into the open air.

"You're processing visual data through magic instead of through your optic nerve," he says, tapping against the side of his head, as if to demonstrate. "Similar to how Necromancers can make a map of the world with dead bodies."

"I definitely did not know that," Alette says.

"Your Necromancer does it all the time, and she has no idea," Zoel says, then gives her a sideways smile, and it's a little heartbreaking.

And it's been ages since Alette's recognized that in herself.

Shit.

"Good news, it's not going to harm you, though you might give yourself a headache if you do it too much," he continues, "bad news, you're definitely going to need to learn to control it, some magical beings will not be happy to be scanned like that and they will start a fight."

Alette desperately wishes all the diagnostic spells still worked in the Headquarters, because this would be a doozy.

Then...

"Shit, Gurlien's going to be rabid about this, isn't he?" she asks. "The College goon, he's going to—"

"Don't see him," Zoel interrupts her, "not until you've discharged this and at least appear normal."

It's sound advice, of course, but still, dread creeps in.

~

AFTER SOME MORE KIND, gentle touch, she dozes off, despite all her interest and excitement, and wakes up to find Axel and Zoel conversing in low tones in the kitchen, Melekai scowling at the table, and Lyra sitting on the ground next to the fireplace.

She blinks at all of them. Someone had thrown a blanket over her at some point.

"Oh good, you're awake," Lyra says, and Alette's stomach turns over with how loud everyone is in the small room.

Then, oh right, now she can hear.

She sits up.

"Did you know your body is so full of electricity your heart keeps on stopping and restarting?" Lyra says, and everyone else stops talking to stare at her. "You're not dying, not really, but your body is pretty confused."

"This is why I said you should be careful," Melekai all but growls.

"She's not going to die," Zoel says, and at least his voice is normal toned, not oppressively loud. A thin sheen of sweat is on his forehead, and given how he's talking with Axel, she guesses that he's appearing to him and that takes more effort than he'd like to admit.

"Was I asleep for too long again?" Alette asks, touching a hand to her ears gingerly. Her hand still prickles, but it's less, like the time spent sleeping gave her a bit more ease in existing.

"Another twelve hours," Zoel says, still normal toned, though he raises an eyebrow at her, at everyone in the room, seeming to check in. "They insisted on checking on you."

Lyra reaches over to squeeze Alette's hand, but a spark jumps at her, almost defensive, and Zoel sighs.

"I'm okay," Alette says, and gets an identical eye roll from Axel, Melekai, and Zoel, which is not great. "I mean, I'm alive, I can think, there's a new form of magic that I can experiment with, I'm okay."

"No, you're not," Melekai says, loud, too loud.

"A, you were literally sparkling with electricity when we came in," Axel says, watching her like he can see right through her. "New form of magic or not, that's spooky."

There's something she missed, something she was unconscious for, she can just tell.

"You're better," Zoel says, thankfully still at a correct volume. "You should be stable in a few days."

"For given quantities of stability," Melekai grumbles, and Alette gets the feeling she definitely missed something.

"So, she'll have new powers, at least she's alive," Zoel snips, aggravated. "I'm happy she's alive, I've found—" he cuts himself off, rubbing his face with his hand.

It's too much, and Alette is immediately aware that she's been in the same muddy pajamas for far too long.

Out of the corner of her eye, she catches movement, and both Spot and Grey are at the back of the hallway, huddling away from the influx of people. Grey's fur is ruffled, standing up on the ridge on his back, and Spot's ears are back and his tail between his legs.

"Can we get me home?" she asks to the silence in the room.

AFTER A BRIEF but furious conversation with Melekai and Zoel, they come to the conclusion that she'll probably be able to get inside as long as Axel's there to code the locks open. The chance of her magic reacting poorly is relatively low, so Zoel helps her to Axel's car, haphazardly parked on something that could charitably be called a driveway.

The outside of Zoel's little cabin is, for lack of a better term, adorable. The logs are rough-hewn but put together with care.

The dogs follow them out, circling them in the setting sun, and Alette's entirely disoriented about the time of day. Not enough time seems to have passed with her being conscious for this to be evening.

The moment she shuts the door behind her, Axel starts driving, rough, down the dirt and gravel road.

"But Lyra—"

"I have no idea how Lyra and Melekai got here," Axel interrupts, "but she didn't ask for a ride, so I think she's fine."

"Oh, you're angry," Alette says, turning to him, instead of the dogs running gleefully alongside the Mustang.

"Of course I'm angry," Axel says, then bites off his words. "A, you disappeared, you were just gone, then your Wight comes by with the 'oh she's fine but she's now altered,' whatever that means, and that he wants us to give you 'space' so you're not overwhelmed, and then Lyra was saying those things!"

She lets him rant.

"And we were being really loud, but you literally weren't reacting and when Melekai and I tried to get you up the magic literally shocked me like it was static fucking electricity," he continues, "so yeah, I'm pissed."

She waits a few more seconds, but he's quiet, driving in silence as they reach the freeway.

It's a familiar freeway, at least. She wasn't too far away.

Zoel isn't too far away.

"In his defense," she starts, and he snorts derisively, "I think he probably saved my life."

"I'm sorry, did you think I was angry with *him*?" Axel says, scowling at the road.

"Well," Alette starts delicately, "yes."

"Honestly, A, going after a rogue piece of magic without backup in the middle of the fucking night and then grabbing it? That's so..." He thumps his hand against the steering wheel, cutting himself short as he pulls off the highway to her apartment.

The dogs speed by the car, tongues lolling out, like they're happy to be out of the little cabin. Like they're happy to be away from the noise and the extra people who couldn't see them.

And Alette can't think of a single thing to say.

Axel remains silent the rest of the short drive, until they pull up to her apartment, where he slams his car door getting out.

He stares mulishly at her apartment, where Alette can see all the magic tracing itself around the handle, before he grabs the doorknob and twists.

It opens, of course, since she recoded it, and he swings it dramatically forward for her.

"See if it lets you through," he says, crossing his arms over his chest.

With a nod, because that is very much not guaranteed, which is terrifying, Alette carefully steps through.

Her magic swirls at her footsteps, chaotic, as extra magic sparks down to the edges of the runes from her shoes.

Like her own house is confused by her.

Gently, Alette crouches down in her own entryway, and the glittering magic swirls around her fingertips.

It half recognizes her.

The chaos grows worse, more erratic, until she rests a hand against the door jam, on the first rune she wrote, and it flares, bright, before calming. Whatever knowledge it's able to glean from her flows deeper into the house and she can control it once more.

With a sigh, she turns to Axel, who's watching with his chin tucked down.

"It's okay, it knows me," she says. "I think it'll be okay with me now."

"Good," Axel says, "because your aunt would be fucking pissed right now."

This pulls her up short.

"All this work she had you put in, all the knowledge you have, and you did something so fucking dangerous you almost died," he says, then turns around, striding back to his car. "Text me if you need something, I'm going home."

Without waiting for her response, he slams his door closed again and drives off.

23

She stands at her doorway for a few minutes, as if that could give her some sort of guidance on how she should feel, or what she should do.

More than anything else, she feels like she should feel something big. Should feel something dramatic.

But instead of anger or spite, there's just an odd pit of exhaustion, like the events of the last few days have carved out all of her normal emotions and replaced them with air.

There's still the detached feeling of excitement, that she'll be able to research this, that there's something new. There's still the grief, deep down below, but it's like there's a buffer between her and it.

It's probably not the healthiest way to process all of this.

Alette's never been one to stress too much about the health of her coping mechanisms, though, and Axel's always burned hotter than her, always coming down out of anger faster. He'll come around, and if she hasn't heard from him in a few days she can reach out.

Though bringing her aunt into all of this is new.

Spot and Grey sit on the driveway, splayed out in the

setting sun, and now that she knows they lay around a house all day, their energy to run around makes a lot more sense.

"I didn't mean to be unsafe," she whispers.

Spot lifts his head at her words, thumping his shadow tail against the concrete.

Her aunt took plenty of risks, took plenty of questionable experiments, and Alette can't quite comprehend a world where Aunt Frisse wouldn't do the exact same thing she did, wouldn't have grabbed the edges of the magic herself and gripped tight, consequences be damned.

With one last nod to the dogs outside, Alette closes her door with a too-loud click, and her magic sparks into the wall, lighting up the runes.

The entire apartment flickers, runes shimmering in and out, like it can't decide how to fully react to her, but she carefully hangs her coat, heading to the shower.

If she's not feeling the things she should, at the very least then she can figure it out while being clean.

LATER, hours later, as she sits and combs oil into her hair, the runes in her apartment flare up, bright, two seconds before there's a knock on her door.

That bright, it's someone it didn't recognize. Someone who hasn't been there before.

Carefully, Alette sets her comb down and fits her glasses on her face, glancing at herself in the mirror. Her hair's still a mess, and she's wearing nothing more than yoga pants and a tank top, but...

But in the last week she's climbed a cliff, been slammed into a tunnel wall, and electrocuted by magic. Whoever's knocking at her door at 9 PM could deal with however she looks.

"Coming," she calls out, tapping a rune to pull down her silencing spell, so whoever it is outside can hear.

At one point, she had a spell that identified all new motion in front of her door, but she had been unable to tweak it enough so it recognized people instead of leaves blowing around.

Not many people come up to her doorstep, anyways. Her neighbors don't know her, and it's set back far enough that door-to-door salesmen aren't generally ones to come up.

Magic still sparks with her every step, and though it's stopped prickling needles into her skin, she's still intimately aware of each motion, of each brush of her clothing.

Her peephole camera shows nothing, but her runes still burn bright, so, keeping a hand on her needle case, she turns her handle.

Outside, stands Zoel, leaning casually against the side of her porch, black curls messy in the wind.

For a second, they stare at each other, before he gives her a quick one-two check out. "Magic not reacting poorly to your house?" he asks with a crooked smile.

She opens the door a little wider, so he can see the rune glowing sporadically against her hand.

"It's responding, but..." she trails off, tapping her fingertips on the rune, and sparks arc from her hand to the rune. "It's letting me interact, at least."

"Better than I thought might happen," he says, and there's something tense in his voice. She'd call it awkwardness, but it's more charged than that.

It's a flimsy excuse to visit her, even she knows that, but she opens her door wider.

"Do you want to come in?"

His blue eyes sear through her, like he knows what she's doing.

She doesn't even know what she's doing.

"Well," he drawls, shifting his weight on her porch, looking at the runes and the magic flickering around her, "I think you'd need to let me in."

Keeping one hand—her miraculously burn-free hand—on the rune, she extends the other to him.

It's a strange way to invite people inside, but not very many people come to her place that don't know about magic, and an amused look flashes over Zoel's face, as her runes flash over him in a heartbeat, learning who he is, before receding past her hand.

"Neat trick," he says, before stepping through her doorway. "We've been wondering how it worked."

He grazes a fingertip to the wall, and the runes flare up around his touch. He studies it, obviously so, like he's just as much of a scholar as she is.

He's handsome.

He's handsome and he's in her space, filling it up like he belonged more than she did.

Dry mouthed, she steps aside, and his hand is still in hers.

"The prickling sensation has gone down a good eighty percent," she says, words falling from her mouth. "Other than the occasional pins and needles, I'd say I'm almost all better."

He turns his gaze back to her, and it takes away her words.

"Your magic might never be the same," he says, voice accented. "If I knew for sure, I would tell you."

She nods, then leads him deeper into her apartment.

Her magic flares up around them both, brilliant and gold, spiraling out from the two of them.

The corners of his eyes crinkle into a smile, before he turns to her. "This place is pretty fantastic," he says. "I knew you had protected it, I knew you had put in a fair amount of magic of your own, but not like this."

"How do you see it?" she asks, the thought striking her like a bolt of lightning. "I made it visible because I wanted to, what does it look like—"

He squeezes her hand and the entire room blooms into gold.

She can see the runes, each individual one, the ones she's scratched out faded beneath them, all layered on top of each other. Magic under magic under magic, with her footsteps trailing along top of them.

"Everywhere I look, I see a little trace of you," he says. "There's no way someone like me would see this and not know, beyond a shadow of a doubt, that it belonged to you."

"And here I crash half the time at the Headquarters," Alette says.

"Why?" he asks, and he drops her hand to step closer to a rune, one she had sketched near the kitchen stove, one to help with temperature modulation. "This place has got to be more comfortable."

"Well, yes," Alette says, watching him as he pokes his way around the runes she wrote so many years ago, a strange shyness welling up in her bones. "Mostly...mostly because my aunt was there."

"And then you didn't leave for a month, when she was gone."

Alette falls silent, and he glances back up at her.

"Grief does strange things," she says, finally. "It was like everyone needed me, and it was easier to be needed there."

She sweeps herself into sitting on her couch. "Lyra and Melekai were confused, Melekai was suddenly human"—Zoel snorts at that—"Axel was a wreck, I had to find my aunt's will, and..." she trails off, and he eventually trails over, sitting next to her on the couch. "It was easier there. Here I am just...myself. There I had actual impact."

"You have impact wherever you go," he says, and they're not sitting so close that they're touching, but she wishes they were. She wishes that she could be touching him, instead of the sudden deep dive into her guilt. "Do I need to remind you of the Ley Line?"

Alette's eyes track his hand, resting against the back of the couch, instead of looking at his face.

"Or is that hard to think about, because your aunt had little to do with it?" Zoel asks, and she snaps her gaze back up to him, and he shrugs, self-conscious. "You have far more to you than just her legacy, than just fixing her mistakes," he says, and there's even a hint of red on his cheekbones, like she caught him doing something he shouldn't. "She was amazing, she was brilliant, she was somewhat unethical, but you're still here and that's...that's more important."

"Did you get a degree in psychology or something?" Alette asks, and he grins at her, like he's embarrassed. "Or did you just pull that out of the ether?"

"I observe people," he says. "I observe and I read and...and people often act in predictable ways."

"So you do study," Alette says, and a dimple appears in his cheek. "That's the definition of studying to me."

"Are you teasing me because you're uncomfortable?" he asks

There's that moment, the moment of hesitation, the moment of wondering, before something clicks into place for Alette.

"Do you want a drink?" she asks, raising an eyebrow. "Can you drink human alcohol?" Not even waiting for his response, she pushes herself up.

"Yes," he says, and she can just feel his eyes on her, as she moves towards her kitchen, "nothing too bitter."

Someday, someday, she's going to have to ask him everything about him. About what he can and cannot do, what he can eat, how he survives, everything.

But something fizzes in her blood, and she doesn't think it's the magic from the break.

She's never been one for beer or wine, so she pours them two small glasses of ruby red port. The port she picks for herself when she's had an overwhelming day, when she just needs to relax.

Relaxing sounds good right about now.

She cheers him with the glass and he mimics the reaction.

"Did Melekai ever share any spirit-made brandy with you?" he asks after a small sip, rolling the glass in his hand like he's examining the color. "This reminds me—slightly— of that."

"First time I'm hearing about it, so no," she says, holding onto her glass like it could give her a bit more courage, "but every culture has their alcohol, don't they?"

"Pretty much," he says, then gives her a slow smile, a mischievous glint in his eye. "If you want to mess with Melekai, find some high-quality brandy and put it in a clay jug, and hide it in his house."

"That sounds like an excellent way to get uninvited," she responds, but smiles at him all the same.

Tentatively, so tentatively she's taken by surprise, he presses his leg against hers on the couch once more, like he's feeling out what her reaction would be. Like he's figuring out what he wants, or what he wants to ask her for.

Alette wouldn't have pegged him as timid, so she takes another drink, then leans into him, her unbound hair falling over her shoulder, and raises an eyebrow at him.

He raises the eyebrow right back.

"So, tell me, why did you come over?"

"Well," he starts, then licks his lips, like he hadn't actually thought she'd ask. Like she isn't the most curious person most people ever meet.

She lets him sit there with the question, leaning towards him, as the silence grows longer.

Finally, after the moment stretches so far that it almost snaps, his eyes flicker to her lips.

"I wanted to see you," he says, voice deep, his vowels round, like he's not attempting to hide his accent, "I wanted to see you and make sure you were still okay."

There's something there she could push, to find out why he would think she wouldn't be okay, but something stops her from speaking again. Some instinct, some pounding in her heart, that whispers something close to hope into her veins.

He rests a hand on her wrist, right at her pulse point. Right where the break had been, right where Terese's magic had curled against her skin, and rubs his thumb across tenderly.

"I considered sending Spot or Grey to make sure you were safe, but I didn't think that would be enough," he continues, words now tumbling out of his mouth, one right after the other, like they were tripping over each other and falling into haphazard piles. "But they would just tell me that you're safe inside, that you're here, and nothing more. I couldn't tell, not without coming here, if you were okay. If you had issues with the magic, if it was choking you or rejecting you. If you were here but upset. If someone else followed you in, instead."

She rests her hand on his arm. The points of contacts send chills up her spine.

"I...I wanted to see you," he repeats. "I wanted to see you with my own eyes, even if I know that Melekai or your alchemist would contact me if something came up, or I hope they would, but—"

Alette leans forward, just enough so she can press her lips against his.

He stills, and for a heart-pounding moment, she lets herself wonder if she had miscalculated, had misread, had misunderstood.

He makes a noise, deep in his chest, and he surges forward, pressing her back down into the couch, his lips opening against hers.

His lips taste of port.

His hand tangles in her hair, and she kisses back with as much force as he's giving her, as if she could win in a battle of strength, and it's glorious. It's glorious, it's sensation, it's more, and—

With a shaky gasp, he pulls away, and his lips are reddened from their touch, his eyes wide.

"I'm—" Alette starts, her mouth dry, not wanting to hurt or harm but wanting more.

He blinks at her, and his hand is still loosely in her hair, like he doesn't know how to react, like he doesn't know what to think or what to do, like she dumbfounded him.

"You're...was that intentional?" Zoel says, before he swallows, and Alette wishes she could sink into the ground with embarrassment. "Did you mean to kiss me?"

"Yes," Alette says, as crisp as she can make it, sitting

back. His hand falls away from her, and she misses the contact. Misses the immediate touch. "My apologies."

"It's...it's okay," he says, his face twisting in confusion, "I mean, yes, it's great, I just..." he trails off, visibly gathering himself, before he smiles, heartbreakingly awkward, and Alette's stomach flips. "That's not something I expected."

"Do you need warning next time?" she blurts out, then shuts her eyes against the embarrassment. "If there is a next time, I thought...I thought you were...flirting."

This is up there with the worst conversations she's ever had with someone.

"I was not...consciously, this time," he starts, "but..." he trails off, and she opens her eyes again to find his blue eyes watching her. "I certainly have tried, before. I thought..." His face twists again, before he shakes his head, and Alette is exhausted just trying to figure out where this conversation is going, before he shifts a bit closer, and it reads intentional this time, like he's inviting her in again. "Alette, you're beautiful. You're beautiful and curious and smart, of course I tried to flirt with you before, I just thought you didn't have any interest back."

"So I just misread this moment?" she asks, and it's still awkward, but a little better. A little like there's still hope.

"I'm not even sure you did," he says, before he leans back in, pressing a kiss to her lips, slow and deliberate. Slow and deliberate and devastating, like this time he's in control, and it makes all the difference.

She could swear her heart is stopping all over again, and the strange magic has nothing to do with it this time.

"I've wanted to kiss you ever since I saw you notice me," he continues, his lips just a whisper away from hers. "I could swear that your eyes saw mine and that my entire self responded."

She leans up against him, stopping his words for a brief second.

"I wanted to kiss you when I saw you out with your aunt and your alchemist, hunting down the demon of Terese, and you looked at everything with the same intensity as you look at a book." He lifts a hand, tucking her hair behind her ear, and everything's slightly unreal, slightly softer around the edges, like the sharpness of the world is gentled. "I wanted to kiss you when you were in my boat, on the island, and you said you wanted to come back, so you could study it better."

It's more than Alette had expected, but still, a curl of warmth slides around her. "I'm pretty sure I was snotty to you on the island," she says, and gets a smile in return. "I was very skeptical."

"Still beautiful," he says, "still beautiful and powerful and looking at everything in entirely different ways," he trails off almost like he runs off a thought and has to figure out where he goes from there. "I'm not...always the best at expressing what I want, but I very much wanted to know you more. Still want that, still want to spend as many moments as I can, as I figure everything out."

"I like that," she says, feeling her own lips curl up into a responding smile. "I'd like that a lot."

She'd like a lot more. But whenever she takes anyone to her bed, they're always shocked when she does, and considering how she just shocked the hell out of Zoel by just kissing him, she doesn't think that she'd be too successful.

She leans up into him, opening her mouth to his, looking for any of that sensation, for anything she could feel.

It's been too long since she's had someone to kiss.

Someone who wants to hold her like this, someone who holds her like she's precious.

His hand touches the side of her face, whisper gentle, and he deepens the kiss. Deepens until she reaches that blissful place where all she can feel is him, all she can comprehend is him in front of her, is his hand against her cheek and his leg pressed against hers and—

Her magic snaps, hard, and they jolt apart.

A spark crackles down her arm, before discharging loud mid-air, and they both stare at it, dumbfounded.

"That's new," Alette says, before she can stop herself.

For a few seconds, it looks like he's torn between smiling and scowling, but eventually his lips curve upwards.

"That's why I thought it best to stop over," he says, before clearing his throat and sitting back, blinking rapidly. "I didn't know if something would set you off."

Alette's cheeks grow hot, and she resists the urge to bury her face in her hands.

Instead, he catches her hand in his, and a shiver of the magic sparks into his palm, immediately soothing.

With another crackle, he carefully grazes her cheek with the back of his hand. The hair on the back of Alette's neck rises and she shivers.

"You are beautiful," he repeats, and it almost sounds like a prayer. "You're beautiful and you have always been beautiful."

Instead of replying, ignoring the pull and crackle of her magic sparkling towards him, she kisses him again, then again, until he pushes her back against the couch, bracketing her in.

The runes in her floors swirl up and around him, like he's meant to be there. Like her own effort and magic can tell how perfect this feels, how solid and real he is against

her skin. At a moment when everything around her seems
ephemeral, everything feels unreal, his hands hold her tight.

He's there. He's there and he's wonderful and with everything else going awry in her life, he's there.

She breaks the kiss just to shed her pajama shirt, and he
spreads his hand across her midsection, and she can feel
every callous on his fingers and every rough part of his
touch. His eyebrows raise and his lips part, like he can't fully
comprehend the view in front of him.

He strips his own shirt over his head, his muscles flexing
with the motion, and it's been forever since Alette was with
someone so...brawny. When most of her available dating
pool is nerdy magicians, one gets used to a lack of muscles,
but...

But he's shaped like he's built to move rock and stone, to
fell trees and build shelter, to climb cliffs and carry animals,
from the breadth of his shoulders to the deep "v" below his
stomach. He's pale, but that's nothing terribly unusual from
people in the Pacific Northwest, though a spare dusting of
freckles sits on the top of his shoulders and a small trail of
hair leads down his chest.

He raises another eyebrow at her, this time challenging.

And Alette's not one to back down from a challenge.

So, she surges up to meet him, open-mouthed, and he
groans against her, before pushing her back onto the couch,
hooking two fingers on her pajama pants.

"May I?" He breathes, almost inaudible over the
pounding of her heart.

"Yes," she whispers back, and he slides off the couch to
kneel in front of her, pulling down her underwear with him,
and Alette's heart catches in her throat.

He presses a kiss against the inside of her thigh, like
she's a thing of beauty and treasure, and chills race down

her arms. There's the barest hint of scruff against his cheek, like he'll need to shave in the morning.

And he's spending the night with her.

With only a flicker of his blue eyes up to her as warning, he pushes her thighs apart and presses his lips against her clit.

She jumps and feels more than hears his chuckle against her. His hand rubs the side of her hip, soothing, so she lets herself...relax. Lets her eyes flutter shut, lets her head rest back against the couch, until all that she is aware of is his lips against her and his tongue inside of her, until she's teased apart and no more thoughts enter her mind.

24

He stays the night, and she wakes up with her cheek pressed up against his shoulder and the steady rise and fall of his breathing in her ears.

Slowly, she pulls back, and he doesn't wake up. His head is tilted back over the edge of her couch, his mouth open slightly, his black curls mussed on one side.

It's startlingly adorable, and startlingly real.

She would never have known he wasn't human like her.

She carefully unfolds herself from next to him, her back and neck complaining from sleeping on the couch but she stretches, popping her back.

It's so heartbreakingly normal that her stomach feels warm.

She hasn't had normal in years. Not like this, not just affection.

Still sleep-clouded, she patters over to her coffee maker, a sleek machine that she'd refused Axel's help setting up, and thankfully no sparks from her fingertips shut it off.

She uses it just for tea, so now it's little more than a glorified kettle

She doesn't know if Wights drink tea, but she does, and it's now been a few days without it.

A few days.

She braces herself against her counter.

A few days without any knowledge of the breaks in the magic, without any knowledge of how Gurlien was ripping apart her aunt's legacy, a few days without any update of Terese or where she might be.

She didn't have a few days to waste.

A spark snaps out, just harmlessly hitting her marble countertops, and she makes herself take a deep breath, then another, until—somehow—she feels the control start to ease back into her bones.

So. If this is how control feels, she needs to sit herself in that sensation, replicate it.

Write up some guidelines for herself and stick to them.

While the tea brews, she approaches her cell phone, making sure to breathe deeply before she picks it up and turns it on.

Still no sparks, but she flicks it to silent so that whatever texts come in don't wake up Zoel, sleeping so sweetly on her couch.

There's an odd pit of protectiveness about him sleeping there.

As expected, messages pour in, panicked ones from Axel and Lyra from the first day, a few businesslike ones from Gurlien, then frustrated and angry ones from Lyra's phone that, if she had to guess, came directly from Melekai without him even signing it.

Then:

AXEL (3:00 PM): Your Zoel told Mel what you did. Are you kidding?

GURLIEN (4:21 PM): The other one told me you went into another magic break, but that you survived. How?

GURLIEN (4:52 PM): Your friend has assured me that you are still unconscious and being taken care of in another location. How did you survive, that should have killed you?

GURLIEN (1:03 AM): Call me when you are able, this is a startling discovery that could have ramifications that need to be explored.

AXEL (2:49 AM): I don't care that you're still unconscious, we are all coming over, Zoel is letting us into his house.

AXEL (3:01 AM) Stop Doing Stupid Shit!!

Then, from less than an hour ago:

AXEL (9:26 AM): I'm still mad. Gurlien wants to see you. Please stop making me run interference.

Alette lets her phone sit while she pours herself tea and takes a few more deep breaths before replying.

ALETTE (9:59 AM): Just woke up. Still sparking some places. Any idea how to explain that?

AXEL (10:00 AM): No.

She steps back away from her phone right in time for a loud spark to echo off her fingertips, uselessly into the air.

Zoel jolts upright.

"Sorry," Alette says, clutching her tea mug as if that'd make her less likely to spark up, "still learning how to control this."

He blinks at her wildly, before staring numbly at the walls of her apartment, then back at her.

"I slept?" he says, voice raspy.

"For at least a bit," Alette says, then gestures at her tea. "Can you digest caffeine?"

He wordlessly shakes his head, eyes still wide, before he pushes himself up unsteadily.

"I've only been awake for about twenty minutes," Alette says, now intimately aware that her hair is still an unbraided mess, "so it might've just been for a few minutes, but—"

He shakes his head, as if shaking loose the cobwebs, before raising an eyebrow with an embarrassed smile. "Wights rarely sleep," he says, clearing his throat from the rasp. "I haven't slept in...months?"

Which would have been right in the middle of Terese twisting all the magic around.

"Do you need any food?" Alette asks, hiding her raised eyebrows by looking towards her kitchen.

Not needing sleep is a new thing. A new bit of information to slot into the ever-filling file in her mind that reads Zoel.

A file that includes he's found her pretty for months.

He blinks a few more times, still looking woefully bewildered, before shaking himself once more. "Do you have any fruit?"

She shakes her head.

"Any fish?" At her continued shake of the head, his face creases into his normal amused smile. "Were you just offering me food to be polite?"

She nods. "I've only shopped once since my aunt died," she says. "Too sad, then too busy."

It's once again more information than she wants to give out before breakfast, but it's too late to pull those words back.

He nods, distracted, before crossing to her and pressing a kiss against her head.

"I need to check on things," he says apologetically, half holding her in a hug. "But I want...to see you. Again. Later."

"Apparently Gurlien wants some information on how I

survived," she says, letting herself lean into the embrace. "Not sure how to explain the electricity thing."

Zoel makes a sound deep in his chest, before holding her tightly for one long second. "Would he recognize Wight magic?"

"I have no earthly idea," she says, resting her head against his chest.

She can hear his heart beat.

He hmmms, and she would give anything to not have to deal with any of the responsibilities in front of her but to stay there forever. Just the two of them, without any outside pressures.

But the world never works like that, so she pulls away, offering what is probably a warbled smile. "Would it endanger you if I went?"

Zoel scoffs.

"What?" She asks.

"I'm a bit stronger than that," he says, with just a hint of bravado.

"I thought I'd ask," she says, reaching for her tea again and taking a sip. "I'd like to see you again soon. Too."

He nods, presses a kiss against her lips, then vanishes.

Leaving her in her kitchen with a whole pot of tea and a fluttering heart.

She swallows hard, then leans back over her phone.

ALETTE (10:11 AM): I can be there in half an hour. If my car works properly with the magic.

AXEL (10:11 AM): ????

ALETTE (10:12 AM): I'll fill you in.

∼

HER CAR WORKS FINE, and Spot and Grey both join her, sprinting joyfully as she drives the familiar stretch into the Headquarters.

The moment she passes over the protective runes, a shiver works its way down her back, and her car grinds to a halt in a rough, shuddering gasp.

"Ugh," she whispers, then grabs her bag and shoves her door open.

Spot and Grey pace at the gate, unable to pass through the wards, and she wants nothing more than to let them. Then to take down the wards in one final motion, open up the compound to whatever magical forces are out there, and let them run wild.

But Responsibilities.

And her aunt had those up for a reason.

She grabs her phone from her console, and it sparks and shuts down in her hand.

"Not helpful," she mutters, before tossing it into her bag, and looking up the long driveway.

Her aunt had first purchased this property before Alette had been born and had built the grand sprawling compound in a way to mostly hide it from view, so the paved path up the hill twists and turns and dips along the property.

The slush has mostly melted off, leaving everything a muddy brown, and it's been ages since she's walked this part of the property. Something tickles at the back of her mind, like there's something there she's supposed to notice, something she's supposed to pick up on, but can't, not quite.

A thin ribbon of magic glimmers in the breeze, healthy, twisting between the trees and fluttering along the side of the road, but that's not it. That almost feels natural, like it was here before her aunt and that it'll be here after even herself.

There's something else.

But no matter how much she keeps her eyes peeled, how much she watches, the rest of her trek is uneventful, and she arrives at the front gate just slightly winded.

She stares up at the front door, the front door that they barely ever use, and sees magic scrawled all over it. Scrawled up and down, in her aunt's elegant hand, some runes crossed out and some glowing more than ever.

She raises an eyebrow at it, then at the security camera that she knows still works.

It's not the same glow and sensation as Zoel showing her magic, but it's also not quite different, either. Like her brush with death and the break once again changed her very perception of the world.

Which is exhausting.

"Okay," she mutters, pushing her hand into the center of the door, into the scanning rune her aunt had carved in years ago.

A spark snaps from her fingertips, but the rune doesn't react poorly, merely turns the lock and lets her in with the same groaning wheeze as a deflating bounce house.

As teens, Axel and Alette had once tried to change the noise it made but had never been successful. Axel had tried to change the very nature of the door, and Alette had tried to charm it so it rang like an old church bell, but nothing had ever stuck.

Once inside, she strides as fast as she can to the elevator, before hesitating, her hand hovering over the button. Because getting stuck in the elevator would be far worse than her car shutting down in the driveway.

"Fuck this," Alette mutters in a way she knows could be

heard by anyone tapping into the old listening spells, and she turns to the mostly unused staircase, huffing and puffing up the set of stairs until she reaches the sterile conference room, completely devoid of any of her aunt's magic.

The grand mahogany door sends shivers down her hands, pins and needles crawling up her wrist, and she's really going to have to learn the rules of all this magic if she's going to be like this.

But after just a moment of puzzling over her, the door swings open, and the full force of the sterile room smacks her in the face.

She freezes, all breath stolen away from her, her own magic sparking and arcing to the ground, stirring up dust around her.

The colored liquid in the equipment now heavily weighs down one chamber, and it drips further into it, drop by noisy drop. The pendulum swings a bit closer to the current day.

Both Axel and Gurlien look up at her, Axel from a pile of papers, Gurlien from what appears to be a pile of rune sketches that even from here give her a strong, off-putting metallic taste.

Axel narrows his eyes, then, obviously, looks back to the papers. Deliberate.

So, he's still upset like that. Good to know.

"So that's what he meant by your magic having issues," Gurlien says, stepping away from the pile of sketches, and immediately the coppery taste of the room declines. "That's...startling."

"Yes," Alette says crisply, narrowing her eyes and trying to read the runes from this far away, but even her glasses aren't that good. "Whatever magic you're doing reeks."

She doesn't miss Axel's eyebrows raising a hair, and him scowling to avoid a smile.

Gurlien instead steps towards her, his brow furrowed, like she's the problem here, before circling her silently.

Her magic sparks out at him, and he jerks back, the spark dissipating inches from his nose.

"I can't control it yet," she says, silently cursing his ability to evade. "But it should go away."

"Describe it to me," he orders, standing a fair distance away, and it's a fair order, one she would give if she was in his place, "use as many details as you're cognizant of."

Alette glances at Axel, but he's studiously reading pages that look like bank statements instead of following along, which must be excruciatingly boring for him.

"I followed the sick magic into the field behind my apartment, and I felt it snap, and I...grabbed the pieces," she says, filtering through her words to be as vague as possible but still accurate, "I woke up and I was like this, two days later."

Again, the eyebrow twitch from Axel.

Gurlien tilts his head at her. "Has there been any magical events in your life that would...fundamentally change you?" he asks, and it's a sharp question. "Some inter- action with magic, something bigger than just the normal things that would come from being under Joyanne?" He paces around again, still a healthy distance away. "Did the demon that was Terese strike you, how she struck him?" He gestures at Axel without even looking over.

"What do you mean?" Alette asks, after far too long of a pause, where she searches for a lie and finds it missing.

"Most magicians would be dead, instantly, if they did that," he continues, "but demon magic...has circumvented some of it."

Axel lifts his eyes to Alette with a raised eyebrow.

"So, Axel could also fix it?" Alette asks, and Gurlien shrugs. "No, that's important to know. We've both been...struck...in different ways, if he could help hold things together, then—"

"I'd have to see the magic to begin with," Axel mutters.

"Exactly, he'd have to see the magic. Moot question. How were you struck?"

And suddenly, Alette cannot care. Cannot care about his reaction, cannot care about how he'll almost certainly be angry, almost certainly want to experiment. How it'll reveal too much.

"She killed me, the Necromancer brought me back, easy." Alette says, crossing her arms, and another spark crackles loud into the air. "That cannot—"

Before she can react, Gurlien sketches out a spell midair and flings it at her, faster than any magician she's seen, and—

The sparks crackle around it before it reaches her, and the spell fragments fall to pieces.

"And I still can't control that," Alette says, pulling herself to her full height and putting as much frost into her voice as she possibly can, "but please refrain from scanning me."

"Yeah, that's rude," Axel drawls, finally setting down the papers, "especially without permission."

She glances at him, he gives her a raised eyebrow, checking in. Seeing if she's sure about this.

"Why," Gurlien breathes out, and he's not angry, his eyes are alight, "why didn't you tell me?"

He takes another step towards her, then flinches back when her magic reacts.

"Why would I tell someone I just met that I had previously died?" Alette asks, letting all her suspicion pour into her voice, letting all of the frustration at all of it seep into her very being.

The magic crackles again.

"I still haven't contacted my actual brothers and told them, why the hell would I tell someone who's just come in and is demanding answers?"

Gurlien leans back, his eyebrows raised.

"I don't know you, all you've done is come in and insult my aunt, insult my best friend, and insult me. Why would anyone tell you something so private?"

Axel sits back, crossing his arms.

Gurlien finally looks away, and she gets the barest of feelings that she's surprised him. Or embarrassed.

"Dying was private?" he asks, after a long moment, his voice pondering. "I would have thought that every moment of it...wouldn't be."

"Fuck off," Alette says, then turns to Axel, nods, and storms back out.

The moment the mahogany doors close behind her, the pressure on her chest lifts, and she gulps in great, heaving breaths.

She's not supposed to be the person who has outbursts like that.

But anger still fizzes in her blood, and she pushes herself away from the doors, down the padded carpet hallway, almost at a run. Like she couldn't get away from the room fast enough. Like every step away from it grants her air, grants her clarity of mind, grants her something resembling calm.

When she was young and more prone to moments like this, she would lock herself in one of the padded foam rooms and let her magic blast wildly until she felt better, but this time her feet take her up the stairs, towards the greenhouse. Towards all the green plants, still cheerfully growing despite the lack of her aunt.

The humidity slaps her in the face when she opens the door, and the moment she steps in she sits down against the glass wall right next to the door.

It's warm, prickly, so she sheds her tailored coat, plopping it next to herself, and lets her head rest against the glass.

It's not her smartest moment, not her most elegant, but she stares up at the cloudy skies beyond the glass.

The leaves of the plants flutter in some unknown breeze, a susurration of noise she didn't know she wanted. She could smell the basil and the sage all the way from the door and the orchids her aunt grew just because she liked the way they looked.

She could smell the damp soil, the green of the grass that grows in lines of sod by the far window, and the beginnings of rosebuds.

Her aunt had used the roses as spell components, had always waited until the petals had shriveled and died, the blossom falling off the plant. Alette had wondered if it was from altruism, but her aunt had never told her.

And now she never could.

Because her aunt was dead and Alette had been the one that was raised.

Tears prickle at the edges of her eyes, but she sniffles those down by sheer force of will and fury, squeezing her eyes shut as hard as she can.

The leaves of the plants rustle again, and this time she opens her eyes to glance up at them.

There's magic everywhere.

Neat, orderly Lines of magic, precisely following the irrigation that her aunt had set up all those times. They pulse in time with her breathing, like just by being there she's influenced them.

Carefully, Alette climbs to her feet, but the magic doesn't move from its neat spots around her ankle height.

She sniffles again and feels crazy, before striding down the rows and rows of plants, the leaves fluttering around her.

The crackling magic inside of her bubbles up, benign sparks discharging in mid-air playfully.

Her chest still aches, still hurts from her outburst, from the sanitation in the room below, but something resembling a smile tugs at her lips.

"Couldn't touch the magic Lines my ass," she whispers, as if the plants would overhear her and judge her.

The Lines pulse around her, so she sits down, right in the middle of the orderly lanes of plants, and lets the magic brush against the bare skin on her arms.

It's healthy, none of the fraying or limpid nature of the other ones, and she can't believe she missed it for so long. That she couldn't see them, couldn't see everything her aunt did, everything her aunt touched.

The magic grazes her arm again, like it's learning, and the sparks inside her crackle near it. And she breathes, letting herself relax, letting her shoulders unwind.

The cold logical part of herself knows she should write a report about this, so it could be studied, so she could learn about it. Learn to use it, learn to be around it, learn what it means.

Figure out if it's because she's spent so much time with Zoel (like Melekai had suggested), or if it's a weird effect of Terese's magic, or because she was at that break. Figure out if there's any lasting danger to her, if she needs to be aware of anything before she acts.

And she'll need to explain it in exhaustive detail to

everyone, make sure that it's categorized, that people know about her, that people know what she can do.

That sounds about as appealing as eating her own coat.

So, she lets herself sit there, breathing in the scent of the soil and the leaves, and just is.

GURLIEN FINDS her exactly thirty minutes later, still sitting on the floor of the conservatory, and it's too precise of a time for her to think that he needed to search for her.

He probably had access to the security cameras, for all she knew.

He frowns down at her, and she refuses to feel small, instead straightening her spine, like sitting on the floor of a garden greenhouse is normal behavior for herself.

"Are you able to complete spells in a timely fashion?" he asks, sitting down on a bench close by.

"What sort of question is that?" Alette asks, blinking at him. She'd feel stung, but it's so bizarre and outside of the realm of what she expected.

"You're experiencing a drastic magical disruption, does that affect your ability to complete spells?"

She squints at him.

"Nobody knows how magic would work combined with necromancy, did it affect your ability to complete spells?" he repeats, sounding frustrated, like she is being the obstinate one. "You had a magical disruption."

"I had no issues after being raised," she says, flat, "except my arm was also broken and that stopped some weaving."

He nods, like that's a piece of the puzzle that is Alette. "Have you done any since the break?"

For a few seconds, she debates being offended, that he's

treating her outburst and upset so clinically, but she's too befuddled by it to consider it seriously.

"I just regained consciousness yesterday," Alette says. "Half the time when I touch my phone, it shuts off. My car stopped working the moment I crossed through the runes on the land. I definitely have not."

And he regards her much longer than she's comfortable with.

"I investigated the break," he says, because of course he did, of course he'd go and snoop around the field behind her house.

A strange stirring of protectiveness over her strange little section of the world shifts inside of her, but she breathes out of her nose, and no magic crackles around her.

"And?" she asks, when it's clear he is waiting for a response.

"Those are the sort of disruptions that are happening all over the area, and we don't want to infect everywhere," he says, sitting primly on the bench nearest to her, like he couldn't comprehend sitting on the floor. "The type that spread, that kill magicians near them, that destroy magic as we know it."

She had guessed that much.

"Yours isn't spreading."

She absorbs this, lets herself feel around with the words, feel around with what he's saying.

"So, we don't need to sanitize," she says, still feeling brittle from her outburst before, "we just get me—and maybe Axel, maybe Jack...the Necromancer's brother"— Gurlien's eyebrows flash up at that—"and we find and stop them."

"That would be an undertaking so large it would burn you up and destroy you," he says, but his face is thoughtful.

"I doubt it'd work—we'd have to have dozens of you working around the clock, and even then if you miss even one, you could doom an entire generation of magicians."

"But it's possible," she pushes, "theoretically. We could try it."

His face remains thoughtful, even after he shakes his head.

"All it would take is one of the main Lines going, and it would be all gone," he says, but he's musing, he's thinking, she's making progress.

"Well, we can protect the main Line?" she asks, shoring up herself to ask Zoel as well.

"I see why Joyanne chose you as her protege," he says. "She never wanted to do things the established way, either." He pushes himself up to standing. "I will investigate, I will research, but I am skeptical. Rest up and get this"—he waves a hand at her—"under control. Whatever we end up doing, it will need a lot more precision than this."

With one final nod, his brow still furrowed, he strides out, leaving Alette with a whisper of hope that she's not used to feeling.

AXEL'S not in the main rooms, nor is he in any of his workshops, and she's not going to be the one to snoop on the security cameras when he clearly doesn't want to be disturbed.

It feels odd, to have had the time she had with Zoel, and not immediately go gossiping about it with Axel, and some remote part of her worries at it like a loose tooth, that he's actually angrier than she thinks. That he won't just come around given time like he usually does.

But the magic still crackles from her fingertips when she reaches for the elevator button, so she tromps down the stairs, the runes written in the concrete walls wavering as she passes by.

Tentatively, mid stairs, she rests her hand near one of the runes, and a spark jumps from her palm, and the rune spazzes, the physical writing jerking in place.

It's not a rune for stability, it's just one her aunt had experimented with, to make the concrete warmer. It generally works, though not to the degree a homesick Alette had hoped.

Beneath her fingertips, the rune pulses like she's just another creature of magic. Like she's supposed to be like this.

It's an odd thought, and she puzzles over it, still leaning her hand against the wall. That there could be something in the magic that is responding to her like this, that it's recognizing something.

It's not quite how the magic recognized Alette at the death bubble, but it's not the most dissimilar. More like it's responding to how she's changed and responding positively.

It leads her down a mental pathway she's not quite sure she wants to follow, not yet. About just how much that incident in the woods could have changed her, and just how much her life might be different.

She's awfully tired of thinking of her life in terms of before and after.

She snatches back her hand, but the rune remains bright.

It's just one more thing she'll have to research.

So, she sighs, kicks open the door back to the slushy outside, and tromps back down to her car at the bottom of the winding driveway.

It sits, sensible as always, out of place among the dead blackberry brambles and the towering spruce.

Next to it, idling, is Axel's shining black Mustang, the engine rumbling in ways it never used to.

Alette stills, raising an eyebrow, and Axel stands from where he was very clearly crouching next to her car.

"Don't let me touch your car, mine stopped the moment I crossed the border," Alette says as he crosses his arms.

"That's why you left it in the way?" Axel asks, which is fair. It's not exactly like he's able to leave.

Probably wanted a drive.

"It's not like I could push it myself," Alette says, mulish.

He takes that, then nods, because even while angry he is a logical person. "You haven't told Nate or Amir you died?"

Now it's her turn to blink at him. "I haven't...no."

His brow furrows, a familiar look, one full of confusion and consternation at her behavior. "Don't you think you should?"

Casually, he gets into her driver's seat and she tosses him her keys.

"They don't know Aunt Frisse is dead," Alette says, and there's a pang inside of her when she says it, even after all this time. "They'd probably celebrate."

The furrow in his brow deepens further, but he tries her car, and the engine crunches, then whines.

With a sidelong, suspicious glance at her, he pops the hood. "You haven't modded the car, have you?"

"I gave it heated seats ages ago," Alette says, which he knew, but if he's going to be bringing her brothers into this, she doesn't exactly want any lectures. "Nothing with the engine."

"If I was Nate or Amir," he starts, and to the best of her

knowledge he hasn't communicated with his family in ages either, "I'd want to know I almost lost my sister."

He pushes past her to prop up the hood, and her magic crackles around her, so she leans away from the machinery.

It's not a fight she wants to have in the mud, but he's the one actively upset with her, so she just crosses her arms as he pokes at her car engine.

There's nothing she can see is wrong with her car, but he makes concerned noises.

"I doubt Amir remembers me too terribly much, he was five when we left," she says, after it becomes clear he's not going to talk to her. "And last time I saw Nate he threatened to punch me if I chose to go with Aunt Frisse."

"They send Christmas cards," Axel points out, not even looking at her. "There's one still on the fridge from this year."

"Nate's wife sends Christmas cards." It's a nonsensical argument, and her magic crackles around her.

Axel stands straight up, narrowing his eyes at her. "I can't see anything, but I can goddamn hear that," he says, referring to the magic crackling. "Just how much did you fuck yourself up if I can hear it?"

"It is very inconvenient," she says, gesturing at the car, "but I'm able to use my phone sometimes now."

He scowls at her, then ducks back at her car.

So. Still angry at her.

"I didn't mean to endanger myself," she says again, as he digs a wrench out of his pocket —because of course he keeps one on him now that he can't magic one—and begins to turn something in her car. "I just acted on instinct."

"Your instincts are fucked," he replies, and there's a thunk inside her engine.

"I stopped it from getting worse," she points out, which

is probably not the smartest thing to say to him, "and we might have a way to stop it more, we don't know."

"And you're going to be just throwing yourself into more and more danger, aren't you?" he says, frustration coating his voice as he slides into her driver's seat again, turning the key. "Are you going to go hunt down more of those and knock yourself out again so your heart stops beating?"

"Lyra says I wasn't dying."

"Heart stopping is still bad!" He thumps his fist on her wheel, and her car horn honks, before he very clearly steels himself, turning the key again.

It whines before the engine turns over smoothly.

"What would your Zoel do, then?" he says, leaving her car running but getting out and slamming her hood shut. "All this work he needs your help for, all this showing up to rescue you, and then you go and stick yourself right in front of a firehose of uncontrollable magic and almost die." He crosses his arms in front of her. "What about finding Terese, she could just fuck the rest of us up. What about Lyra and Mel, the College could find them, and no one would be able to protect them or anything."

"I don't...I'm not trying to get myself killed," she says, breathing out hard through her nose, but the magic crackles around her fingertips all the same. "I don't want to go down that path again."

"Yeah, but you're sure not doing much to stop it from happening." He throws her car in reverse, rolling it down the hill until the front tires roll out of the line of runes.

Almost immediately, Spot and Grey appear, circling her car and sniffing at it.

"Don't you think it's good," Alette starts, and he shoots her such a venomous look that she raises an eyebrow at him, "that you could hear the magic?"

"Sure, focus on that," he says, leaving her car idling and stepping out. "Try not to fry your spark plugs this time."

She takes that as a win, climbing into her car, and despite the energy crackling all over her, it doesn't shut off.

Axel stands there, scowling at her.

"I said I'm sorry," Alette says, rolling down her window.

"No, you didn't," he retorts, then sighs. "Go talk to your Zoel, see if there's any way you can control this shit. And answer the texts so I don't have to deal with Asshole alone."

And with that, he turns on his heel, stomping over to his car and slamming the door on it.

25

T he almost overwhelming need to let the magic crackle over her builds and builds as she drives away from the Headquarters until she pulls off of the road to a dirt parking lot, letting herself breathe hard out of her nose.

She kicks open the door to her car, stomping out on the damp dirt. It's a trailhead for one of the million walking paths in the area, and thankfully bereft of any people.

There's a thin strip of magic barely visible up the highway, fluttering merrily around, but she's not here for that, instead turning her back on it and facing the trail.

Spot immediately circles around her, shoving his nose in her palm, then flinching back when a crack of magic sparks onto his nose with a yelp.

"Sorry, boy," Alette says, though she finds it difficult to put anything into her voice, "I didn't mean to."

He gives her such a wounded look she would have believed she kicked him or something, before the two dogs slink off.

Great.

One more thing in her life that's angry at her. One more thing that happened outside of her control that hurts people around her, that doesn't care about her intentions, that does nothing but harm.

The crackle builds up against her chest, a strange pressure that doesn't feel healthy, and she squeezes her eyes shut against it.

It's—obviously—affected by her emotions and the swirling knot of frustration in her isn't helping, isn't making things any better, but no matter how much she controls her breath, tamps down on the upset, it doesn't go away. It doesn't lessen. Like all of her emotions she can shove into various little boxes just boil over, just bubble and froth until there's nothing she can do.

She can't stop that magic from breaking, she can't stop everything from always going wrong, she can't bring in Terese, she can't get the College to back off, she can't even stop her best friend from being angry at her.

She couldn't stop her aunt from dying.

With more force than necessary, she yanks her survival pack out of her trunk, throws it on her back, then tromps the few feet onto the trailhead so she's not visible from the road and then...

...Then she lets go.

Lets go of all the strange electricity around her, lets go of the crackling sparks. Watches as they collect in her hand, then snap around into the air, like little ineffective fireworks.

They sparkle, popping and jolting in the air, hitting pockets of moisture and bits of air, and they're beautiful, swirling around her.

The pressure in her chest doesn't lessen, but tears prickle at her eyes.

Of course that wouldn't work. Of course something that seems like it would make her feel better, doesn't.

She sits down on a tree stump, the moss icy from the cold. Sparks still swirl around her, snapping at everything but affecting nothing, and she buries her face in her hands.

"There's easier ways to call me," Zoel says from only a bit away, and she jumps, her magic sparking out.

He's standing just down the path, comfortably dressed in a soft-looking sweater, his brows drawn together and watching her.

She sighs explosively and the magic crackles around her again, but she can't find words. Can't find things she's supposed to say.

"I...wasn't," she starts, after far too long. "I mean, sorry."

He shakes his head, dismissing her concerns. "I figured."

"Why is it doing this?" she asks, holding out her hand, showing him the magic crackling around it. "I thought this would make it better, but it's not."

He steps closer, until the magic snaps out at him as well, but he shrugs it off, unaffected. "I take it you're upset?" He sits on a large boulder directly across the trail from her, and her magic arcs over the dirt path to him, but he doesn't flinch away.

"Gurlien just wanted to ask me questions about how I'm still alive," she says, wearily, "and whether or not I could be useful to him."

He straightens his legs across the trail, and if anyone truly wanted to cross the path they'd be right in the way, but the cold weather and remote location deters most of the hikers in the area.

He watches her with those kind blue eyes.

"Axel's mad that I put myself in danger," she continues, feeling like she's about to start blubbering, which just won't do, so she takes in a big, gulping breath, and it does nothing. "Gurlien still wants me to destroy everything my aunt touched, my car didn't let me drive onto the Headquarters with this magic shit, I can't find Terese, I can't control this, I can barely help you, and—"

"You're helping me a lot," he interrupts, but his face is soft, like he's just listening.

"And I can't do anything." As if to punctuate her words, the magic snaps out, loud. "I even zapped Spot's nose and upset him."

"He'll be fine," Zoel says quietly. "He gets zapped by much more malicious things, he's just being a baby."

His words don't quite help, so she buries her face in her hands again, and he nudges her foot with his shoe from across the narrow trail.

"Do you want to see something beautiful, something no human has seen?" he asks, voice still soft. "It won't help the magic, it won't help the people you've angered, but it's something you can look at while feeling those things."

"Can it help me actually help you?" she asks. "Can it help me actually make a difference?"

He shakes his head, but stands, offering her his hand.

And she can't feel any worse, so she takes it.

Keeping her hand in his, he tugs her away from the trail, through sparse underbrush and slush, until he leads her to a rock outcropping, one of the many black stones that decorate the area.

"I found this one year while patrolling," he says, leaning his free hand against the icy stone. "Near as I can tell, a Wight hid it centuries ago, sealed it away from humans, then didn't tell anyone where it was."

The knot in her chest still sits, but curiosity starts to worm its way through her bones.

"This won't hurt it?" she asks, raising her hand, where static magic still crackles dimly.

It's lesser now, after the short walk.

"That's natural magic, this is natural magic, like draws to like," he says, and it's a familiar refrain. "If anything, it'll appreciate it."

He drums his fingers against the stone face until his entire hand disappears into the rock.

Ah. An illusion.

"I find it hard to believe that no human ever rested against this stone and slipped in," Alette says, as he deftly steps directly into the rock, keeping a grip on her hand.

It's surreal to see her hand vanish into solid stone, but she doesn't feel anything different, just Zoel's grip in hers.

So, she takes a deep breath, the pressure of tears still behind her sinuses, and ducks inside.

There's a brief sensation that her ears are going to pop, before they clear, and she opens her eyes to an entirely different world.

Crystals glitter in dim light, reflecting off of every surface, shimmering and shining. Two softly glowing spots of light hover.

The air warms the skin on her cheeks, just enough to take the chill of the slush from outside.

Tucked against one corner is a simple couch, a rough-hewn table and two chairs, and an austere-looking bed with an old fashioned quilt.

But no dust decorates the stones, and no dust feathers over the quilt or the table, like it's untouched.

It had obviously been someone's home.

Zoel's watching her, and she blinks.

"Wow," she says, which is wholly inadequate, "and you just found it?"

"I think the guardian of this area a few generations before me made this," he says, stepping easily through the space. There's even a throw rug on the stone floor, leaving his footfalls silent. "I maintained it, replaced the bed and the quilts, so that if someone had the need..." he trails off, shrugging. "I like having safe places where I can retreat, if I need."

She reaches out her hand, touching one of the crystals. Its edge is smooth, pristine, like a museum-quality piece.

"These don't naturally occur here," she says, tapping her fingernail against the surface of the crystal. "I've never seen..."

"Oh, it's entirely crafted," he says easily. "I once saw some hikers walk by with cave measuring equipment and completely miss it."

"Interesting," Alette says, because it is, and she lets her fingertips drape on the glittering gems.

Her recently healed fingertips, the ones that had been burned, feel almost too sensitive against the surface.

But she doesn't move, just sits with the sensation against her fingertips.

"I was worried, when magic started to break, that this would be gone," he continues, "and that all this hard work would vanish, but I think it's safe unless the main Ley Line goes."

"Gurlien talks a lot about that one, too," Alette says, turning back to him. "That if it goes, all magicians will lose powers or die."

"And that's why I am keeping track of it," he says, "and any instability, any strand of worry, I'm going to try to fix."

He lifts her hand to his mouth, pressing a kiss on her palm.

"The world is dire," he whispers, "everything is in danger, but you are also hurting."

She resists the urge to snatch her hand away.

"I'll live," she says hollowly. "I think the grand state of magic is more important than my hurt."

Though it sometimes doesn't feel like it.

"It's not going to collapse in the next hour," he continues. "You can let yourself be upset."

She wants to snap at him, she wants to refute it, but instead she looks out at the glittering crystals. They're a myriad of colors, blues and pinks and greens and purples all reflecting the light.

"Here." He pulls her over to the couch, and she lets him. "The danger of the world does not stop this from being beautiful."

He's correct, she knows he's correct, but the pressure of tears mount against her face again.

He sits down next to her, wrapping his arms around her, pulling her tight. His hug is warm, even warmer than the bespelled air, and the sweater is soft and the threads aren't scratchy and—

Before she can stop herself, she buries her face into his shoulder, and feels herself start to shake.

Feels her shoulders tremble, feels her hands grip his sweater as if it could save her, and feels how solid, how real he is against her. How strong his shoulder is, how steady his arms are around her.

And tears bubble up in her eyes, and this time she doesn't try to tamp them down.

His arms briefly tighten, so she presses her face harder into his shoulder.

And she cries.

She cries for her aunt, who she never thought would appreciate any tears being shed. She cries for the strange knot of stress sitting behind her breastbone, that doesn't ease no matter what she does. She cries from the frustration, that the Headquarters no longer works how she wants it to work. She cries for the fight with Axel, for the anger she can't really fix.

And she cries for the confusion, for the turmoil of emotions inside of her. For the magic that's still swirling around her, the magic she used to be able to control and wield however she wanted, and now sparks around without her input.

For her lack of control. In everything. There's so precious little that she can actually do, can actually control, that the loss of it comes at her in great rolling gasps of pain.

Zoel does nothing, his arms just wrapped around her, tight but not constricting, solid but not threatening. Just...there.

And for a period of time—seconds or minutes or hours, she cannot tell—she just cries, and he just holds her, in a glittering room of magic and crystals in the middle of the woods, so close to the Headquarters and yet so remote. Until, somehow, her tears subside, leaving her brain feeling scooped out and hollow, but the knot in her chest lessened.

His arms still around her, he swipes the pad of his thumb against her wrist, and it's a familiar motion, and she realizes with a jolt of embarrassment that he has been doing it the entire time she's been there.

"Sorry," she mumbles, pressing her forehead into his shoulder. Her eyes sting, of course, the awful gummy sensation of too many tears shed.

"How long has it been, since you cried like that?" he asks, and this close she feels the rumble of his words in his chest.

She doesn't want to pull back.

"I don't...think I cried, after Aunt..."

"You think?" he asks, but there's no heat to his voice, no pressure. "Alette, you need to mourn, you can't keep everything in like that.", He holds her by her shoulders, pulling back enough so she can see his brilliant blue eyes, and he keeps his gaze on her. "No wonder you're hurting."

"It's not like I've had the time," she says, taking the moment to wipe under her eyes, and comes away with the mascara from the morning streaked across the back of her hand. "And Axel had it worse, and there was Melekai to adjust, and then the magic"—she sniffles, and it's gross and undignified, but he's giving her such a soft look—"it's not something I have the luxury of doing."

Her voice breaks.

He nods, not in agreement, but understanding.

"And Aunt Frisse would hate me crying over her, and this"—she lifts a hand, and a lackluster crackle of static discharges between her fingers—"doesn't help."

He captures her hand in his, and the spark hits his hand instead of the air, and the prickle immediately soothes.

"When I first noticed the magic breaking," he starts, and his deep voice fills the crystalline room, "I thought there was no way it could be as bad as it is, so I ignored it."

She lifts her chin at him, listening.

"I found a few small things and repaired them, but I thought they were anomalies. Nothing terribly threatening. I didn't...I didn't reach out for help, long after I should have, and I don't know how much damage I caused." He turns her hand over in his, a gentle steady motion against her palm, like his attention on her could solve his problems. "I didn't begin to even study it in depth until far too late, and it had already killed a small community of other Wights up in

Prince Rupport. If I had paid attention, if I hadn't dismissed it, they would still be alive."

Her lips part, but she finds her words to be gone. There's nothing she can say that would make up for that, nothing she could do to help.

"After they died, I couldn't...couldn't grasp it,"

"Did you know them?" Alette asks.

"Only by vague relation. But after that..." he trails off and swallows, his Adam's apple bobbing, "I rushed in too fast."

The words hang in the still air.

"I rushed in too fast, did more damage than I knew, and people were hurt. If I had stopped, if I had given myself time to think...I probably could have stopped this as a threat weeks ago. Before it started to affect more people, before it started to break down your Headquarters, before they started to twist and become unmanageable by me alone. I wouldn't have had to ever involve you." He places his hand on her fingertips, where the burn once resided. "You would have been safe, you wouldn't have had to deal with the inter-loper at your aunt's home, and no magic would be breaking."

She leans against him on the strange couch in the crystal room.

"That's a lot of blame for someone who's not at fault," Alette says, letting her words collect inside before speaking. "You couldn't have predicted."

"I might've," he says, the corners of his lips tugging down, before he shakes his head, as if to banish the thought. "But that's not the point. My point is to—"

"—to take it easy?" Alette says dryly.

"To give yourself time to actually process, to actually think of what needs to be done. If you rush in and run your-self dry..." He sighs. "There might be something we're both missing, some way to solve the problem that's out there, that you're so stressed with responding to the immediate that your brain hasn't stumbled upon yet."

Alette lets herself lean more against him, and a less dignified person would have called it a snuggle, but instead of examining that further she...thinks. Mulls over his words like she would a new piece of evidence, like a previously uncovered bit of research.

It's not that she's entirely unaware of the physical aspects of stress on a human body, or of the phenomenon that people think of their best things when letting their brain relax, but it's never something she's considered applicable to herself. She's the sort that excels at cramming, at filling her brain and her schedule to the brim, until all that pours out is excellence.

But...

A stray bit of magic sparks up off her hand, hitting one of the crystals and reflecting away, shimmering through the room.

And the moment it does, Zoel leans over, pressing his lips against hers.

She considers pushing him away, she considers leaning back, as kissing her while she's still snotty and tear streaked can't be the most pleasant, and she really prefers to be in pitch perfect condition when she makes out with someone, but—

But his lips are soft against hers, and all of a sudden, everything inside of her sings. Like a bell that has been rung, every part of her thrumming with the realization that this is what she's been wanting. That this is what her entire being has been waiting for.

And for once, she doesn't ignore it.

She grabs at his hair, twisting her hands into his curls,

kissing back with way more force than is actually necessary, and he grunts in surprise. In between one tantalizing moment and the next, he opens his mouth to hers, his tongue gentle against her lips.

And she's done with being gentle.

She meets his gentleness with fierceness, with a possessiveness that surprises even her, and a lack of dignity that almost certainly will make her blush later.

But right now, right at this moment, all that matters are the points of contact, the incredible heat of his mouth, and his hands settled on her hips.

Before she gives herself a second to doubt herself, she straddles him on that small couch in the strange room, still kissing him.

"This," he mumbles into her lips, in between kisses and presses, "is not what I anticipated."

"You just said to let your brain think about other things," she retorts, and he smiles, heartbreakingly close, before her lips capture his once more.

She lets go of his hair, just long enough to pull at the edge of his shirt, and he leans back to shed it, before kissing her at the sacred point where her neck meets her shoulder.

She exhales, half between a sigh and a ticklish laugh.

He's strong, she knew he was already, but the dim light from the glittering crystals just casts everything in stark relief. Thick muscles frame his broad shoulders, like even beyond the magical work he does, he lifts weights or logs in a forest, and a dark line of hair trails down his stomach.

On the back of his shoulder lays a tattoo, brilliantly dark against his skin, a winding whorl of leaves and vines and thorns, and she splays her hand against it. His skin is warm, despite the winter outside of their be-spelled paradise.

She opens her mouth to say something, but he kisses the

hollow of her neck and the thought immediately flees her brain.

He unbuttons her coat, flicking the buttons aside with deliberate motions, revealing the entirely sensible blouse underneath it.

"Here," she says, breathless, and lets the coat fall from her shoulders, then pulls her shirt over her head, leaving her in just her bra in front of him.

It's a far cry from a sexy bra, but still he exhales as if she has gifted him with a beautiful vista.

She shivers, once, even though it's not cold in the slightest. His hands are warm against her skin, gripping at her waist, as he kisses his way down her chest, as if the answers to the world lay between her breasts, and all she wants to do is let him explore until he can find everything.

She twists her arm behind herself, unclasping her bra, and he cups her with both hands, immediately there.

"You're beautiful," he mumbles, pressing a kiss against her chest and sparking up something deep inside of her.

And some magic, but it crackles away, harmless to them both.

"You're beautiful," he repeats, as her hands splay over his chest, with the hard muscle and the trail of curls leading her down, "you're beautiful and I can't believe you're here."

Instead of answering, she just pulls his head back by his curls and kisses him deeply. As if her life depends on it, on this fervent connection and fast motions.

And she wants more.

Of course she wants more, it's been too long and too much has happened since she's been held like this, since she's been wanted like this.

She lets her hand drift to his belt buckle, and he hesitates, just slightly, beautiful blue eyes blinking up at her.

"May I?" she asks, caught halfway between wild want and a strange bashfulness.

"Of course," he says, and his voice is breathless, rough. "Whatever you want to do to me, I'm yours."

She arches an eyebrow at him. "That's a dangerous thing to say."

He just smiles sideways back at her, and she's straddling him on his lap, completely topless. "I like this idea of danger much more than your usual."

While speaking the words, he undoes his belt, then teasingly undoes the top button on his pants.

"Anything I should be aware of?" Alette teases, and he grins at her widely. "Any sudden surprises here?"

"That," he says, and his accent rounds out his words, "is entirely up to you to decide."

So, she kisses him, shedding her slacks as fast as she can, and he tugs her over to the bed, and the lights overhead twinkle and glimmer on the stone and crystal, and she's never felt something so perfect in her life. Never felt something so in tune, so completely right, so completely natural, as this moment feels. Like the whole world stops and shines a spotlight on them right there, to illuminate how she is meant to be.

She guides him onto his back and her hands shake, just a bit, before he catches her palm in his, threading their fingers together.

The magic sparks, crackling off loud, but nothing changes, drawing a smile from them both.

"I guarantee that will stop, after a while," he murmurs, and he's a beautiful sight to see, black curls spread out on the pillow beneath his head, his jaw tilted towards her. Like even like this, he's drawn to her.

It's a heady idea, so she straddles him, and he breathes

in, a sudden intake of air, like he didn't expect that, even with the two of them naked together.

He's perfect.

He's built, she already knew that, merely by the hiking and rock climbing she's seen him do, and under the dim lights every bit of him is illuminated, and every bit of him is perfectly designed for her.

"You're amazing," she murmurs, then briefly closes her eyes in embarrassment, "you..."

He leans up, capturing her mouth in his, and she lets him take her away. Lets him push inside of her, until all she can feel and all she can tell is him.

26

After, she snuggles up against his shoulder, their sweat cooling in the air, and she lets her eyes flutter shut.

"Is that a thing?" Zoel murmurs, and she presses her face into his shoulder. "Do humans really fall asleep after that?"

"No," she mumbles against his skin, "it's just..."

He presses a kiss to the top of her head, to where stray black hairs have escaped her braid, and she can't bring herself to care anymore.

He throws his arm around her, and it's just even more comfortable.

"So, would you call this more of a hidden room or a pocket dimension?" she mumbles, blinking her eyes open to stare at the crystals, and he chuckles, a sound that starts deep in his chest. "What, it's a question."

"Amazing," he says, but there's no heat to it. "I think hidden room. It's still here, even when I'm not in it."

She props herself up on her elbows. "And pocket dimensions aren't?" she asks. "You would think they'd exist even while empty."

"But spatially"—he waves his hand at the room—"it's always in this stone, it's roughly the same size as the boulder, and if you shift the boulder, you shift the room." He gives her a brilliant smile. "I tried. It stayed the same."

"You moved a however-ton boulder just to test a theory?" she asks, and she's teasing, but it might be the most attractive he's ever been.

He shrugs, and it's gloriously naked. "I didn't understand it. I wanted to. I had time."

Time.

One thing they probably didn't have too much of.

"Where's the next tangle?" she asks, pushing a wayward strand of hair out of her eyes. "Where's the next thing for us to fix?"

He sighs, and for a split second she can see a twinge of sadness in his eyes. "It's impossible to tell which will break next," he says, and he pushes himself up as well, reaching for his shirt and shrugging it back on, "There are tangles all over the place, but we should let you..." he trails off, like he's at a loss for words, "finish recovering."

"Would it affect it?"

"Probably," he says, and he tenderly hands Alette her clothing, before he hesitates. "How could you tell that the one next to you was about to break?"

"It woke me up," she says, twisting her bra back on. "I was dead asleep, but it woke me up, and it was outside my door."

"There wasn't a Ley Line outside your door before," he says, and she can see the cogs turning in his brain, "and while they do travel, not usually that much."

"So, it sought me out?" she guesses, and her mind is off

running, chasing down thoughts and ideas and connections faster than she can track. "Could it tell somehow that I could hold it in place?"

"That would suggest the other magicians could as well," he says, catching her line of thought and reeling it in, "that the magic itself is drawn to those who can help it, or might be able to."

"Only they couldn't, because they were dead when you found them," she continues, and he nods, "or they might've, just not enough..." she trails off, still only half-dressed, and tilts her head at him. "Zoel, is there anything else that might've helped me survive that? Besides the necromancy stuff, anything else?"

"There must be, or else every break would have had a magician at the center of it, trying to fix it," he says, buckling his pants back up. "And they weren't all raised, we're pretty sure we know all of the ones that Lyra raised, and there aren't any more Necromancers active in the area right now."

"And you said my aunt couldn't help," she starts, shimmying her way into her slacks again, "so it's not a sheer power factor."

"That could've helped you survive," he muses, before shaking his head. "No, it wasn't a power factor, but they all..."

He trails off, staring blankly at the glittering geode around them.

"They all..." Alette leads, throwing on her shirt and swinging her be-spelled coat around her shoulders.

He shakes his head again, as if trying to dispel his thoughts. "It's too easy, but they all knew the others of the land in some way."

She raises an eyebrow at him, because that seems very much not the easy answer.

"The one in NorCal, he had a ghost haunt his house for the last decade, they communicated very well," Zoel says, but his face is twisted, like it's leaving a foul taste in his mouth, "the one in Idaho, he knew the Wight of the area, they were..."—he gestures between Alette and him —"close."

"Understood," Alette says, her cheeks flushing.

"The one in Oregon, I knew him somewhat well, he would find ways to clear experiments with me before trying to break something down," he continues, "he would give me written documentation, and would change things if I said they needed to be changed." He falls silent, blinking out. "And you."

"And me." Alette sits next to him on the bed, pulling on her shoes. "And I'm the only one who lived?"

"And the only one who's actively touched Ley Lines before, who actively charged into a break without backup, and who's been gifted a boon by a spirit of the land." He touches her breast pocket, where the perfect glass marble still sits next to her needle case. "But you can't be everywhere."

"So, it's the natural magic, broken by a human slash demon combination, and needs humans plus natural beings to fix," Alette says, tying her laces, "with a really bad death rate."

"For breaks," he interjects, "if we get them before the break, it's fine."

Another thought sparks off of her mind, skittering away.

"Zoel," she starts, and he raises an eyebrow at her tone, "I know you told me to not pursue this"—his lips thin—"but you've...communicated with Terese. She's where the damage originally came from."

He's already shaking his head. "She tried," he says, dark,

"but whatever was left by the demon makes everything worse."

Alette worries her lower lip, but nods. "Ominous, but glad that she's...enough of a sane person to try to help."

"Oh, I would not call her sane," he says emphatically. "Whatever was left behind is definitely not sane. Not destructive, but not sane."

"I'll figure out how to tell the College, to get them off my back about bringing her in," Alette says, and doesn't miss his eyebrow raising again. "Give them something to consider, some good news in all of this, that at least they don't have someone running around trying to end the world. Still."

"That was their interest?" he asks, guarded.

And Alette gets the sudden thought that he's not going to like this next bit. That whatever she says next could destroy whatever little bit of joy they had created, this little pocket of happiness.

"They don't want the breaks to spread," she says, as neutrally as she can, "they've charged me with finding out how to get it to stop."

He leans against her, just the two of them on the bed, and she tries hard not to close her eyes and give in to the want to remain there forever.

"That's logical," he says, still guarded, and he rubs his thumb across the back of her hand. "I doubt I would like their methods."

Alette just looks away, shaking her head.

And when she can't look him in the eye, she tells herself it's because of everything being so truly overwhelming.

∾

THE NEXT FEW days pass in a haze of sleeping too much, of no texts from Axel but an annoying amount of texts from Gurlien, of the dogs stopping by with various tokens of affection (flowers, a translation guide to the scrolls, and even a perfectly chiseled out crystal from the cave).

And the inactivity leaves Alette on edge.

It always has, ever since she was a child, but now, crackling with unknown power and the world possibly falling to pieces, she feels like she's going to vibrate out of her skin.

~

27

On the third day, she plans ahead, keeping a folded-up piece of paper by her door, so the next time she hears the vague sounds of dog toenails on concrete, she throws the door open, and gets immediately rewarded by Spot jumping all over her in joy.

"Yes, yes, I'm okay," she mutters, even though she had seen the dog through the window just the day before. "I'm doing better, please tell Zoel I can do things again."

Just in case, she tucks a folded-up piece of paper into Spot's collar, as she's still somewhat unclear about how much the dogs understand her, and Spot shimmies at her with enthusiasm, before setting down a bag of scrolls at her feet.

She takes a step back right as a crackle of magic escapes her fingertips, but now she's able to tell, she's able to predict when it's happening, and the dog doesn't slink away from fear.

"See," she says seriously, and this is what just a few days

of solitude do to her, she's talking enthusiastically with a magical dog, "I can control things now."

Spot wiggles at her, tail thumping, before he turns and sprints into the day, shadows trailing after him.

And Alette doesn't know how long it'll take for him to receive his message, doesn't know how long she'll have to wait, and she resists sitting down on her porch until she gets a response back.

She bends to pick up the bag of scrolls—much smaller than previous ones, and the translation ledger is tucked right next to it—and her phone beeps.

LYRA (4:21 PM): How are you feeling?

Alette blinks at her phone, and it's such a foreign question in everything she's been thinking about.

ALETTE (4:22 PM): Fine. Still a bit overcharged. Bored.

LYRA (4:22 PM): Wanna come over?

LYRA (4:23 PM): Mel's out with Axel and I want to investigate the Buggees again. Mel gets all sad face when I suggest going.

It's not the smartest thing she's thought of in the last few days, but she immediately reaches in, grabbing her purse and her car keys.

"Do you want to walk or drive?" Alette asks the moment Lyra opens the door to her tiny mobile home.

"You're less sparkly," Lyra says, opening the door wider so Alette can step through. "Heart's not stopping."

"It never hurt," Alette says, bending and greeting Lyra's cat, who immediately preens at her. "Did Axel say he was mad at me? He's still mad at me."

"He didn't, but I gathered," Lyra says, pulling down her

jacket from the coat hook. "He only seeks out Mel when he's truly pissed off." She grabs her cane, then gestures towards the door.

"I can drive—"

"And walking is good," Lyra interrupts with a scowl, so Alette relents.

It's a brisk walk, during one of those days that feels like the first whispers of spring, where there isn't warmth in the air but there is promise. Something between a breeze and a scent, extolling them that the ugly winter may soon be over.

And Buggees is...different.

The whirlpool of magic still sparks everywhere, the boards are molded over and the concrete still grimy, but there's a change in it, in everything about it.

"When did you see this change?" Alette asks, staying far away, though the golden needle in her pocket grows warm at the proximity.

"A few days ago, Jackson stopped by and mentioned the gas station looked really weird," Lyra says, and she's staring pensively. "I think Melekai would have an aneurism if I went in, don'tcha think?"

"Absolutely," Alette says fervently, but takes a careful step forward. Not enough to get close, but just enough, so the taste of the decaying magic fills her nostrils and crawls down her throat.

"And Axel would probably refuse to speak to you ever again, if you did," Lyra continues, which is a very valid point, and Alette takes a step back. "Though..."

Alette reaches her hand out, the hand that was burned but now healed, her palm flat, and a spark of magic discharges from the magical tornado to it, completely harmless.

"Doesn't even hurt," Alette says, though Lyra's eyebrows are raised. "Not even a tickle."

"Sure hurt when I came back and tried," Lyra says, and Alette needs to give Lyra more credit, of course she's smart. "Mel keeps on saying that the magic is changing you, I think this is what he means."

Alette spares a thought of how weird it must be for Lyra to be living with a former demon, then immediately disregards it because she's slept with a magical creature of the land and she very much wants to do it again.

"But it's not hurting me," Alette repeats, then holds out the hand again.

More sparks fly from the tornado, hitting each of her fingertips, hitting the sensitive, too new skin, like it remembered.

And she knows she's not supposed to personify magic too terribly much, but it's like the tornado feels bad.

"I have an idea," Alette starts, raising an eyebrow at Lyra, "but I think telling the guys would be bad."

"Would I be considered one of the guys here?" From out of nowhere, Zoel appears, and both of them jump.

Right. Because Lyra can just see them, and always has.

"Probably," Alette answers honestly, and his handsome face splits into a grin, "but I think this can be fixed."

"Does he look any different to you?" Lyra asks, peering at him. "Because he just looks like a normal human to me."

"Thanks," Zoel says, and there's only a trace of sarcasm there.

"He looks human to me, too," Alette says, and gets rewarded with a dimple from Zoel. "Look."

She holds out her hand again, and immediately the sparks connect to her fingertips.

Zoel regards that, then turns to Lyra. "Is her heart stopping again?"

"Nope," Lyra says, popping her 'p' sound.

"Well," Zoel starts, "that's always a good sign. Hold out your other hand, and you tell me if her heart stops again."

Alette does, and more of the magic immediately hits her hand, creating a bridge between the two.

"Seriously, don't feel anything," Alette says, but her heart feels alight at just seeing Zoel. At the prospect of doing something useful. "Nothing."

Both Zoel and Lyra watch her, thoughtful, and she raises an eyebrow at them.

"Something I can't see?"

Zoel just watches the magic hitting her hand, a strange look on his face. "I have an idea."

"I like ideas," Alette says, and he squints at her, before returning his gaze to the magic.

"I'd do it myself, but this one has already shown that I can't, I've tried. This will...not be that safe," he says, and it's mostly to Lyra. "If needed, how adept are you with healing outside of death?"

Lyra's mouth forms a perfect 'o'. "Not very."

"Hmm." Zoel's lips thin, before he very deliberately meets Alette's eyes. "This is dangerous—"

"—I gathered," Alette interrupts.

"—But it might work, and it might solve this break, instead of keeping it in stasis." He tilts his head at her, and she wishes she could read his expression better.

"How dangerous?" Alette asks, and another crackle of magic meets her fingertips, almost ticklish in its intensity. "I'd like an informed opinion."

His lips twitch, almost a smile. "Do you see any strong

threads in there? Not just all the static, but anything thicker, like it's a main conduit of energy?"

"That doesn't answer the question," Alette murmurs, before she focuses back on the swirling maelstrom in front of her, searching for patterns.

At first, there's nothing, just chaos and magic everywhere, but the longer she looks, the longer she lets her eyes relax, the more...controlled it seems. Like amid all the chaos, enough electricity hits each other, coalescing into something larger.

"Maybe," she says, not taking her eyes off of it.

"If you try to thread it," Zoel starts, and she can hear the thought process in his voice, "there's an even chance that you might be able to control it, therefore stopping all the decay and the instability, or..."

Alette keeps her eyes on the crackling, vague cord, her heart pounding.

"Or it might try to harm you, snap out at you and throw you around," he continues. "I doubt it'll kill you, it might make your magic more unpredictable, but it might recognize you."

She hears Lyra taking a step back. "So basically exactly what Axel wants you to avoid," Lyra says. "But with the possibility of making a difference."

"And if I can make a difference here, I might be able to make a difference elsewhere," Alette murmurs.

Zoel shifts closer to her, and she's intimately aware of his every motion, like he's brilliant against her senses, even without her taking her eyes off the storm.

"It's your choice," he murmurs to her, leaning so close she can almost feel him. "I'll be here, regardless, to help afterwards, but this has to be your choice."

And that hardly takes any thought.

Telegraphing the motion to the magic in front of her, she reaches into her breast pocket, tugging out the golden curved needle without pulling out the rest.

"If you burn my hands again, I'm gonna be cross," she says aloud to the magic, and Lyra has to smother a giggle, but if the magic at the death bubble had reacted the way it did, there's no reason this might not. "I want to help."

Again, the needle sings in her hands, all the way down to her core. Sings with the possibility of magic inside of her, in front of her, of the world around her.

Zoel whistles underneath his breath.

"Tell me what to do," she orders, and the needle is warm in her hand, pleasantly so. Like it recognizes that this is where it had been changed, and is eager to go back in.

A spark snaps to the gold, and it shivers against her fingertips, but does not melt, does not react against her.

He grabs a fistful of her jacket in his hand, a very literal anchor, keeping her firmly stationary. Like he expects the magic to draw her in, to lock her in place like it did the last time.

"Avoid threading the smaller sparks," Zoel says, clearly bracing himself, "the gold won't melt, but the smaller sparks are uncontrollable and angry."

The larger cord certainly seems angrier, but she nods.

"I'm going to stand back," Lyra says, but it's not out of any condemnation, more of a stark practicality. "If anything goes wrong, I'll be out of the way."

"And you can call Axel and Mel if it does," Alette says, even though that'd rain down anger upon her. "And keep your cell phone functional—mine's still not happy with me."

Then, before she can lose whatever will she has in her,

before the nerves and the skepticism have time to set in, she lashes out with her formerly injured hand, and pulls.

Immediately, the hand goes numb, jerking her forward before Zoel gathers his footing and keeps her back, but the stream of magic flows around her hand like a rushing river, like she's merely a stone plopped into a place in water.

It blocks out all sound from her ears, everything but the harsh crackle of the magic, the electricity snapping everywhere.

She can't see her hand in the sparkling maelstrom, can barely feel it, but watches until the cord of crackling energy gets close, before, with more courage than she feels, she jerks her hand upright, closing her fist around it and yanks back.

It's coarse, rough like an ancient rope against her hands, and the numbness gives away to a strange sensation, halfway between pain and rubbing a piece of velvet the wrong way.

It tugs, as if resisting, as if trying to complete its circle in the whirlpool, but she grips it tight, so tight the individual strands spark and crackle around her, like driven through a wind.

And immediately, she understands what caused the whirlpool, what the tangle in front of her is. That when Terese had expelled her magic there, all that time ago, instead of creating the bubble, instead of just using what had been around her...

She had reached somewhere else. She had reached somewhere else and now all the magic wanted to do is get back to where it belonged.

Alette exhales, past the strange pain, leaning back against Zoel's hand, even though the only sound she hears is the crackling of the static.

No wonder the magic was angry. No wonder it was distressed.

No wonder it's so foreign.

She draws her needle over to it, and it spasms in her hand.

"Zoel," she starts, even though she can no longer hear her voice, "Zoel it's just displaced."

Her mind sparks off in many directions, spiraling away on what this could mean. Is all the volatile magic just from somewhere else? Is it as simple as untangling what should be there and what shouldn't? Is that why the death bubbles stayed there, not letting anything decay?

So, she exhales, pulling the cord through the eye of the needle, sparks crawling in on the edges of her vision, until—

With a bang, the moment her needle has the thread, the entire maelstrom in front of them pulses outwards. Explodes.

It tosses Alette back like she's a rag doll, tumbling her into Zoel and slamming them back into the decaying concrete that once was Buggees.

He makes a sound of surprise against her, but the wall merely crumbles around them, softening the impact.

Her ears ring and she shakes her head to clear them, before the needle in her hand pulses warm.

"What—" she says, and she can hear her voice again, her hearing's back to normal, she has feeling in her hand, and—

The needle glows. Actually glows, the strong cord of magic now a whip-thin thread, bright and vicious and seething with anger.

And the maelstrom is gone, only a few spare sparks crackling over the rebar and plywood.

"Are you okay?" Alette whispers, half to Zoel, half to the magic held in her hands.

Behind her, Zoel groans, before shifting in the rubble, gray dust in his black hair, but he sits up, looking profoundly disoriented.

"I'm..." he trails off, staring at the needle in her hand, blinking. "That's...impressive."

"So, I'd say that's half a success?" Lyra calls from across the parking lot.

Alette climbs to her feet, completely covered in the rotting concrete dust, and the magic coils around her wrist, wrapping tightly like a snake, scaly and possessive.

"Huh," she says, dumb.

～

THEY MAKE it back to Lyra's mobile home, and the magic doesn't let up its grip on her wrist, right where Terese had broken her bone so many months ago, and Alette half listens as Zoel rambles with theories.

It's so angry, at its confusion and at how lost it feels, and she knows that she's reading far too much into it, personifying it, but...

The moment she crosses in the door, Lyra's cat immediately skitters to run under the bed with a thump.

"Can we...find where it belongs?" Alette asks, finally interrupting Zoel's musings. "That's why it did that, that's why it reacted so strongly when I went in the first time."

"So, is magic a sentient thing now?" Lyra asks dryly, sinking into her big green armchair.

"It's far from that," Zoel starts, "but of course it has emotions, it has wants, why else would the immediate sense of death call out to you?"

Lyra falls silent, giving a nod to him.

"Could this cause everything?" Alette asks, letting a fingertip lay on the cord of magic. It pulses. "All the tangles, all the death bubbles not decaying, everything?"

Zoel reaches forward for the hand with the needle in it, and the cord of magic sparks at his touch, angry.

"Right," Alette says, rummaging one-handed through her pocket for a spare strip of linen, and quickly begins to stitch it into place.

It resists her at first, before she tugs it into place, and it slides smoothly into the weft.

"This should make it—in theory—neutral for transportation instead of wrapped around my wrist," Alette explains, mostly for Lyra's benefit, "but really, is it?"

"All of it, no," he says, and there's a perturbed look on his face, like watching her magic is somehow disturbing for him. "Some was definitely caused by Terese just grabbing the magic around her and trying to fix herself, but..." he trails off, his face thoughtful. "You said it felt like a hole in the world?"

"Yeah," Alette says, focusing on her stitching, on the familiar motion of weaving the thread into the cloth. "Different from the death bubble you showed me."

"It started out as a death bubble," Lyra says. "That's what she did to me, remember?"

Alette briefly glances at Zoel, who frowns, the furrow in his brow deepening.

"That's not good," he says. "That means whatever magic she did isn't just tangling everything, isn't just suffocating everything, it's ripping into things. Ripping barriers between magical places..." He wavers his hand, like he's trying to find what he wants to say.

"Like it's ripping the fabric of space and time?" Lyra says sarcastically, but Alette's stomach drops.

That's exactly what Gurlien had been saying.

"Closer," Zoel continues, brow still furrowed. "The state of magic, at least, can't sustain it without drastic repair—" he cuts himself off, looking over to Alette. "Or they'd spread."

28

Hours later, the thread still glowing angrily in its linen cloth, she spreads it out on her dinner table, the runes rising up and shining around it.

So, not a threat, or her magic would never let it through her wards, but definitely not happy.

She sits at her dining room table, staring at it. If it is spreading, if it is moving that fast, then...then she doesn't know what to do.

She doesn't know what to do, when faced by all this exact evidence of something angry, of something malicious, and she stares at it for too long, her eyes aching and her face feeling like she crawled out of a desert.

If all of the breaks, the ones they've found, transform into that, and it spreads, then—

She pushes herself up, folding the piece of linen back on itself and tucking it into her pocket, and looking towards the back of her apartment. Towards where the Line woke her up only a little more than a week ago.

IT'S a short walk to the point, even though it had seemed so long in the middle of the night, but with the glow of early twilight it barely seems to be the same. Spot and Grey join her, a more sedate tromp through the meadows and woods than anything else.

And it's easy to find the break itself.

All the grass, already dead from the ices of winter, is blackened, crumpling into dark ash, and the trees nearby are charred from the blast.

And deep in the middle, there's the barest hint of a crackle of electricity, an almost imperceptible ball of static.

Alette exhales and she crouches next to it, hovering on her heels.

A spark from her hand snaps out at the ball, not changing it at all. Like it didn't have enough mass to be changed quite yet.

It's a far easier and smaller break to deal with, at least at this time, and Alette's not entirely sure if it's because she had once been at its center or if it's just too new to cause real problems.

"Spot," Alette starts, and the dog perks his ears up at his name, "go get Zoel."

Spot immediately dashes away, leaving Alette with Grey, who sniffs at the edges of the break with something approaching suspicion.

It's less furious, less lethal feeling, so she just crouches there, watching, until she can sense someone approaching.

It's still a new sensation, like discovering a color she didn't know previously existed, but she holds as still as she can until they're almost next to her, and she lifts her gaze.

To see Terese, pale and colorless, standing there. She's clutching her jacket close to her, like she's chilled to the bone.

Alette freezes, then consciously relaxes.

"Are all of them like this?" Terese asks, and her voice is small. "All the breaks, all the places where the magic snapped and shattered, are they?"

"I don't know," Alette responds, studying Terese. Her cheekbones stick out against her skin, like she hasn't had enough food, and her fingers tremble.

Terese crouches down, next to the edge, her boots crushing the ash, her eyes tracking over the break, like there are hints of magic she alone can see, before her gaze snaps up to Alette, alert.

"You've already notified Zoel?" Her tone lilts up, musical.

"Working on it," Alette says.

"I saw what you did to the gas station," Terese continues, almost sing-song, and the hair raises on the back of Alette's arms, before Terese sits back. "Do that more."

"That's the idea."

They both sit in silence, as Alette's mind races on something, anything, to say, and Terese just watches her with an unflinching gaze.

"Zoel is kind," Terese says, finally, "You shouldn't let him die."

"I'm not - what?" Alette blurts out, "I'm not going to -"

Terese stands again, and there's that same little frown on her face, the one that haunts Alette's nightmares. "I can only imagine what all of you magicians want to do to these problems," she says, immediately drawing Gurlien to Alette's mind. "Zoel doesn't deserve that."

As if she just wanted to say that, Terese nods at her, then vanishes.

Alette rocks back on her heels, then swallows down that fear, her heart pounding, and sits there, until the familiar sound of Spot crashing through the underbrush echoes around her, with Zoel following behind.

WITH MUCH LESS EFFORT, she threads her needle with the hint of electricity, then takes Zoel back to her apartment, but they're both too exhausted to do anything besides fall into bed with each other, and she sleeps as the dead.

She wakes up with him stroking her hair back, his hands whisper light in the dawn sun, and doesn't want to move.

"Did you sleep?" she asks, pushing herself up on her elbows.

He shakes his head, though his curls are rumpled on one side. "I rarely need to."

She watches him in the still light, and there's something wonderful in the moment, of seeing his beautiful blue eyes blink back up at her.

"This is going to get worse, isn't it?" Alette whispers, not wanting to give the words too much volume. "The magic, the breaks?"

His lashes catch the light from her glowing runes as he looks down. "I think so."

She nods, then, instead of getting up, instead of getting to work, she rests her head against his chest, so she can hear his beating heart.

"We'll figure it out," he whispers back, his hand tangling in her braid, "we'll figure it out."

AXEL (9:08 AM): Asshole has a theory. Wants us to meet in the greenhouse.

ALETTE (9:09 AM): I'll be there.

AFTER A FEW MORE SOFT kisses and gentle touches, Zoel leaves to go find the next break, to see if he can untangle it himself, to try her method of neutralizing it, taking a few pieces of her linen with him.

And Alette carefully folds the captive magic in her own strips of muslin into a protective carrying case, then daintily steps out of her apartment to find Spot and Grey lounging in the sunlight on the concrete.

"Aren't you two supposed to be fearsome creatures of death and foreboding?" she asks, nudging Grey with her boot.

He responds by licking the air at her, still lounging, so she steps over them to her car.

It's a short drive to the Headquarters, and this time, when her car shuts off the moment she hits the runes, she just immediately throws it in reverse and rolls enough down the hill to where she'll be able to start it again without Axel's help.

Hopefully.

The magic in her linen grows warm, twisting the threads, angry, and she places a careful fingertip against the cord, until it calms down enough that she's certain it won't combust in her bag.

Because if Gurlien has ideas, so does she.

And maybe, just maybe, he can see this idea and accept that the sterilization won't be necessary.

In the hike up the hill, past the berry brambles and the mud, the strip of magic is pulled taut, instead of merrily fluttering.

Torn for a split second, Alette rests her hand on it, feels its aching pull towards the Headquarters, and in between one moment and the next she gets a flash of dread, a flash of something akin to pain, to confusion. Nothing severe, but...

But definitely not what the magic in her place should be doing.

She cranes her neck up, and it's the strip of magic that leads directly into the greenhouse, barely visible from this angle.

"Of course," she mutters, and, giving the magic what she hopes is a reassuring pat, continues up the hill. The strip of magic pulls towards her, following her up.

The logical part of her brain knows that's not what happens with normal humans, but after everything else, after all the changes, she's not going to be distressed by something like this.

AXEL GLANCES up at her just long enough to acknowledge her arrival when she steps into the greenhouse, but he's too busy scowling at Gurlien to do anything more, to say anything else.

"But if she really cared about this plot, she'd have put actual protections instead of laying what amounts to live wires around—" Gurlien cuts himself off when he finally notices Alette standing in the doorway.

And in his hand, balled up and a mess of tangles and distress, is the Line that had previously been so well laid in the rows.

"Drop that," Alette snaps, striding toward him. "Drop that right now."

"Oh, so you can see this." Gurlien twirls to face her, yanking the Line even more. Static frizzles down the cord.

No wonder it's in shock.

"Let it go!" Alette says, and his fist closes even tighter around the Line.

A small spot of electricity snaps out of it, but neither Axel nor Gurlien notice.

"Do you know how much danger your aunt put everyone in, by letting this"—he shakes his fistful of magic at her—"just where someone could trip over it and cause something catastrophic?"

Axel looks between the two of them, eyes sharp. "Alette, what do you see?"

"And this one just doesn't believe me and tried to stop me," Gurlien continues, and his blond hair hangs over his forehead, unkempt in his anger.

"He has a fistful of magical Line that Aunt Frisse very carefully laid in place up here," Alette says, deliberately slowing down her words, all of her attention laser focused on the magic in his hands, "and is in real danger of causing another break if he doesn't put it down. Right. Now."

Axel takes a step back, sitting hard on the bench. He knows her tone of voice.

Gurlien scoffs. "Meddling in this is what caused the breaks to begin with, I'm just removing the hazard."

The magic in his hand pulses, but he doesn't react, like he can't even see it.

"And you shouldn't even be able to tell," he snaps, "you shouldn't be able to see a single bit of this, you're just a spell weaver, and a mediocre one at that—"

A rumble echoes through the building, sharp and sudden, and Axel grips the bench, but nothing happens, just the creaking of the glass around them.

Alette stares, hard, at Gurlien.

"What was that?" she asks, pouring as much of her aunt's imperiousness as she possibly can into that sentence. "We don't have earthquakes up here."

"I don't know," he says, and his eyes are so wide that she believes him. "We need to see the edge of the property."

The ball of magic tumbles from his hand, unresponsive but for the frizzles of static running down.

THE ROCKS where the seam meets are jagged, like they broke apart all anew, and the concrete has crumbled, revealing bare rebar.

And, along the reddish haze, there's a rough thread of magic, like a paracord, glistening and sickly. It lays limp on the ground, like it can't muster up the energy to move, to be at the correct height.

Alette sucks in a breath.

"Is it me, or did it damage the rocks more?" Axel asks, looking between her and Gurlien. He knows exactly what he's asking.

"Definitely," Gurlien says, and he ventures closer, stepping unaware on the rope.

It shifts underneath him.

Alette shoots Axel a look, and he raises an eyebrow at her, and she wishes that they had developed a code between them like Lyra had developed with her brother.

But neither of them are mind readers, and Alette needs to get Zoel in here, quick, if the entire building is going to shake down around them because of Gurlien's insane tactics.

"We need to deal with this," Gurlien says, grim, and he

hesitates his hand above the exposed rebar. "Alette Jyoshti, can you do that spell I sent, I will do—"

The rope shifts underneath him, and he's unaware of it, as it twines around his ankle.

"Stop," Alette blurts out, and he freezes. "Come out, you need to step back."

The rope crawls up his leg like a vine, and the entire thing glows red, sickly.

There's a bit close to her, and she drops to a crouch, grabbing at it.

It spasms in her hand, and spasms on his leg.

Gurlien flinches, like he could feel that. Like he hadn't been so insensitive to the magic in the greenhouse, but this, this he could feel.

She locks eyes with him, before slowly taking out her needle from her case.

"Can you step out?" she asks deliberately. Like how she would talk to a wounded animal, how she would coax a frightened child.

"Where did you get that?" he breathes, eyes focused on the gold in her hands. "That shouldn't be possible."

"That is so not the important question right now," Alette says, before throwing a glance to Axel. "Axel, you know where the paint thinners are in the basement?"

The magic pulses in her hand, like it's telling her to hurry, and she really doesn't want another break, right here, where who knows if she'll live.

"Yes," he replies back, already heading towards the entrance.

"Splash it on the painted protection runes on the walk-way," she orders, and his eyebrows flash up, but he turns on his heel.

"Stop!" Gurlien calls out. "You can't do that, it'll open this up to all sorts of other creatures—"

The Line tightens around his leg, creasing the fabric of his slacks, and he cuts himself off.

"That's the point," Alette snaps, "I'm going to try to keep this stable enough until help gets here."

"The creatures of the land can't help," he says, but his face is pale.

The strip of magic pulses red, an almost visible light, and they both fall silent. It's stretched thin, like it's fraying apart, and she's seen this before, she's seen this too recently.

"Try to step out," Alette says again, but when he tries, it just tightens, jerking him back into place.

"If you take down the runes," he continues, and there's something akin to panic in his eyes, "then anyone could waltz right in. Terese could detonate it. Any random demon can blast you out of existence."

Alette just focuses on the strip of magic, and her fingers sweat against the gold needle. "I'll deal with that later."

"Magic could flood in," he says, "it could flood in and react to all the shit your aunt put everywhere, it could destroy this whole place." When she doesn't answer, he tries to jerk his foot out again, but it won't let him. "All this magic around, all this corrupted magic, could ruin us all. Could kill us all."

Carefully, as carefully as she can without threading from the fraying Line, she pulls some power from the air, twisting it into a gossamer string through her needle.

Without knowing what she's doing, she wraps the thread around the frazzled Line, like it could reinforce it. Like she could do a patch job until Zoel could get there, until this is stable enough to at least pry it away from Gurlien and kick him out.

He watches her, eyes wide. "How are you even doing that?" he asks, and his voice wavers. "You're just a spell weaver, you shouldn't be able to."

She pushes the sweaty hair out of her eyes, not answering.

It's fussy work, and her heart pounds and the Line pulses with each loop and knot she ties. It's achingly slow, it's achingly terrifying, and the magic resists her, almost lashing out in anger.

After one such knot, he flinches, then his hand flies up, sketching a spell, almost too fast for her to track, but—

It's a sanitation spell.

"Stop!" She jerks herself upright, catching his arm midair, and her own magic crackles, snapping around them. "You can't."

And the moment the words leave her mouth, the ground beneath them shifts, as if falling, and the protection runes that she wasn't even aware that she could feel, vanish.

She inhales, sharp, and the wild magic all around surges up, filling up her lungs and her veins and her skin.

A tree cracks around them, the foundation of the very stones shuddering, and Gurlien lets out a wordless noise of terror.

Alette stills, the flush of magic and sheer power trembling in her hands, burning against his skin until he jerks out of her grasp. "I said, you can't."

Gurlien's eyes are wide, wide and panicked, but the Line twisting around his leg falls away, and he stumbles back, away from the exposed rebar and the concrete.

Alette lets him, lets him scramble back. Her heart pounds with the magic around her, and the electricity snaps in her fingertips.

"What are you?" he demands, disgust coating his voice. "What did you do to become this?"

"That's rude," Axel says from behind them, and another small bit of Alette relaxes, that whatever earthquake they felt didn't injure him. "It looks to me like we just saved your life."

Gurlien takes one shaky breath, then another, then straightens like a rod made from righteous fury imbeds in his spine.

"You have to get rid of this," he commands, with a hand gestured at her, "it's consuming you and your entire sense of self, you need to purge the area, purge every bit of magic and creature from this earth until this. Can't. Happen."

"No."

After speaking the words, the magic crackles in her hand, and he takes another step back.

"I won't," she continues, putting as much ice into her voice as she can, "I'm not going to be the one to ruin this, to kill all the people."

Something happens on Gurlien's face, something ugly and vicious, and he snaps his attention to Axel.

"Did you know I could fix you?" he spits out. "I could restore all your powers in an instant, everything you lost, but your friend refuses to do things my way."

Axel inhales, an involuntary gasp of air, and Alette's stomach drops.

"All she had to do from the beginning was just help me, and she refused." Pulling himself to his full height, he brushes himself off with shaking hands. "You're not going to stop me from fixing this, Alette Jyoshti," he says, and there's fury in his voice. "It'd be easier with your help, but you're not going to stop me."

And with more dignity than he has, with a torn pant leg

and burns on his upper arm, he turns on his heel and strides away, leaving the two of them in silence.

Axel remains silent, long after Gurlien disappears into the Headquarter buildings, and when Alette turns to look at him, his face is startlingly blank.

"Axel..." Alette starts, then trails off, because what can she actually say?

"You knew?" he asks, voice just as blank as his expression.

She opens her mouth to reply, but all the command and power she had just wielded withers away.

And his face crumples.

"Axel, it was a choice between genocide and you getting your powers back," she says, and her stomach is falling, falling so far she doesn't know if she could ever recover. "I couldn't...I couldn't justify that, no matter—"

"I know that!" he yells, and his voice echoes over the forest, over the limp magic and the decaying concrete and the exposed rebar. "God, I know that, but you...you knew. And you didn't say anything."

He's right. He's absolutely right.

"I didn't want to get your hopes up," she says, lame, well aware that it is a wholly inadequate response. "I thought it'd be cruel, to tell you and then...not."

He turns away, grabbing at his hair with his hands, pulling at it. "What, A, did you think that I would all of a sudden demand that you kill people? Did you think that I would do that?"

"I..." Alette trails off, then crouches back next to the limp magic, because maybe, just maybe, she could repair that.

"Is that why you haven't just kicked him out?" he snaps. "I saw the will, you could."

It's too many questions, it's too much, and she squeezes her eyes shut, hand on the magic, instead.

"Did you really think that I would be that selfish?" he asks, and this time his voice breaks.

"I didn't know what to think," she replies, and it's the truth, at least. "I didn't know if he could, or if it was possible, or if it was just a fucked up thing he said to try to get me to cooperate." The magic in her hand, at least, pulses slightly. It's not dead, it's not angry, it's just...limp. "I just thought it was cruel."

It settles in her bones, suddenly, that there might be no way to fix this. That she might not be able to ever repair this, after holding this from him.

From the look on his face, he's thinking the same thing.

"If you had told me," he starts, and it's the tone he only uses when he's trying desperately to control his voice, "then maybe I could have helped you deal with all of this emotional shit. We were supposed to be friends."

The words settle in the dirt and icy mud between them like a bomb.

Alette squeezes her eyes shut, and by the time she opens them again, he's walked away.

29

A lette doesn't know how long she's been sitting there, loosely gripping the strip of magic, but a flutter of a breeze moves the hair across her forehead and a strange scent fills her nose.

She glances up, and Zoel is standing a few feet away, his brow furrowed.

"You took down the barriers," he says unsteadily, like it takes something from him to acknowledge that. "Anything can come here now."

She nods, unable to fit words past the lump in her throat, and he strides over to her, folding himself up next to her.

"What's wrong?" he asks, and it's so kind, it's so perfect, that tears prickle at the edge of her eyes.

Instead of waiting for her to answer, he lays a hand on the strip of magic, and it pulses, stronger than anything else, against their hands.

"The magic...it was upset," she starts, and it's wholly inadequate, so she shakes her head. "I lied to Axel."

He settles in next to her.

"I didn't tell him, and now he's..." she trails off. Angry seems too simple, pissed seems incomplete. "I messed up."

"Probably," he says, and it's so easy for him to say, that she turns her face into his chest, presses her cheek against him. "People do." He strokes her hair back, away from her forehead, tender.

"He's like my brother, and I should have just told him the truth from the beginning," she says, and it feels like she's baring a wound, like she's daring him to poke at it, "but I didn't. I should have."

He doesn't stop the soft touches.

"I should have just said everything, been completely...I dunno. Honest. I don't know," she says, and she's not making sense.

Carefully, ever so carefully, he pulls away from her, so he can look her in the eyes. "Alette," he says, with way more care than she deserves, "yes."

It almost hurts.

"Yes," he continues, but it's gentle, "but that's okay."

She shakes her head, but can't put into words what she means.

"It's okay," he continues, "because you're allowed to make mistakes, you don't have to be the most perfect all of the time, and your mistakes don't make you less."

She shuts her eyes, now immediately thinking of the secrets she's kept from him, the untruths and the half lies.

It brews in her, something dark and brutal.

"Yes, telling him would be better," Zoel continues, soft, and the magic in their hands warms, friendly, "but you can't expect yourself to be perfect. Not all the time. Let yourself make the mistakes."

"Maybe that's just what I do," Alette starts slowly, as if

she'll stop herself if she slows down enough. Give herself enough space to stop before it gets bad.

His face twists.

"Maybe I'm just the person who lies. Who keeps things from people, until it hurts them." The words fall out faster. "Maybe I'm just as bad as...as Aunt Frisse..."

He picks up the magic, with her haphazard mending job and string wrapped tight. "This isn't bad," he says, running his fingers over the repair. "You've lied to me?"

She can't answer that, not directly, it's too fraught. "Kept things from you," she hedges.

Still holding the magic, he stands, extending a free hand to her. "This disappears into the building, we need to fix that before we fix this break."

She takes his hand, clutching tight. "The College wants me to sanitize the area."

He stills, blinking down at the strip of magic.

"They think it'll stop the break from spreading. From breaking the rest of the world."

Still looking at the strip of magic, his blue eyes not meeting hers, he inhales. "Will you?"

It hurts. That he doesn't know for sure.

"God, no," she blurts, "this entire time I've just been trying to find something. Anything. Besides that."

He takes a moment, visibly so, when he just looks down at the magic in his hands, before he lifts his eyes to hers.

"Show me where this leads?"

So, she does, pulling him towards the greenhouse, past the broken stones and rusted rebar, past the molding blackberry brambles, and he's silent the entire way.

One of the glass panes of the green house has shattered, probably when the magic fell and the foundation shook, and the shards glitter on a row of the orchids. She'll have to repair that, too, or they'll wither in the cold before too long.

There's a glimmer of movement, at the edge of the broken glass, and she catches a glimpse of a spirit, like the edge of a rainbow, poking through.

The strip of magic still lays in a tangled lump, inert from Gurlien's actions. No more are the neat, orderly lines of the planters, instead a mess of bad intentions and dire dramatics.

Wordlessly, Zoel sits near it, teasing the knots apart, just like he did the first Line on Shaman's Point.

A spark flashes from Alette's hand, useless.

"So we need to stop him," she blurts out, flopping down into a seat next to him, cross-legged and undignified. "He said it's easier with two people, but that he'll do it alone, and—"

Zoel holds up a hand, and she falls silent.

"Sanitation spells aren't something one person does lightly," he says, his voice tightly controlled. "Did he give a time frame?"

The wisp of a spirit she saw, barely the size of a fox, pokes his nose deeper into the greenhouse, ears back. Like this is new territory and terrifying all the same.

"No," Alette says, again more than useless. "He wanted me to sanitize the mess out there, when it had him trapped, but I..." She holds up her hands, to gesture like sewing, but the spark snaps off again, ruining her point. "I had Axel take down the wards so we could call you instead."

He nods. "It called me and every other spirit of the land, that's for sure," he says noncommittally. "Don't be surprised if people or things come investigating. They've never been allowed on this land."

He hands a loop of magic to her, just like how he did on

Shaman's Point. It's squishy in her hands, almost off-puttingly so.

"Sanitizing that mess would have done little besides harm him, harm you, and render this building uninhabitable," he says, and his voice is soft. "That shows a surprising lack of forethought on his part."

She begins to untangle the loop he hands her, and he sits back on his heels, watching her.

"I'm sorry I didn't tell you," she says, and it's bare, like she can't reveal anything more.

The loop falls free, then pulls taut, jetting towards the outside instead of falling back in the neat and orderly lines.

It's not the brilliant display of the Ley Line at Shaman Point, it's not a majestic culmination of hours upon hours of working, but it glitters all the same, a melancholic chord struck inside of Alette.

He sighs, and it's weary, more than it should be. "You probably shouldn't be feeling that," he murmurs. "That's not something that humans feel."

Alette nods. Between the magic still crackling from her and the warnings from Melekai, she put that together a long time ago.

Misery seeps into her bones like the damp seeping into her clothing from the automatic misting of the plants.

Zoel sighs, again, and she never wants to hear him make that noise because of her, but he leans towards her, wrapping his arms around her, so tight it's almost painful.

She presses her face against him, until the pressure behind her eyes is indistinguishable from the sensation of his touch.

"You really should have talked more, shouldn't you?" he says, and his voice is wistful. "All of this sitting in your mind, and you couldn't talk it out."

She nods against him, and his hand strokes up her arm.

"I'm sorry," she repeats, and the words feel like not enough, never enough. "I'm sorry, I should have...I'm sorry."

It's silent for a few moments, as the wisp of a spirit pokes around at the glittering shard of glass, and he clutches her against him.

Her aunt didn't apologize for much, but when she did, she instilled in Alette to always, always try to make it better. To try to push aside any pride, until all that's left is the want to repair things.

Alette can't see a way to repair this. To repair anything.

So, she pushes herself up, and wipes her eyes as surreptitiously as she can.

"What do you need me to do?" she asks, and her voice warbles, a far cry from her confident self. "I don't...I don't know what you need me to do, but tell me, and I'll...I'll figure something out."

His face twists.

"I'll figure out how to stop him, to fix all the magic, to stop this decay, to stop anyone who wants to come in and change this, I'll work with whoever, just—"

He presses his lips against hers, and Alette falls silent.

"I need you to talk to me," he says seriously, and it's such a small request, so small in the grand scheme of things, that she must be mishearing him. "I need you to not shut me out. I need you to be honest with me, even...even when you think I wouldn't want to hear it."

It takes her breath away, and he tucks a strand of her hair behind her ear. His blue eyes watch her, steady and serious. Like this is what is important right now.

"After...after we figure this out, after this is all gone, I want you to trust me with all of your secrets," he continues, voice grave. "I don't want to be cut off from all of this. From all of you."

She's not quite sure she's been all of her to anyone, ever, and she teeters on the edge of terror, like a balancing act on a cliff. Where all she has to do to escape to safety is to step back on the rocks, back on solid ground.

But that'd be without him.

So. She lets herself fall. Lets herself lose her balance.

"Yes," she says, but this time, her voice actually sounds like her. "Yes. I...will."

His face breaks, and he pulls her in tight, still sitting on the ruined ground of her aunt's solarium, with cold wind whistling past the shattered glass.

She doesn't know how long they sit there, with his arms around her, but by the time they lean away, her tears are dried sticky and chilly from the air and the sun is lower in the sky.

"We do need to stop him," Alette says, and her voice rasps, like she's been yelling this entire time. "I don't know when he's going to do it, but..."

Zoel's already nodding, pulling her up to standing with him. "I assume it would make things worse if we just kill him? For you?"

"Probably," Alette says, with a twinge of regret. "The College..." she trails off, trying and failing to find something actually positive to say. "I mean, they could probably come and drag me to prison for refusing to comply, especially if all of the magic breaks."

He gives her such an unimpressed look. "They could try." But his face settles into something halfway between grim and determined. "Let's go stop this threat, then we deal with the next."

30

A fter all the untangling of the knot in the greenhouse, the spot of broken concrete and rebar is...lesser. More of just physical distraction instead of any magical malaise, with the edge of a scent of nature creeping back in.

"Was this...was this entire thing caused by my aunt's manipulation?" Alette asks, letting herself lean against him.

"Possibly," he murmurs, nudging some of the blackened dirt with the toe of his boot. "Her death probably more so."

She leads him down through the Headquarters, and the runes on the walls, all the little bits of magic that made it work, are all dark. Inert.

Like bringing down the wards brought everything down.

She trails her hand down the long familiar hallway, but none of her aunt's magic responds to her. Her own magic sparks at the touch, but it falls on dead paint and cold tile walls.

Like that one act erased all parts of her.

"Even though it's gone, this is masterful work," Zoel

murmurs, the hand on her back twitching. "Every part of this is designed to keep people she doesn't want out."

Alette throws him a glance, but besides the small lines around his eyes, his face is unbothered. "Does it hurt you?"

"No?" he says, surprised. "I mean, it's not the most comfortable, but it's not...bad."

"Interesting," Alette murmurs, and her hand trails over a rune, and it gives her a jolt.

She stops in her tracks, staring hard at it. It glows, ever so slightly. A simple light spell, to add onto one of the ones that replaced the fluorescent lines.

One she wrote, as practice, when she had been maybe fifteen.

Zoel doesn't say anything, but his hand on the small of her back is gentle. Kind.

She lets her fingertips drop away from the wall, allows herself one second to breathe, then pushes onwards.

"You stayed here?" he murmurs, trailing his fingers on the wall after her. "For that entire month?"

"Pretty much," Alette says, lets her eyes flicker to his, to his study on the wall, to how completely inhuman he is. "I don't know if Gurlien's still here, I don't know what he'll do if he sees you, he may attack—"

"He could try," Zoel says, but he regards her seriously. "Show me where you stayed?"

There's something vulnerable, something uncomfortable in his stance. Like he's so outside of his comfort zone that he's searching for something, anything, that he could find that could be familiar.

Alette had never formally taken an apartment or a room, not like Axel, but instead she primarily crashed on the couch in one of the many libraries her aunt hid around the complex.

Thankfully, it's far away from any of the built-in apartments of the sprawling complex, and even if Gurlien—or Axel—retreated deeper within the building, they were unlikely to encounter them.

So, she leads him down the winding staircases, to the section of the building built later, after the grand ballroom and the experimentation rooms. Towards the part of the building that always felt more like home. More like a school than a proto-military headquarters or scientific station. A place where she could sink into books, sink into knowledge, and not worry about anything else.

There's less runes this way, her aunt relying on proper construction techniques and wiring more than anything else.

And the knot in her chest eases, just a little bit, as they encounter less dead magic.

"This is more like you," he murmurs, as they wind their way through the brick and staircase-lined rooms, past the room she kept her more magically inclined sewing projects. Past the shirt she had cut out but never stitched together, past the jacket she had been making for her aunt, past the knitting project she had once attempted.

Finally, she pushes open the library room, with its giant couch and about half her wardrobe neatly folded in the corner.

There's a wisp of magic that hadn't been there before, but it vanishes the moment they enter the room, like it's running away.

And Alette lets herself think, for just a moment.

"You saw that, didn't you?" Zoel says, and his voice isn't quite grave, but it's near.

She nods, compulsively folding the blanket she had left hanging over the edge of the couch. "I know enough now that that's not normal, isn't it?" She watches him from underneath her lashes. "All of this, it's changed me."

Saying it so blatantly sits odd underneath her skin, but after everything that day, after everything she's felt, saying anything else would stick out.

"I don't know," he says, equally solemn, tracing his fingers down the spines of the books. The entire room is lined with bookcases; grand, dusty bookcases with tomes as old and useless as anything in the world.

She loves this room, for reasons she never really put into words.

"There had been rumors, myths, that whenever Wights would become close to the humans, that the humans would fundamentally change." His hand lingers on a dark leather book, one that teenage Alette had read many, many times. "And our myths said that's how the first magicians came to be, from a human that befriended a Wight, until they could see a part of the world that only the Wights could before that."

Alette lets herself sit on the couch and watch him, lets his words and his voice soothe something inside of her, something left too raw for the world.

"Some say it happens when a human interacts with too much wild magic, too many Ley Lines, that sort of thing, and some myths say it's when a human forgets that they weren't here first." He glances away from the books, finally, to where she's sitting. "I was more concerned with solving the breaks than giving weight to ancient myths."

It sounds like a confession.

"Well," Alette says, lifting a hand and letting a spark crackle from her fingertips. "I think I'll need you around to teach me how to control this."

He smiles, a tentative, heartbreaking smile, then sits next to her, leaning his head against her shoulder.

A small moment of peace, of silence, before her phone beeps, startling her so bad she almost jumps.

AXEL (4:21 PM): Gurlien just left. Said the line was breaking, and he would fix it.

AXEL (4:22 PM): FYI

Zoel jolts up straight. "I would have felt it, I would have—"

She stands, sudden. "He kept all his equipment in our grand ballroom," she says, out of the need to say something, anything, to move past her emotions of the moment. "All sorts of readers for checking the stability of magic."

He jerks to his feet and she pushes herself up, out the door, striding out. "Take me to it," he says imperiously, but there's a quiver of fear behind his voice. "I need to see what it is.

The elevator doesn't open, so she leads him through the stairs, past the dead warming runes. If they survive all of this, if nothing else happens, then she'll have to open up the place for a construction crew. For someone to actually come in and fix it, make its functionality actually last beyond the inhabitants.

One problem at a time.

With her heart in her throat, she pushes open the door to the grand ballroom, and Zoel sucks in a breath, jerking back from stepping inside.

"He cleaned this room first," Alette says, and Zoel nods, queasy. "Set it up so his equipment—"

She gestures, and the glass contraption still drips, the large reservoir now entirely full of the dark blue liquid.

"I can't go in there," he says, his voice tight, "I can't go in there and never will."

Alette nods, swinging inside, the acrid stink of the sanitation making her eyes water, and...

And the date on the glass equipment is just the next day.

"Zoel?" she asks, and her voice quavers, beyond her control. "Zoel, his reader..."

"What is it?" he asks, still from the doorway, and it's like she's looking at everything through a haze.

She shakes her head, as if that could clear the malaise from her vision, but it just blurs further. "He has a reader, for the stability..." She has to take a shuddering breath, and it doesn't help, the stink too bad—

"Get out of there," Zoel's voice reaches her, sharp, cutting through the harshness, and she stumbles back towards the door, until his arms reach out and grab her.

The moment she's past the large double doors, the air clears and she gasps, bringing in something, anything, approaching clean air.

"He has a piece of equipment," she says, between breaths, "that measures the stability of the final Line."

His brow furrows, before it dawns on him. "How could he have measured that without me knowing?" Still, he straightens, eyes unfocusing for a split second, before he shakes his head to clear it. "I can't teleport to it, not this close to..." He waves his hand towards the room behind her, and a knot of terror sits in Alette's stomach.

If that's how she reacts to just the small sanitation spell, when she didn't before, what changes had already happened to her and—

She firmly pushes the fear aside, to be dealt with later. One problem at a time.

She straightens with him, ducking her head into a nod. "I used to be able to be in there, this is new," she says, shaking her hands out. "Can you be in a car?" Without waiting for him to answer, she strides off to the staircase, but he matches her steps.

"Yes," he says, voice round, not even trying to hide his accent, "it'll take about thirty minutes to reach it from here."

"I'll speed," Alette says, and her magic sparks out, crackling in the air around her. Like her surety lends her more power, and it has to go somewhere.

Her car is at the end of the driveway because of that power, but...

They breeze past another spirit poking at the dead runes in the staircase, but besides a nod towards Zoel, it leaves them alone.

She throws her shoulder into the door at the bottom of the staircase, and it grinds, but opens.

"If he does that spell there..." Alette trails off, striding across the muddy grounds.

"He'd kill us all," Zoel says grimly. "He'd die, I'd die, any spirit would die, Lyra would be powerless, Melekai might —" he cuts off, his eyes unfocusing again, like he's checking in on something.

The difference in the magic outside is astounding. The very air breathes with it, the leaves fluttering with the power, like this is the first bit of life they've had in years.

For all she knows, it might be.

"What do we have to do," she starts, as they head down the steep hill, "if it's about to fragment?"

He gives her a wild-eyed glance, and she gets the sudden understanding that he's scared. That he's terrified, and he's only keeping it together because she's there.

"Whatever we can?" he says, and there's a curl wayward across his forehead, hanging over out of place. "I'll repair, we'll untangle, something, anything—"

ALETTE (4:42 PM): Go evacuate Lyra and Mel. If this goes bad, they should be far away.

"Tell them to head East, until they pass the mountains," Zoel says without looking at her phone, and he's blinking, fast, like he's keeping track of too many things not in front of them.

ALETTE (4:43 PM): Head towards Spokane. Cross the Cascades if you can.

AXEL (4:44 PM): On it.

With so much power swirling around her, she lets her hand drift to her breast pocket as they make their way towards the end of the driveway, and the little wrapped up square of linen grows warm with the magic that once killed her.

AXEL (4:50 PM): You should still try to be safe.

She breathes that in, along with the power and the energy all around her. They might not ever be that close again, but there's something there.

They finally get to the edge of the property, to where her car rests, and both of the dogs sit primly on either side of it.

At the edge, in the mud of a giant spruce tree, is Terese. Her colorless eyes fix unwaveringly up at the Headquarters behind them, terror etched into each line of her body.

Alette hesitates, but Zoel pushes past her. A problem for a different time.

"There's something still blocking me," Zoel says, once past the barrier that used to be the wards. "I don't know what it is, but there's something blocking me from tele-porting."

Alette throws open the door, shouldering her way in, and Zoel does the same, and despite the urgency, despite the hurt in her heart, it's still so bizarre to see someone so unreal sitting in her own car.

But now is not the time for musing, not the time for poetic realizations, so she throws her car in reverse and drives.

ANY OTHER TIME she would have gloried in the sensation of driving fast, of sitting next to Zoel, but all she can feel is a thrumming, terrifying need to get there sooner.

The dogs sprint happily along the car, like this is another adventure. Like they have no idea what could be going on.

At one point, Zoel vanishes, then reappears a few seconds later.

"I got some Wights to evacuate," he says grimly. "Not most. One might come for backup."

She doesn't know how he did that, or how he knows, but she nods in return.

"The ghosts won't leave, and the spirits are moving, but slow," he recites, like it's some horrid responsibility in his bones, "and Mel is packing up Lyra and their cat." His eyes unfocus, before he blinks them back. "Terese is refusing to leave."

"One of these days," she starts, and he leans his head over to listen to her, as if desperate for her words, "you need to explain all of this to me."

"I will explain whatever you need," he breathes. "We make it through this, and I will never stop explaining to you, you will never be without something new to learn."

Briefly, she reaches over and squeezes his hand, and he grips her hard in return.

"Can you make Spot and Grey run to safety?" Alette asks, releasing his hand to rest it back on the steering wheel.

She's speeding, and if someone catches her it'll be bad, but—

"They won't," Zoel says, voice laced with grim knowledge. "I've tried to banish them before, they refuse."

"So, we have to succeed," Alette says, and he gives her a wild-eyed glance. "If they won't leave, we just have to succeed."

He reaches over, gripping her thigh as she drives, and takes a deep breath. "I can teleport there, now," he says, dark. "I don't know how long I'll be able to."

"Go," Alette says, and he disappears with a curt nod, leaving her all alone in the speeding car.

31

There's already a car at that remote cove with the pebbles and stones and crystal blue water, but both Zoel and Gurlien are nowhere to be found.

Alette throws open her door, and the power immediately pulses through her, dizzying in its intensity. Like the entirety of the Line pinpoints her down, pressing against her sinuses and filling her veins.

It's vivid, so bright she doesn't know how she could have ever missed it, how she could have never seen it before, but it's just another marker that she's changed. That something inside of her has changed, somewhere in all this new magic and new ways of exploring and the breaks and the Lines and everything in between...has been irrevocably changed in all of this.

Both the dogs sprint out towards the ocean, splashing into the water and streaking across the beach, ears back.

Static crackles around the edges of the Line, and her heart goes cold.

"Oh," she breathes, and, unbidden, tears spring to her

eyes. Like the very emotions of the Line impress into her, and it, too, is scared. Is sad.

And this time, she knows what that feels like.

Carefully, she pulls out the golden curved needle from her needle case and unravels the strip of linen.

The protective magic within it curls around her wrist, unbidden, pressing against the spot where her bone had broken, and the strip flutters to the ground, devoid of magic.

Next, the strip with the angry, displaced coil, and it snaps itself against Alette, brilliant and fiery.

And the needle in her hand pulses warmth and understanding.

The two dogs disappear behind the cliff face in the cove, down the pebbled beach, parallel with the Line.

It's the same sense of fear, of sadness, of seeking comfort as the Line behind her house, but magnified by a thousand. Instead of a whisper for help, it's a goddamn screech against all her senses.

And somewhere, Zoel and Gurlien are out there, and she doesn't know what they are doing. What state they are in, if Zoel is trying to fix it, if Gurlien's trying to take it all away.

It presses against her, and all she can do is swallow down the panic, keep her needle in her hand, and follow it along the rocky beach.

She doesn't know how it could have gotten this bad, and a snap of electricity sparks at her, only to be met with the same crackle that's inside of her. Like it sees itself in her, and her own self responds.

Which does not bode well for her if it breaks. If her own magic thinks it's a part of it...

She steps carefully along the stones in the beach, towards a downed tree, and, somehow, everything comes into view. Like the magic had been trying to hide it from her, had been trying to stop itself from scaring her.

Gurlien's standing in the middle of the rushing river of magic, and it swirls all around him, ruffling through his flaxen hair, crackling over his skin and his fingertips. One hand is raised up, some sort of spell in it, of which she can't tell.

There's too much magic around for her to even have a prayer of telling the type of spell.

Both the dogs circle him, growling, and by the look on his face, Gurlien can see them. Spot's ears are back, his eyes glow red, and his teeth flash in the glow of the magic.

There's so much magic. It fills her nose, fills her chest, blurs out everything in her eyes, until the entire world is viewed as if past a gauze.

And the world crackles.

Gurlien spots her, she can tell the very moment his gaze falls on her, like the Line itself points it out. Lends her awareness.

She can't see Zoel anywhere.

"Where is he?" Alette asks, and she doesn't need to shout, the Line itself carries her words.

The magic stills in Gurlien's hands, like the Line itself is trying to stop him, and it resonates something inside of her. Some sort of command, some sort of recognition of what she needs to do.

"Who?" Gurlien says, and he has to yell, the noise crackling over all of him, and she can taste the fear radiating off of him.

He knows, too, that he'll die if he completes this.

Alette continues forward, and the magic pushes against her, as if looking for reassurance.

All she can do is hope that she can give it.

"The Wight who came here first," she says, and both the dogs turn to her, then back, and growl.

He lifts his hand, resuming the magic, and the entire Line convulses in panic.

"Stop," she says, breathless, but her words reverberate around her, "you need to stop."

"It'll break, you can feel it almost break," he yells. "It'll ruin the entire world."

She locks eyes with Spot for a split second. "Where is he?"

Spot turns away from Gurlien to point, leg curled up, nose jutting out.

The magic doesn't want Alette's eyes to stray, but she forces them.

Half obscured by a boulder, so all she can see is a mess of black curls and a slumped shoulder, is a prone figure.

She can't tell if he's breathing.

"How do you command them?" Gurlien asks, and his voice is desperate, like he's grasping at the distraction with both hands.

And Alette sees her way in. Sees her way through this, even if Zoel lays unresponsive. Even if all her instincts tell her to go to him, to leave the magic, to leave Gurlien where he stands.

"They're friends," she pitches her voice down, though it still carries, and she takes another step.

The magic crackles, ripping pieces of her hair out of her braid and whipping it across her face, but Gurlien hasn't lifted his hand back up.

"They're friends, I can't let them just die," she says, and her own magic snaps around her, mixing and swirling with the natural magic in a frenzy. "You finish that spell, and—"

He takes a big, shuddering gasp, as if he's feeling all the

pressure from the Line as well. "I don't...I don't know if I have a choice -"

"It'll kill you," Alette continues, stepping forward, and the magic twists around her, so loud she can barely hear her own voice, barely hear her own breath. "You need to stop, we'll figure something out, we—"

And with a clap of thunder she feels in her bones, the Line snaps, shattering apart between one second and the next.

It crashes into her, knocking the air out of her lungs and the ringing from her ears, like she's been plunged into deep water.

Almost like dying once more.

The stones underneath her feet shatter, knocking Gurlien to the ground, and the downed tree splinters apart, as if it is nothing more than paper to be shredded away.

Somehow, through all of it, she can hear Spot whimpering in fear, and they're huddled near Zoel.

And Alette's in the middle of it, and her heart's still beating. In the middle of the coursing river, electricity spiraling around her, so much magic she can't even hear anything.

But this time she has her needle in her hand, and the whisper of magic against her wrists, and the pressure of a hundred lives against her chest.

She grasps out, not that she could ever hope to contain it, not that she could ever hope to thread it in her needle, but grabs the edge of the Line.

It's like trying to grab a car engine, and it jolts against her hand. Sparks blast across her, down her bloodstream and across her heart and through her other hand.

And the other side of the split is within reach, so she slams her hand down on it, and all sound stops.

She inhales, and it's as if the magic is choking out all of

her air, but nothing changes. The destruction settles, the crackling sparks swirl around just her, and the stones stop their shifting.

Her lips part, but there's too much moving through her, too many things for her thoughts to make sense, her mind running too fast, too fast for her to track.

And over, next to the boulder, she sees Zoel shift. Sees him stir, push himself up.

She gasps, but the air burns down her lungs, and it's something like breathing through an engine.

If she lets go, he'll die. The dogs will die, Gurlien will almost certainly die, there's no way she'll survive...but Zoel. Zoel will die.

"No," she whispers, and she can't hear her own words, but she blinks back the spots in her eyes, and the magic twists its way around her, crawling up her body and wrapping her tight, like it could squeeze out the ability to save itself.

And the protective magic around her wrist, from the bubble that could have killed her, twinges.

It's not like she has an idea, it's not like she has some brilliant plan, something that she's thought over and over again until she could find nothing wrong with it.

But what she has is some will.

And she pours that will into that twist of protective magic, still tight against the point of the break, nudging it towards the needle still held between her fingers. Towards the gold that had been smelted in such a break and then re-forged by wild magic.

The protective magic moves easily, like it knows her well enough by now to bend to her mind, and it slithers into the palm of her hand, warm and dry despite the breakage in the dam that was the magic.

And even then, she could feel the want of those wayward strands. The want to help, the want to protect, the want to somehow fix things. The want to be close to her, the strange sense of inhuman and detached wonder.

Without moving out of the jet engine blast of the magic, in complete silence, Alette threads her own needle with the bit of magic, and the entire blast thrums.

It wants her to do this, too.

"Okay," she whispers, though she cannot even hear her own words, and her head is light, so light she wouldn't be surprised if she floated away—or has brain damage—once she is out of the onslaught. "Okay, I got you."

From across the rocks, hazy through the magic, Zoel sits up, stumbles to his feet. Magic pours from him, swirling around her, adding to the strip in her hand.

And, with the magic in her needle and the Ley Line coursing through her, she connects the two sides.

Thunder claps, loud, and she gets tossed aside like a discarded doll, and all sounds smash back into place.

The dogs are howling, someone is screaming, the magic rumbles like a train, and—

Alette lifts herself up off of the broken stone, just long enough to look at the Ley Line, and it courses, loud and confident, like a river crashing through a canyon.

With no break.

Her hand spasms, and the golden needle clatters against the black rocks, and she passes the fuck out.

32

T his time, when she wakes up from being inside a break, everything definitely hurts and everything is awful.

Strong hands smooth her hair away from her face, strong hands with a hint of calluses, and something deep inside her knows that they belong to Zoel.

She turns her face towards the hands, pressing her cheek into them, and they briefly pause, before softening against her face.

There's a thudding in her back, her arms tremble despite being prone, and her head pounds, but each little bit just brings her forward from whatever sleep she had, pulling her exorbitantly along towards consciousness.

"Alette," Zoel whispers. "Alette, it's okay."

Everything feels very much not okay, but she forces her eyes to blink open.

The world blurs around her, and she blinks, but everything's still too far away.

"I got you, I got you," Zoel whispers, and her head is

cradled in his lap, and they're still on the broken stone, and—

She jolts upright and pain slams into her, but she steels herself, gritting her teeth and blinking through it.

His face swims into view, out of focus, and she jerks her hand to her face, but her glasses are gone, the familiar gold frames missing from her face.

Her fingertips crackle with static, bright points of pain, and it's almost reassuring.

"Glasses?" she mumbles out, and her mouth is mealy, not working like it should.

She can hear herself this time, but it's far away, tinny, like she's whispering through a solid wall.

Zoel snaps his fingers, and her head swims trying to follow the motions, but Spot dashes into her line of sight, gently dropping her glasses in her lap.

Spot. The dogs are alive, too.

Ignoring the dog spit and the dust on her lenses, she fits them on her face, looking back at the Ley Line.

It surges, a smooth unbroken beam, like nothing had ever happened before.

"We fixed it," she says, words falling from her lips, before she turns back to Zoel. "We fixed—"

There's blood all along the side of Zoel's face, streaking from his hairline and dripping over his chin, but his blue eyes are clear.

Her arms tremble, but she lifts her hand to his face. "You're hurt."

"Alette," he starts, then pulls her into an embrace, and she's shaking, every part of her is shaking, but there's a thrill of success, a thrill of the magic being exactly as it should, a thrill of being alive and being next to him.

"If this worked," Alette says, and it did, she can feel in

her bones that it worked and that it's safe, "then we can repair everything. For good."

He grabs her face with both of his hands, and electricity snaps around her, but he kisses her, kisses her like he'll never kiss anything ever again, like his entire life is poured into the kiss, poured into this single gesture of affection.

So, she clings back to him, and sparks crackle from her fingertips and the pain presses ever closer to her, but they're alive.

IT TAKES a while before her legs are steady enough to climb to standing, but he throws his arm around her, letting her lean against him. He tucks her needle into her pocket, her hands still trembling too much to grasp the delicate instrument.

Everything still sounds muted, like there's cotton over her ears, but she totters on the shattered boulder, and the Line presses against her again.

This time in thanks.

"We're going to need more of the death bubbles," Alette says, and her words still feel fumbling. "Find more, stitch them together." But it's a solid feeling, a plan that feels right, that rings true. No longer the catching up, no longer the half-panicked feeling of always being a step behind.

"You're going to recover first," Zoel says, but there's amusement in his voice, something fond, so she presses her face against his shoulder for a long second, before—

On the other side of the demolished down tree, Gurlien twitches enough to draw their gaze, and she freezes.

Zoel stiffens, then relaxes, obviously so, against her.

Gurlien flinches, then sits up, panicked, and there's

blood against the sleeve of his white shirt, and his eyes widen when he sees Alette, then looks up towards the coursing, strong Line.

"Where is it?" he blurts out, and she can see the whites all along the edges of his eyes. "Where's the Line, where's the magic, how are you still alive, tell—" He waves his hand, in a familiar snap of a spell motion, but nothing happens.

He stills, staring at his hand, then does the action again. Nothing.

"Where's that Wight, where are the shadow dogs, what happened—" His voice catches.

Zoel sighs, then steps away from Alette for a brief second, vanishes, then reappears. Alette doesn't stumble, but it's a near miss.

Gurlien recoils back, and he's clearly, obviously injured, obviously concussed, and Zoel crouches near him.

"You've had an injury," Zoel says, and despite everything, his voice is kind. Kind to this person who hurt him, kind to this person who almost destroyed everything.

Gurlien scrambles back in a panic, repeating another hand motion, an offensive spell meant to hurt, but it does nothing.

No magic, not even the barest hint of a sparkle.

"You should get to a hospital," Zoel says, standing back up, leaving Gurlien staring down at his hands. "You were next to the major Ley Line when it exploded, you're lucky if all you have is a loss of magic."

He turns back to Alette, and she nods to him.

"Let's go," Alette says, and the Line pulses against her, happy.

~

ZOEL HELPS her to her car, and it's been just enough time that her mind is rolling. Is twisting and moving along, creating plans and spiraling down experiments, fueled by hope. Sparks crackle up her arm, visible and loud bits of pain, but they have hope.

Next to her car, the black Mustang is parked, and she almost hesitates, but—

"This, this is what I told her to be careful of," Melekai says, grumpy, and he's sitting on the car trunk, and Lyra's next to him, face serious, and Axel—

Axel leans against his car, rolling a pen between his fingers, and his brow is furrowed, but he's not quite scowling as they step into view.

With a quick brush against her arm for warning, Zoel steps away, disappears, then reappears. Lyra blinks at him, and Alette can see how she's tracking his injuries.

"We found out a way to fix everything," Alette blurts out, and Melekai's eyebrows raise. "We can stop all this instability, everything."

"Your heart's better this time," Lyra says, solemn, which isn't exactly comforting, "but something's different."

"Obviously," Melekai retorts, and he's scowling at Zoel. "I told you—"

Alette shuts her eyes from the squabbling, lets them trail off, not tracking their arguing.

"They wouldn't evacuate," Axel says, and she opens her eyes again. "Something about providing backup, something about not letting you go alone."

He's looking down, in the gravel of the cove parking lot, instead of at her, tapping the pen against his car.

"I take it you charged right into danger again?" he asks.

"Yeah," Alette says, lifting her hand, and a spark snaps out, loud, "but I think I saved everything."

He nods, before scowling, like he used to do when they were teenagers and something pissed him off. "I still don't like that."

"That's fair," she says, honest, and he smiles, just a smidgen. "I'm gonna keep on doing it."

He mulls on that, and she lets him.

Her magic still swirls around her, and Zoel is right there, arguing something with Melekai. There's blood on his face, still, but he's alive, he's vivid.

They're all here. They're all alive. Magic still exists, Gurlien can't sanitize, and they know now how she can save everything else.

"Is it safe to hug you?" Axel asks, small. "Melekai said he could see you almost die, and Lyra couldn't tell where you were at all, and all I could see was a tree explode and rocks crash and—"

"Oh, come here," Alette says, and pulls him into a hug. "Ow, not that hard—"

He lets her go, laughing, and Alette can feel Zoel's eyes on her, alight, and everything is alright again.

Out of the corner of her eye though, something moves, and after all that, her heart jumps in her throat, but nobody else notices.

Deep in the trees, however, is a hint of colorless blond hair, and Terese stares out at them, her mouth pulled into a thoughtful frown.

Alette stills, and Terese's eyes flicker to her, before a quick shake of her head, and she stares out towards the Line with something resembling sadness.

So Alette breathes out, looking back to Zoel, and lets her be.

EPILOGUE

It's been three weeks, and her magic hasn't calmed down yet, not exactly, and they've nearly run themselves ragged running down and repairing small breaks, but Zoel deems it stable enough to take her somewhere as a surprise, then whisks her away to the beach at Placer's Cabin near Shaman's Point.

The Line they repaired shines bright, brilliant even in the sunlight, and glimpses of magic glitter like rainbows in the beauty of a spring day.

The ocean laps lightly against the shore at high tide, shimmering in the sunlight, but it's abandoned, no other cars. No way of walking to the island.

"Now, I promised you something," Zoel says, his hand on her back. Her magic sparks at his touch, but it's a friendly motion now. "Here."

He rests his hand against his side, like he did all those months ago, but this time—

The magic unfolds in front of her, vivid and glittering, the sand swirling around the base, until a low, beautiful canoe forms.

"That's a lot more impressive when I can see it," Alette says, and he grins at her, and she could go her entire life without being tired of that grin.

He offers his hand to her, and she takes it, climbing into the boat, and he pushes them off, until they're sailing through the shallows of the tide, the water sparkling beneath them.

THE END

SNEAK PEAK OF "THE GIRL WHO CANNOT DIE"

Near as she can tell, Terese has died twenty four times in the last seven months, and she's tired of it.

She's tired of a lot of things.

Like how she still can't control whatever hellish magic that got dumped on her somewhere between being possessed and then un-possessed, like how her body still doesn't process all the normal things like being hungry or being sleepy in any way that she can easily interpret, like how she still doesn't have a place to call an actual home, and like how she's not sure if she's actually spoken to another human in well over three weeks.

She thinks she has. But again, not sure.

Because, see, she's been losing time, and it freaks her the fuck out.

It's different from The Possession, it's far different from the Demon that had forced its way into Terese's mind and body and ruined everything, but the part of Terese that's left that still shrieks about her overall health and safety tells her that losing track of time and where she is is definitely a symptom of something Not Good.

So when Terese finds herself in her favorite safety tunnel, bleeding suspiciously from a wound on her side into the dust of the rock floor, her dog Izzy calmly asleep on the blanket Terese scavenged a while back, and no memory of taking either of them there, she takes a moment.

The area is little more than an abandoned maintenance tunnel for a long since forgotten railway company, with crumbling rock walls held up by aged wooden beams. Graffiti decorates wherever a clean enough rock face presents itself, the long ago scrawlings of teenagers.

It's also incredibly silent, remarkably mild in temperature, and she can hear anyone coming.

She rests her head against the rock wall, and it stretches at the wound.

It's not like she could go get medical treatment. Not when she's had multiple fatal injuries and popped right back up. Not when pain still wracks her bones whenever she moves wrong.

Not when being in unfamiliar places still makes that tickle of panic crawl down her throat.

ALSO BY ALESSA WINTERS

The Magic of the Living and the Dead

The Girl Who Brings The Dead

The Girl Who Has Already Died

The Girl Who Cannot Die

The Ghosts of Riverside County

A Ghost of Her Own

A Ghost to Haunt Her

Summer Merman Series

The Man of the Lake: A Merman Romance

The Man of the Isle: An Alaskan Merman Romance

The Paranormal Organization Series

Marked By The Demigod

The Succubi's Choice

Katya and the Young God

Follow her on twitter at @writerLyn

Want a Free book? Sign up for her Newsletter here and receive a
previously unreleased Novel!

Printed in Dunstable, United Kingdom